UNTOUCHABLE

A NOVEL BY

Peter S. Berman

ISBN-978-1-7335160-0-6

Published by Merseyside Press
Contact us at **merseysidepress@gmail.com**

Visit the author's page on Facebook at **Peter S. Berman**, or check in with us on Facebook at **Merseyside Press**.

This story is dedicated to my grandchildren Max and Charley. Someday you'll be old enough to read my books, and here's hoping you enjoy them.

***

This book is also dedicated to my dear friends Greg and Lois Good. They have helped me form and shape my stories by listening to my ideas and reading my first drafts.

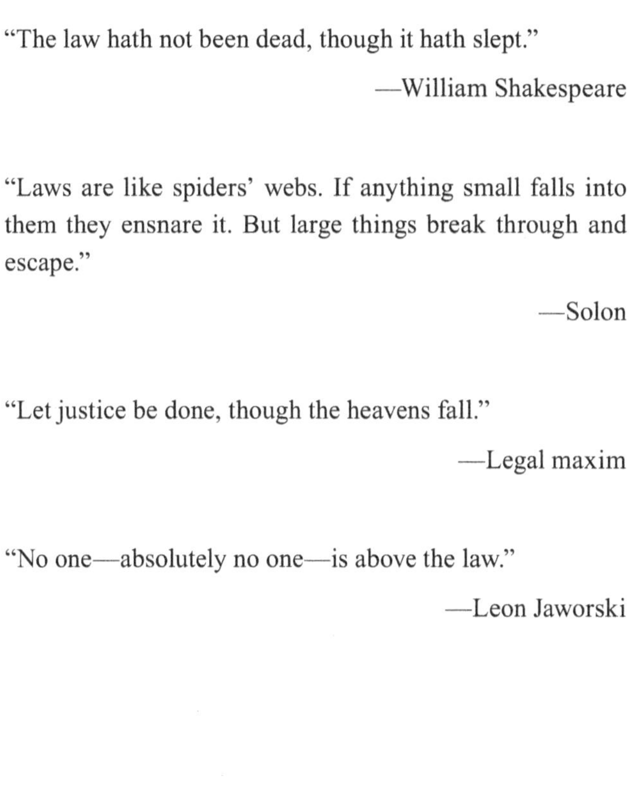

“The law hath not been dead, though it hath slept.”

—William Shakespeare

“Laws are like spiders’ webs. If anything small falls into them they ensnare it. But large things break through and escape.”

—Solon

“Let justice be done, though the heavens fall.”

—Legal maxim

“No one—absolutely no one—is above the law.”

—Leon Jaworski

Contents

AUTHOR'S NOTE

This novel is a work of fiction in its entirety. With a few location exceptions, all characters, settings, dialogue, incidents, and other story elements are wholly imaginary. Following an old literary tradition, I have honored some of my friends by using their names to identify fictional characters, but there is no connection between my imaginary characters and my real-life friends.

Any resemblance between the fictional contents of this book and real people is strictly coincidental. As for governmental institutions and business locations around the world, many of them are included to give the story the feel of realism.

While this story is complete fiction, it is based upon the very real problems that detectives and law enforcement officials encounter when investigating cases that are cold.

The first draft of this story was completed in 2008. At that time, the involvement of diplomats, Istanbul, and Saudi Arabia's Royal House of Saud was purely coincidental. I cannot see into the future.

(Smile)

Or maybe I can…

OTHER NOVELS BY PETER S. BERMAN

HIDDEN AGENDA

*

WEB OF BETRAYAL

*

MONEY FOR LOVE

*

ABDUCTED

*

THE STRANGLER'S KNOT

These books by Peter S. Berman are available at
amazon.com and other fine retail outlets worldwide.

UNTOUCHABLE

PROLOGUE

May 21, 2010

Matt Kirk waited patiently for his change while the young sales clerk, a Hispanic girl with waist-length black hair and large, brown eyes, held on to his ten-dollar bill while she spoke in rapid Spanish to someone on her cell phone. He assumed that she was talking to her boyfriend because her comments were flirty while she negotiated a time and place for them to get together once her all-night shift was over.

She glanced up at Kirk and rolled her eyes in mock displeasure. She was acting as if the call was a nuisance, but he knew that her gesture was just a sham. He smiled to himself. His very presence at the cashier's counter was interrupting the flavor of her phone call.

Finally, when she realized that she could delay him no longer, she told her boyfriend, "*Lo Siento.*" (Hold on).

Kirk tapped his fingers on the counter and pointed at the money in her hand.

She put down the phone and said in English, "I'm sorry officer. That was a customer who wanted to know if we carried milk?"

"Cuánto cuesta?" he asked her. (How much?)

Her confusion was immediately evident, followed by the unnerving realization that he had spoken to her in Spanish and that he probably knew what she'd been saying to her lover.

He smiled to himself. She would have no reason to suspect that he was bilingual, for he was tall and pale skinned, with sandy-blond hair and a sprinkling of freckles across the bridge of his nose. To her way of thinking, an Irish looking cop was not likely to be a Spanish speaker, but like many of the new breed of officers within the ranks of the LAPD, Kirk had grown up a product of the LA private school system where Spanish was now a part of the primary school curriculum.

If you were to ask him about the wisdom of learning Spanish from childhood on, he would be the first one to tell you that being bilingual was a skill more relevant than ever before in a city that was now predominately Hispanic.

"Hable usted Espanol?" she asked. (Do you speak Spanish?).

"*Si*," he told her with a smile and a wink. "*Una lengua nunca es suficiente.*" (One language is never enough).

Now reeling from her embarrassing mistake, she quickly handed him his change.

"*Gracias, senior,*" she told him.

"*De nada.*" (You're welcome.)

He pocketed his change, grabbed two steamy cups of black coffee from the countertop, then made his way to his patrol car that was parked in a slot out in front of the *AM-PM* convenience store.

Before opening the door, he slowly glanced around and took everything in. The sky was cloudless, the temperature balmy, and there was a smattering of stars visible in the night sky. The streets of Westwood Village—a sleepy hamlet adjacent to the University of California in Los Angeles—were all but abandoned. He checked his watch. It was three-fifteen in the morning, a time when very few people were out and about. And while the busiest part of his shift was behind him, the real struggle would now begin. It was the battle against boredom, the true hallmark of the early morning watch.

Kirk was a *Policeman II* training officer, and his partner for the current deployment period was a rookie named Christopher Talafiero. He was a state college grad, Italian by background, who rode mountain bikes and surfed when he wasn't on the clock. Kirk referred to him merely as *Kermit,* a name he reserved for all of his trainees, for Talafiero was fresh out of the Academy and still on probation, with eyes as wide as saucers, and an eagerness to please. But each of the trainees shared a universal characteristic...all were *green* when it came to policing experience; hence the nickname *Kermit,* borrowed from *Sesame Street's Kermit the Frog.*

This particular *Kermit* was a nice enough kid; head shaven, crisp blues, shiny new boots. Big and robust, a very quick understudy, he knew when to ask the right questions. He was one of the few who intuitively understood what the job entailed. He never showed fear and always seemed to use his common sense which was somewhat unique among his peers, for most of the current crop was just back from Iraq or Afghanistan, and few, if any, had the initial restraint that was needed to make a quick transition to civilian policing.

Talafiero was waiting patiently in the passenger seat, his head on a swivel, scanning the empty streets for anything unusual or strange.

Kirk stifled a laugh. He'd get over that soon enough. This job was all about experience, and once you had it, you instinctively knew when it was time to go on alert.

"Black, no sugar," Kirk said as he handed Kermit one of the coffees through the open passenger side window. He then walked around to the driver's side and settled in behind the wheel before shifting his glance back over to the kid.

"You getting used to these early mornings yet?"

The rookie smiled. "Not yet, sir. I'm still having trouble falling asleep in the afternoon. Sometimes, I just lay there for hours."

Kirk nodded. He took a large sip of his coffee, then added, "Darken your bedroom, lower the lights gradually for an hour or so before you lay down, and use a sleeping mask to cover your eyes. It'll help—"

Their radio suddenly chirped:

"Any unit in the vicinity, and Fifteen A Twenty-one..."

Kirk paused mid-sentence, now focused on the radio call. It was a *hot shot* directed to their unit.

"A woman screaming. Four-one-two-one Gayley Avenue. PR is out in front and will direct you to the apartment. Fifteen A Twenty-one... handle Code Three."

Kirk pitched his coffee out the window, snapped on his seatbelt, fired up the engine, roared out of the parking lot, and hung a tire-screeching turn onto Westwood Blvd. The kid had followed suit and somehow managed to dump his coffee without spilling it in his lap.

A Code Three call meant that red lights and sirens were authorized, so Kirk said, "Pop the cherry, Kermit. We're right on top of it."

The rookie flipped on the overhead red flashers.

"Siren, sir?" he asked.

"We're too close. If we sneak on in, maybe we can catch *someone* in the act."

Kirk slid them through a high-speed turn onto Gayley Avenue and calmly said over the noise from the engine, "Tell 'em we're coming in from the West."

The kid keyed the mike.

"Twenty-one to Control. We're on top of it, coming in from the West. Our ETA is...?"

"Thirty-seconds," said Kirk. He floored the accelerator as they shot through a four-way stop.

"*Thirty-seconds*," the kid repeated into the microphone. His voice showed no signs of stress.

"Roger that, Twenty-one. All units, Twenty-one is thirty-seconds out and coming in from the West."

"This is the street," Kirk said as he made a quick turn. "Stay sharp. It's probably mid-block."

The rookie keyed the mike again:

"Fifteen A Twenty-one: show us Six on scene."

"Roger, Twenty-one. All units. Fifteen A Twenty-one is Code Six at the location."

By calling in *Code Six* all the other responding units would know that they had arrived and were getting out of their car.

Kirk was proud of the kid. A Code Three run would normally hype-up most rookies, but this one was as cool as they came. His adrenalin was apparently under control, and his voice was steady and devoid of any emotion.

Very professional, he thought, *but let's see how he handles things from this moment on?*

Their headlights picked up a small group of people standing out in the middle of the street. Kirk looked over at the kid.

"Take a deep breath when you bail from the car and take everything in. Let's find the Person Reporting (PR), and once we know what we're up against, we'll decide if we should wait for our backup."

The kid sighed audibly.

"You okay?" Kirk asked.

"Yes, sir. I'll follow your lead."

This kid must have been military, he thought. *I'll have to ask him about that when we get a little time.*

Kirk killed the overhead flashers and pulled up next to the people in the street. There were five of them, all huddled together, and one, an elderly man, stepped up to the driver's side window.

"Over there!" he said excitedly. He pointed to an upstairs window of what looked like a duplex apartment. "She was screaming for help. It was awful!"

"Did you call it in?" Kirk asked.

The old man nodded vigorously.

Kirk listened intently, but there were no more screams.

"How long since you heard the last one?" he asked as he climbed out of the car. He pulled his nightstick from the holder on the door and slipped it into the ring on his belt.

"Five, maybe ten minutes ago." The old man's voice was trembling. He was in his pajamas, and his body was shaking. "Please, hurry!"

"How many people live up there?" Kirk asked.

An older woman stood just behind the old man. She was also in her pajamas which were covered by a thin, tattered robe. She said, "Carrie is a student at UCLA. She lives alone. We live next door. The screaming was terrible, officer. It woke us up. You've got to get up there and help her!"

Kirk nodded, his adrenalin was now pumping, but he willed himself to resist the urge to start running for the stairs that led up to the second story.

"Does she have a back door?" he asked.

"It's off the kitchen," said the old man. It appeared he had once again found his voice.

Kirk sighed. He looked over at the kid. Was Kermit ready to cover the back alone? Then again, if a suspect was still inside, he'd need someone to watch his back when he went through the front door.

He made up his mind; safety first. He'd take the kid with him up to the front, wait until the back door was covered by others, then he and the kid would go in.

Now that he had a plan firmly in mind, he reached for his microphone button, intending to transmit a request for arriving units to secure the back of the building, but the old man grabbed at his arm.

"She's a very lovely girl, officer. Very kind. Her father's a policeman, just like you."

Kirk held the old man's stare while his mind tried to process what he'd just heard.

Her father's a cop?

Oh shit!

He started to run with the kid close behind. He keyed the transmit button on his shoulder mike:

"Fifteen A Twenty-one, we're going in the front! Have a unit cover the back!"

The entrance to the apartment was at the top of a long staircase. Kirk took the steps two at a time and pulled out his handgun just as he reached the top step.

The rookie was right on his heels.

The front door was closed. Kirk pulled out his flashlight, and the kid quickly followed suit. There were no clear signs of a break-in, and when Kirk tried the handle, he discovered that it was locked.

He put his ear up to the door, but no sounds came out of the apartment. He considered their options. Knock and wait for someone to answer, or take a chance and kick it in? A cop's daughter had been screaming for help...*the decision was instantly made.*

"I'm gonna kick it," he told the rookie. "You ready to go?"

"Shouldn't we wait for our backup?"

Kirk blinked in disbelief. "Her dad's a cop. We're going in!"

Kirk faced the door. He could feel the beads of cold sweat as they rolled down the back of his neck. He gestured to the rookie to take the left while he would sweep the room from the right. The kid nodded, and with flashlights and guns in hand, Kirk booted the door and charged right in.

"Police!" he yelled.

The living room was pitch black, and the light from their flashlights floated like ghostly spirts over the furniture and open spaces alike. Everything seemed to be in order. There were no signs of a struggle and no one in sight.

"Police officers!" Kirk yelled again. "Anyone home?"

There was no response.

In the distance, he could hear several sirens approaching. That would be their backup heading for the rear.

"We clear it," he said over his shoulder to the rookie.

They slowly moved through the front room, making sure that no one was hiding there or could come at them from behind.

When Kirk's flashlight found the door frame to the kitchen, he paused for a moment to peek in. It was empty. But he spotted the back door, and it was open halfway. He pointed that out to the rookie before they continued their search of the apartment.

He walked past a bathroom on the left while the rookie went in and checked it out with his light. Kirk moved towards the bedroom door, and in the glow from the flashlight, he could see that it was open just a crack. Inside the room it was dark.

"Police officer!" he yelled. He pushed at the door and shined in his light.

A lone female was lying face up on the bed. Her body was still, and her eyes were wide open. She didn't move. It didn't look good.

Kirk scanned the rest of the room with his flashlight while the rookie moved in to check the closet, but the suspect or suspects were nowhere to be found.

Kirk flipped on an overhead light and keyed his shoulder mike.

"Fifteen A Twenty-one."

"Twenty-one go."

"Send paramedics to our location. Possible 187 (homicide). Suspects GOA. (Gone on arrival). No description. Back door open. It may be the route of escape. Notify the Watch Commander. We'll secure the scene."

He walked over to the bed, holstered his weapon, and felt the throat of her neck for a pulse.

There was none.

He stared down at her body. She was completely naked and one of her wrists was fastened above her head to one of the posts on the wooden headboard. The blanket and top sheet had been pulled all the way down and were now draped over the foot of the bed. He shined his light around the room. It didn't look like a struggle. He spotted a framed photo on a nearby desk. He walked over and studied it in the glow of the overhead light.

It was a picture of her posing with a uniformed LAPD officer and a woman who might have been her mother. He had the feeling that it must be her dad.

He exhaled slowly, then turned back towards the body. When he got to the side of the bed, he said to Kermit, "Can you see the blood vessels in the whites of her eyes?"

The rookie stepped closer, looked down, then nodded.

"The capillaries are broken," said Kirk who used his flashlight beam to make the ruptured capillaries more visible. "It's called *petechial hemorrhaging.* It means that the possible cause of death was likely manual strangulation."

The rookie nodded his understanding.

Kirk wanted to cover her up, to give her some dignity back, but any change to the scene might destroy a critical piece of evidence. He didn't like it, but he had no choice. She was gonna have to stay just the way she was.

But what he did have was the power to keep the curious from gawking at her, and as long as he could control the scene, that's precisely what he intended to do.

"Okay, Chris," he began. It was the first time he referred to the rookie by name; a sign of the respect that Talafiero's performance had just earned him. "Walk out of here very carefully and wait at the top of the front stairs. On your way out, watch where you step, and don't touch anything. Let the paramedics in, but no one else, and I mean *no one*: no uniforms, no plainclothes, no brass. I want this crime scene to remain pristine, and to make sure that it does, we're gonna lock it down tighter than a gnat's ass. And when the paramedics do show up, remember to log in their ID's." He turned to face the kid. "You got all that?"

The rookie didn't move. The girl's body still had him transfixed and his face was noticeably pale.

"Your first dead body?" Kirk asked.

"No sir, I saw bodies during my tour in Iraq, but that was war. Nothing at all like this."

So, he was military after all. That explained a lot.

Kirk looked back down at the victim.

"Take it all in, Chris, and remember what it feels like. You never want to lose that sickening feeling. It's what makes us different from the people who did this."

The kid stared a moment longer, then made his way out of the room.

Kirk looked down at the victim. She was so young. Her eyes, wide open, were devoid of light and staring straight up at nothing. Kirk shook his head and inhaled deeply while a feeling of profound sadness washed over his soul.

"Don't worry, little one," he said in a soft voice. "I'm here now. No one's going to hurt you anymore."

ONE

Six Years Later

Jennifer Donahue took one last drag from her cigarette then pitched what remained of it into the toilet before blowing out the smoke in the direction of an open bathroom window. She was completely nude and seated on the edge of the bathtub, one foot held up against her chest, lost in thoughts about her life and where things seemed to be going.

"You okay, babe?" came the voice of a male through the door of the nearby master bedroom.

She snapped back to the present and began fanning the remnants of the smoke in the air with her hand.

"I'm fine," she replied, but her voice betrayed a weariness that the rest of her body felt. She briefly wondered if he was going to come in, then quickly discarded the thought. They hadn't been together long enough yet for all the barriers to break down. A closed-bathroom door could still create her refuge of solitude, a place where she could pull herself together and have a cigarette if she wanted to.

"You coming back to bed?" he called out.

"I'll be out in a minute."

She slowly got to her feet, flushed the evidence of her transgression, then stepped up to the sink, brushed her teeth and gargled with mouthwash.

She studied her face in the mirror and sighed heavily. She was thirty-eight years old, and while she knew she had it going on—downright sexy when she pulled it all together—she was starting to exhibit the first signs of aging. The tiny little wrinkles at the corners of her eyes had her concerned. She might soon have to give some thought to starting up with Botox injections, but that was only part of her worries. Her clock was ticking, she still wasn't married, and the life she really craved was quickly passing her by.

She ran the cold water from the tap, splashed it on her face, then patted it dry with a hand towel. With another quick look in the mirror, she put on a robe, then headed for the door and braced herself for where this current mood of hers was inevitably going to take her.

She'd been seeing Zachary Hunter for almost three months. An ER doctor who practiced his craft at Cedars-Sinai Hospital, they had met when he tried to save a robbery victim who tragically did not survive a brutal attack. He was tall and handsome, but not one of those self-absorbed, self-anointed *surgeon gods* who wielded the knife while holding the lives of others in their hands. He was kind and easy going, and that, for her, had been a significant attraction. But what really got her motor racing was the way he always seemed to look at her. His gray eyes were knowing, warm, and sincere, and they pulled her in like a magnet.

The two of them had shared a cup of coffee after that first fateful surgery, and from that moment on, she'd been hooked.

The sex with him was great, but as good as it was, she wasn't yet willing to move into his place. Both of them were pursuing demanding careers, and the outcome seemed to be entirely predictable. Not enough time together, resentment, the feeling that things were going nowhere for her—their relationship had reached a definite crossroads, one that she was now getting ready to face.

She had dealt with relationships like this before. When she worked as a street cop and later as a detective, maintaining relationships had been decidedly difficult. But if she thought it was tough while working Sex Crimes, it became ten times worse when she transferred into Homicide.

At WLA's divisional Homicide Unit, she had spent most of her time in the learning curve. That left her practically no chance for any kind of a personal life. After that, when on loan to Robbery-Homicide Division, the pressure of immersion into a single, high profile case had precluded all but very limited dating. A transfer back to WLA—where she paid her work-time dues again—was followed by a permanent slot back at RHD, and it was here that she finally felt that she was where she belonged. She had tried once again to move on with her personal life, and while she was happy to have met a man as special as Zach, the nature of his career and the time that was needed for her to work homicides was taking a heavy toll on them both.

She could sense that they were already drifting apart, and as tired as she was of the havoc that working murders had taken on her life, she knew that she couldn't give it up. And Zach, for his part, was certainly no better. In addition to the surgery's he handled at Cedars every day, he was also on call four nights a week for difficult cases at *Children's Hospital* in Los Angeles.

Both of them knew when they first hooked up that things were going to be tough, but for her, it was verging on the impossible. Theirs was a relationship based on text messages, occasional phone calls, and quick get-togethers, maybe once or twice a week. It left her feeling lonely and taken for granted, and that was not what she wanted. She hated the fact that it made her feel cheap.

This relationship was going nowhere fast, and just recognizing the truth of what it was had put her in a sullen mood. But she didn't really want to find herself alone again, not yet anyway, and in her present state of mind, she was worried that she might say something stupid that would bring it all up again. So rather than deal with it now, she would call it a night and go back to her place and give herself time to think things through.

She walked out of the bathroom, and in the semi-darkness of his room, she began to collect her clothing

"What are you doing?" he asked, sitting up in the bed. "Aren't you going to spend the night?"

"I can't," she lied. She flashed him a tight, weak smile. "I've got an early meeting tomorrow morning, and I really need to get some sleep."

He sighed, a gesture that said more than words ever could, and she sensed that he was wondering how long this could go on?

"Will you call me later?" he asked. He had made no effort to stop her; a disappointment that stung.

"I will," she said, "this afternoon."

He nodded in silence, then said, "I'm doing the best I can, Jen. I'm trying to make our schedules work."

"I know you are," she told him as she pulled up her skirt and zipped it closed. "It's my fault too."

She finished dressing, walked over to the bed, leaned over and gave him a kiss. As she started for the door, he called out, "You know, it's not just for the sex. I mean...I'm happy just to hang with you."

She hadn't expected him to say that and it went a long way to soften her mood.

"I just don't want to be taken for granted, Zach," she told him.

"You never will be," he replied.

She sighed, turned around and returned to the side of the bed.

"Maybe I can stay a little bit longer."

He smiled, pulled her down and held her in a bear hug.

"Do you really need to get some sleep?"

She laughed and ran her fingers through his hair

"That depends on what you have in mind?"

TWO

Donahue hurried off the elevator on the fifth floor of the Police Administration Building (PAB), the headquarters for the LAPD in downtown Los Angeles. She nodded to two passing plainclothes detectives, one of whom turned around to talk to her, but she waved him off, pointing to her watch. She was already forty minutes late.

She used her ID card to enter the cavernous RHD squad room filled with several dozen double rows of waist-high cubicles. Very sleek and modern looking, each row contained ten cubicles, each of which included built-in storage, file drawers, a computer screen, and an ergonomic office chair. Throughout the room, there were stacks of brown cardboard boxes filled with case folders and papers. Written on the outside of the boxes, in large black letters, were the numbers for the cases and the names of the dead.

At this early hour of the day, the squad room was full of detectives. Some worked the phones, many were involved in discussions with their peers, and others were typing away at their computers. Most of them sipped at strong black coffee, the lubrication that helped to keep them all awake.

Her partner and mentor, Ulysses S. Gibson—called *Gibby* by those he was close to—was seated at his desk, pouring over one of two very thick blue cover volumes of a homicide book.

He stood out from most of the other detectives because of his penchant for sartorial splendor. His skin was the color of coffee with cream, and the wrinkles at the corners of his eyes and mouth were the product of a frequent and a generous smile.

She arrived at her desk, dropped her purse in her chair, and removed her holstered weapon from her belt. She wore a dark black pants suit and a white silk blouse. Her comfortable black loafers, while unflattering, were an absolute necessity, since high heels were impractical for work in the field.

She locked her handgun in the bottom drawer of her desk, then glanced over at Gibson who seemed to be focused entirely on his work.

"Hey, there," she said.

He was wearing a pair of reading glasses that were perched precariously on the tip of his nose while he studied the pages and photographs. He didn't bother to look up.

She knew right away why she got the cold shoulder. Gibby was a guy who kept to a schedule, and he was right to expect her to do the same.

"Sorry I'm late," she said.

That got his attention. He stopped his reading and looked up.

"Tough night?" he asked.

She mustered a smile and gave him the smallest of winks.

"Actually, it was quite nice."

"I'm glad to hear that. Did you get any sleep?"

She felt herself blush.

"None of your biz, nosey."

"Well, well." He pulled his glasses off and studied her face. "I'm going to guess that's a *no*?" He could sense her discomfort, and it made him smile.

"Had your coffee yet?"

"On the way in." Her eyes strayed towards the files on his desk. "What's that?"

He closed the folder he'd been reading and placed it on top of its companion volume. Together, the two volumes were almost five inches thick.

"The Captain dropped these on my desk this morning," he told her. "It's a cold case that he wants us to look at while we're waiting for our number to come up."

Homicide teams at RHD were assigned to duty shifts the same as they were in the respective divisional stations. If your team was up and a new case came in, it was yours to handle. And during your downtime, if there was any, you did what you could on the older, unsolved cases.

Gibson stroked at a thin gray mustache that graced his upper lip. He prided himself on being a meticulous dresser. This morning he wore a well-tailored light gray Brooks Brothers suit with a crisp white shirt, leather suspenders, and gold cuff-links. His black loafers had a military shine, and his pale yellow necktie was matched to the handkerchief that peeked out of his left breast pocket.

"Since you've already had your coffee," he began, "you can look it over and see if there's anything for us to work with?"

He held out the heavy files which she took from his hand before walking with them back into her cubicle. She cleared the rest of her desk, moved several small-framed photographs of her mother to the side, then took a seat and opened the first volume to the table of contents.

"Is it interesting?" she asked over the top of the waist high partition.

Many of the unsolved cases, generally referred to as *stranger on stranger,* had no workable leads, so she could only hope that this one would be different and that perhaps there was a chance that they could solve it.

"Actually, it might be something we can sink our teeth into," he said with a smile. It's a rape-murder out of West LA division, your old stomping grounds. Happened just about six years ago. You might even remember it? The victim was the daughter of an LA cop."

"Is this the Ryson case?" she asked looking up.

His eyes widened with surprise. "Did you work it back then?"

"Not directly. I was uniformed patrol at the time, and I was on days, so it didn't come in on my watch. But everyone out there worked the streets for weeks, talking to informants, following up leads. The whole division was involved."

Donahue felt her shoulders droop. Her decision to spend the night at Zachary's condo was going to cost her dearly today. She was exhausted, but on balance, the fun had been worth it.

"I'll get right on it," she told him.

Ever since they started working as a team, Gibson had been her mentor. His years of experience at working high profile cases made the work she did before RHD seem like a stint in the minor leagues. He was clever, thorough, and dogged when it came to following up leads. She felt lucky to be learning at the feet of such a true investigative virtuoso.

Her first experience working with him involved the shooting death of a wealthy businessman. The accused, a District Attorney named Jeremy Hart, had gone on trial for the killing of his girlfriend's husband. What she learned during their work on that case—about life and about the moral code of her partner—had helped her mature into a thoughtful seeker of the truth. But while she knew she had the skills to go it alone, there was still a certain comfort factor in knowing that

Gibby was taking the lead. In this arena, there was no substitute for experience, and what Gibson brought to the table, money couldn't buy.

He watched while she got herself settled, then slid his chair back from his desk and looked over in her direction.

"I hate to disturb you now that you're finally working, but we really need to get going."

Her head popped up, and she gave him the once over.

He smiled mischievously, then looked at his watch.

"We've got a meeting set up with the victim's father in just about thirty minutes, so it's time to hit the road."

Donahue shook her head. He was subtly calling her out again for coming in late.

"You might have said something before I got settled in," she muttered.

He placed his hands together, fingertips touching, and smiled again.

Donahue sighed.

Well, it's my own damn fault. I guess I'll have to try and read the files in the car.

She unlocked her desk drawer and pulled out her gun.

"Is her father still on the job?" she asked while she strapped her weapon to her waist.

Gibson nodded. "He's a Lieutenant now, assigned to Vice. He's working out of West LA."

Donahue realized that the assignment to WLA was the act of a grieving father. He had obviously transferred into the division where his daughter had been killed to do what he could to find her killer. It didn't surprise her that he'd done it. In his shoes she would have done the same thing.

Gibson slipped on a gray fedora and pulled the brim down to just above his eyes.

Donahue smiled inwardly. She watched him check his appearance in a small hand-held mirror that he kept in his top desk drawer.

"The hat looks good," she told him. "Very fashionable. It does a great job of concealing your bald spot."

He locked eyes with her before he treated himself to a smile of quiet confidence. Her good-natured teasing was nothing new, so he let it pass without comment.

"Can we get another cup on the way?" she asked. She could feel herself starting to fade.

"Only if you're buying?"

"Oh? Was it my crack about your bald spot?"

He tilted his head and studied her carefully.

"What bald spot?"

She rolled her eyes. *This was going to be a very long day.*

"I'll meet you down at the car," he said. "Oh, and Jen, don't forget to bring the homicide books."

He's treating me just like a rookie, she thought. She pursed her lips but kept her mouth shut. She wasn't going to humor him by taking the bait.

With her gun now secured on her hip and her purse slung over her shoulder, she picked up both of the homicide books and followed him out the door.

THREE

Donahue glanced out the window. The day was crisp and clear, and the temperature seemed headed for the upper seventies. She was momentarily struck by a passing fantasy, one that had her lying out at the beach in Santa Monica with a Mai Tai in her hand.

Don't I wish...

She cut off the thought to keep from becoming even more depressed. Instead, she opened the first volume of the two murder books to learn what she could about the Ryson girl's murder.

The first page consisted of an index that was broken down into sections that were designated by alphabet letters. Donahue knew the set-up by heart, so she flipped directly to the section that held the photographs. She needed to put a face to the victim's name to make the case seem fresh and real.

The first picture was an eight by ten glossy encased in a plastic sheath. It was taken at a party of some kind, perhaps a sorority or fraternity bash, for there were numerous other college-age kids holding beers and cigarettes while gyrating on a dance floor. In the foreground was the victim, Carrie Ann Ryson, age nineteen; a strikingly beautiful California girl with long blond hair and a beautiful figure. In the photo she was mugging with several girlfriends, and the look on her face was joyful, as if she didn't have a care in the world.

Donahue could still remember those days. It was the innocence of youth, a time full of fun and adventure with very little in terms of responsibilities.

Oh, how sweet it had been!

But for Carrie Ann Ryson, those days had come to a tragic, grinding halt when the realities of life in a world of good and evil had paid her an unwanted visit. Someone sorely needed to atone for this outrage, and Donahue hoped that with a little luck and a lot of hard work, maybe someday they actually would.

According to a narrative report written by Tony Salerno, one of the original detectives, Carrie Ann had been the only daughter of Michael and Laurie Ryson. At the time of the murder, Laurie was employed as a registered nurse who worked at Tarzana Regional Hospital, while Sergeant Michael Ryson worked in an undercover capacity out of the Venice Vice Division.

Carrie had been raised in a tract home in Simi Valley, a bedroom community just beyond the Los Angeles County limits. It was a sheltered enclave, far from the big city problems; densely populated by intact families, many of whom were cops who understood that the hours of daily commuting were a worthwhile trade-off for the opportunity to own their own homes.

When interviewed by detectives, both parents told officers that their daughter was a high school honor student; a varsity soccer player—lettering three years in a row—who had dabbled in high school theater, having had small roles in both her junior and senior years. Upon graduating from high school, she moved from her home to UCLA to begin her college education. In her second year as a Bruin, her parents allowed her to live off campus in an apartment on a quiet, tree-lined street. On the morning of the murder, when patrol officers first discovered her body, they had the good sense to lock down the scene. Aside from the detectives assigned to handle the case, only essential technicians had been allowed to view the body, so the risk of contamination had been significantly reduced.

Donahue got a lump in her throat. Apparently, one of the patrol officers who discovered Carrie Ann had taken his duties to heart. He'd done what he could to protect the victim's dignity, apparently refusing entry to a long list of nosey supervisors who had dropped by the scene out of morbid curiosity. *Good for him*, she thought, but knowing first hand about the vindictiveness of some of the LAPD brass, he had probably paid the price for his insolence.

She looked at his name...*Matt Kirk*. She would remember who he was and maybe someday she would have a chance to do him a real solid.

She knew both of the detectives who handled the initial investigation. The lead role on the team had been assumed by Tony Salerno, a tenacious and meticulous investigator with a solid reputation for thoroughly working his cases. His partner, Archie Morse, had the reputation of a loose cannon, frequently going off on tangents. But Archie's ability to grasp the big picture very early on in a case made him an ideal foil for the doggedness of Salerno's plodding ways. Together, the two had a high clearance rate, and the fact that this one was still unsolved was not a good omen, for had there been any kind of a decent lead, she was sure that these two men would have worked it to death.

She found Matt Kirk's initial crime report. It wasn't much, but it gave her the details of what happened through his perspective:

We received an initial call of a woman screaming, at 3:17 a.m. We arrived on scene at 3:21 a.m. and were met by neighbors who had heard the victim screaming for five or ten minutes before we pulled up. That would possibly place the time of death between 3:06 a.m. and 3:21 a.m. After waiting a short time for a backup to arrive, we entered the location, a triplex apartment building, by way of the front door. The front door was locked and secured, and after knocking and getting no answer, we identified ourselves and forced entry. A search revealed the deceased lying on her bed in the bedroom. The back door was partially open, an indication of the likely route of egress. The victim was secured to the headboard by one hand. The method used to secure her was a flexible, plastic handcuff.

She pushed ahead to a summary written by Detective Archie Morse. Carrie Ann had been out at a nightclub earlier in the evening. A lot of work had been done to find a connection between the club and her death, but nothing had turned up.

Too bad, she thought. *That would have been where I would have started looking too.*

She flipped over to the section with the crime scene photographs. There were eighty-seven, and they were arranged nine photos to a page, starting with the outside pictures of the neighborhood, the building in question, the walkway and stairs up to the front, the exterior of the front door, and the damage caused by the breach.

The photos then shifted to the interior, beginning with the living room, the kitchen, the open back door, the bathroom, and finally the bedroom.

From a study of the photographs up to this point, Donahue noted that the shrubbery in front of the building was cut low, not affording anyone an opportunity to hide below the windows undetected. That would significantly reduce the possibility of a surprise attack by a stranger as she walked up the pathway to her front door. The apartment was generally neat, a few clothing items left lying around, but that was not unusual for a college-age girl. The dishes in the sink were minimal, no signs of her having entertained, and there were no apparent signs of a struggle: no overturned furniture, no broken or out of place items.

Donahue's first impression—*the killer was someone she knew.*

The next set of photographs made the case real. The wall of separation that usually allowed her to think of the body as mere evidence was torn asunder as she studied the pictures of Carrie Ann laid out on the bed in death.

She was on her back, left hand over her head, secured to the headboard of her bed by a plastic handcuff, the kind that police used for making mass arrests.

Hmm, she thought. *Did anyone consider that a cop might somehow be involved?*

The sheets and blankets were pulled down to the bottom of the bed, and her clothes, or what she probably had been wearing, were thrown nearby on the floor. Her eyes were wide open in that blank, frozen stare that only the dead can display.

Donahue shuddered. It was always the eyes that got to her, the telltale sign of the finality of the act.

There was no blood visible in the photographs, a fact that had her really puzzled. Didn't Carrie Ann fight? Her one hand had been free. One would think that she could have done at least a little damage to her killer.

The clothing told a very different story. It was found on the floor right next to the bed. Her shirt was partially torn and inside out. Her bra had been opened, but the hooks were bent as if the person removing it had simply torn the two halves apart with a great deal of force. She'd been wearing a pair of blue jeans, and while the snap and zipper appeared to be intact, the pants legs were inside out, as though someone other than the victim had pulled them down.

Had Carrie Ann been drunk or drugged? It might explain why the body showed no signs of a struggle. Had her killer put her into the bed in that state? Had he been the one to undress her, or had she drunkenly removed her own clothing? And if she had been drunk, had she opened the door without thinking?

That could explain the absence of any signs of a break-in. But what did it say about the victim?

She studied the pictures, then skimmed over the ninety-day reports that were written and added to the file every three months for as long as the case was still open.

Twenty minutes later, she turned her head towards Gibson. "Did you get very far in these files?"

He kept his eyes on the road. "I got through most of it."

"So, what do you think?"

He smiled tightly. "I think there are a few ways we can go. For one, it says the boyfriend had an alibi."

Donahue nodded. "He was at home with his two roommates studying for an exam."

"Exactly. Doesn't that strike you as strange?"

"Not particularly. When I was in school, I pulled more than my share of all-nighters."

Gibson chuckled. "Maybe you did, but not everyone has your sense of commitment. Remember, we're talking about 3:00 am. Maybe his roommates were fast asleep. In fact, maybe they studied in different rooms." He looked over again. "He could have slipped out, gone over to her apartment, and something went seriously wrong." He shrugged. "It's certainly worth a follow-up."

She looked over at Gibson. "I'll read the entire file later when I get time, but I'd be willing to bet that they ruled the boyfriend out on the basis of the DNA."

"DNA?" Gibson asked.

Donahue nodded. Apparently he hadn't gotten that far in his reading.

"There was semen. And, of course, a lot would depend on where the semen was recovered, its motility, and the last time the boyfriend claims they had sex."

"Were the results ever entered into the system?"

Donahue nodded affirmatively. "Yeah, but they got no hits."

Gibson had no immediate response. He too had only read over the summaries, so he wasn't yet conversant with all of the details.

"I'd forgotten you worked on those kinds of cases," he said. "Maybe you're right. Maybe the boyfriend is a dead end."

Not wanting to dampen his spirits, she replied, "You may still be on to something. When we have time, I'll look it over carefully and see if there's something relating to the boyfriend that got overlooked."

They drove in silence for a while. Behind her sunglasses, Donahue felt her eyes starting to close.

"You got any ideas on what we should do?" he asked, looking over.

Her eyes popped open.

"Not yet. I'm just mulling it over in my mind."

Gibson smiled. He knew she'd been dozing off.

She sat up straighter. "But I will say this. Considering that her father is one of ours, I have a feeling that the case got worked pretty hard. I think our best bet might be to re-interview the people who were working at the nightclub where she hung out that evening before she was killed. Maybe someone saw something or thought of something after the fact that they never got asked about?"

"That's a long shot," Gibson said, "but it might be worth the effort."

Donahue continued, "Also, she had her left hand cuffed to the headboard. We can do a MO run and see if we can find something similar? That might give us a place to start."

A *modus operandi* computer run was a way to check if other crimes were on file that had similar characteristics or distinguishing features that would indicate a uniqueness pointing to involvement by the very same person or group.

Gibson smiled. "Not a bad start for someone who partied all night."

She allowed herself a self-congratulatory smirk. "Imagine how much better I'd be if you let me have a power nap."

Gibson smiled, switched lanes and then pulled off the freeway.

"Where are we headed?" she asked.

"I thought we'd stop and get a cup. You're paying, right?"

Gibson pulled into a Mobil station, took a five-dollar bill from Donahue that she reluctantly fished from her purse, then made his way into the building to get their coffees. Donahue stayed in the car, reopened the file, and began to read the pages more carefully.

As the father of the victim, the Lieutenant would know quite a lot about the case, and it wouldn't do to have her falter on any of the facts. You never knew when you might end up working for the man, or worse, when he might end up on your promotional board.

She chuckled to herself.

I should have gone home and gotten some sleep last night. God is making me pay for being such an easy mark.

* * * *

The West Los Angeles Division was basically a windowless facility with all the charm of a concrete bunker. Built during an era when security was foremost in the minds of its planners, the façade was a duplicate of a design that was created for the more active and dangerous divisions of the South and the East of the city. Not that WLA didn't also have the potential for security problems...it did. There were gangs throughout the division, generally fewer and less violent, and except for occasional flare-ups, they were usually under control. But the bulk of the geography within the division was made up of some of the most expensive real estate in the city: including Westwood Village, parts of the coastline, Bel Air, Brentwood, and Century City. For the most part, these were sleepy bedroom communities and eminently safe. But when something serious happened in the land of the wealthy, people paid attention, and what ensued in these sacrosanct communities often took on a heightened sense of importance. The Ryson murder was one of those cases, and the failure to solve it still rankled with those in power.

Both Gibson and Donahue clearly understood that this visit to the father was as much about raising the PR flag as it was about getting any useful information.

After parking and going into the station, Gibson knocked at the door to the Lieutenant's office and Ryson invited them in. Introductions were quickly made and he gestured them to a pair of wooden chairs placed in front of his desk.

Lieutenant Michael Ryson was a hard-bodied, unshaven man whose brown hair was unkempt. His green eyes were cold and steely, but the kind that missed nothing and remembered everything. His shirt was an oversized, white and blue pinstripe, open at the collar, tails untucked. His sleeves were rolled up to just above the elbows where they did little to conceal a large set of biceps, the product of regular weight training. His blue jeans were faded, slash cut at the knees, loose fitting over his square-toed, black leather boots. The look he presented was that of a Hollywood-hipster; a film industry wannabe, *de rigueur* for fitting in with the LA nightclub scene.

"We do a lot of undercover work in my unit," he said by way of a simple explanation. His eyes locked on Donahue's. "I understand you used to work here?"

He's done his homework, thought Donahue.

She nodded. "WLA patrol for three years, Sex Crimes downtown for two, back here for one in Homicide, on loan to RHD for a case, back here for another stint in Homicide, then the call to go to RHD full time."

"Congratulations," Ryson said with a smile. "Your rep is outstanding. Not many ever make it that quickly to the big-time."

Donahue tried to conceal her delight. They were off to a very good start.

Gibson leaned forward in his chair. He tugged at the crease in his slacks.

"Lieutenant, let me start off by saying how sorry we are that this happened to your daughter. We'll do everything we can to see if we can pull up a lead."

Ryson nodded. "I appreciate that Gibson. Your Captain speaks highly about both of you. I'm sure you'll do a good job."

Gibson nodded as a moment of awkward silence settled in between them. Ryson's reference to the Captain meant that the two men had talked, and Gibson suspected that they now had the case because Ryson believed that the detectives at WLA were getting nowhere, or worse, had lost interest.

"So, what would you like to know?" Ryson finally asked.

Gibson made a point of opening his pocket-sized notebook while he pulled out a pen from his inside jacket pocket.

"Did you get involved in the initial investigation?" he asked.

"Not officially, of course, but I got regular briefings from the Captain out here and later from my Deputy Chief."

Donahue was now sure he was conversant with every single fact. In his situation, she knew she would be too.

"Was there anything that you feel didn't get a good look?" she asked.

"Not really. Once they ruled out the boyfriend with DNA, I figure it had to be someone she met at the club. She went dancing that night with her girlfriends, but from everything I know about my daughter, she wasn't the type to pick up guys." He rubbed at the stubble on his chin. "And yet, since there wasn't any sign of a break-in, I can't really figure out what happened? But I guess the one thing I do know was that it had to be someone she knew."

Gibson looked up from his note-taking. "Would she ever leave her doors unlocked?"

Ryson shook his head. "Not a chance! She was raised by a cop, remember? She knew the risks of doing something like that. Her doors were always locked."

Donahue agreed. Most young women were careful when it came to that. She shifted her weight in the chair.

"So," she said, "you think an acquaintance or friend from the club might have followed her home?"

"Either that or someone she knew from school who lived in her neighborhood or was passing by when she got home from the club," he replied.

"Would she have invited him in?"

"Possibly, but the girls she went over there with said she was alone when she left the club, and as I told you, I knew my daughter pretty well. I doubt that she would have invited just any guy in, particularly late at night, unless she knew him really well."

"So what would make her open the door?" Gibson asked.

Ryson pursed his lips. "Not a day goes by that I don't think about that very question, but honestly, I've got no answer. It could have been an authority figure, but that's just speculation."

"You mean like a cop?" Donahue asked.

Ryson nodded. "The flexicuff always bothered me. She might open the door for a cop, but as far as I know, she didn't know any guys who were on the job." He shrugged. "So, my best guess is still that it goes back to the nightclub."

She had a thought, but didn't want to bring it up with him until she got a better look at the file. *But what if someone put something into her drink, then followed her to her residence?* She made a note to herself to check into that just as soon as she had the time.

Gibson creased his brow. "Did you do any nosing around at the club?"

"I started the very next night." Ryson squared his shoulders. "And of course, I was told to keep away, but I went in anyway…*undercover.* No one there knew who I was." He paused for a moment, lost in thought. "In fact, I was sitting at the bar one night when the two IO's from WLA wandered in. They stood right next to me but never figured out who I was."

Donahue leaned forward. "Did you come up with anything?"

"Not really. I began to peg all the regulars, and after awhile, I hit them all up. But no one remembers her being with anyone. Hell! Most of them never even saw her there. It was pretty much a big, dry hole."

Gibson sensed that they had all that Ryson had to offer, so he flipped his notebook closed and slid it into his pocket.

"I want to thank you for meeting with us, Lieutenant," he said. "I know this isn't pleasant, even after all this time."

Ryson nodded and Donahue could see the lines that pain had etched into his face.

"How have you been holding up?" she asked with concern in her voice.

"I get by," he told her. He crossed his arms and hugged his chest. "It may not be in your file, but my wife filed for divorce six months after our daughter's death." He shrugged. "I guess I'm probably to blame. I got lost in my own investigation, so I was never home to help her try to work our way through our loss."

"Where is she now?" asked Gibson. He decided it might not hurt for them to talk with her, too.

"She passed away last year," he said, and recognizing their shocked looks, he added, "Breast cancer."

Oh, man! thought Donahue. He's really been through the mill.

He shifted his glance back and forth between them. "I suppose my anger is still what keeps me going. It's why I'm still on the job."

Donahue had seen this type of reaction before. In the face of a violent crime, some people did things that were very self-destructive. And sometimes the anger they felt was the only thing left to hold on to. She just couldn't imagine how she would feel if something were to happen to the people she loved.

Gibson gave her *that look,* the one that said that it was time to go, so she gathered up her purse and they got to their feet.

"Thanks for your time, Lieutenant," Gibson said. "We have another appointment that we have to get to."

Ryson nodded and shook their hands.

"I appreciate your stopping by. I know I haven't been much help, but if you need anything, including manpower, just give me a call. I've got a lot of friends in the Department and I'm owed a lot of favors."

Gibson nodded. "We'll let you know if something comes up."

"I'd appreciate that."

They made their way out of the office and to the car.

"So what do you think?" Gibson asked. He started the engine and guided it past security and out to the street.

"I think he's right," she replied. "The key to this case is gonna be with the club."

"Maybe so, but let's not get tunnel vision on this. I want to look at the boyfriend again, just to be sure."

"We will. Just as soon as we get back, I'll tear apart the stuff on the DNA."

Gibson put on his aviator sunglasses. "Before we go back to the station, let's roll by the nightclub in Westwood. I'd like to get a look around before we start our interviews."

FOUR

Westwood Village, the community that grew up around the campus of UCLA, was for the most part composed of low-rise buildings full of retail stores, fast-food restaurants, and a couple of bars. And while it had changed somewhat over the years, it still retained the character of a sleepy little township, one that resisted the temptation to go high density like most of the other areas in the city.

Gibson parked their green Ford Crown Victoria in a red zone in front of a restaurant on Westwood Boulevard. They were a good two blocks from the entrance to the UCLA campus.

"Uh, oh!" said Donahue as she looked around. "What happened to *Club Darkness*? It's gone."

She glanced up at the new name on the wall above the awning.

"What's that sign say?" she asked. She shielded her eyes from the sunlight that was pouring in through the window. "*Café Bojule?* I wonder when the place changed hands?"

Gibson scanned the neighborhood. "Looks like another addition to the trendy wine-bar scene."

She looked over at Gibson and said, "We can go in if you want, but I doubt if we'll get a sense of what it was like back then."

"Let's try it anyway," he told her. "I spoke with the owner this morning. He says he'll be happy to show us around."

"Well, well! You're just full of surprises." She opened her door and climbed out of the car.

Gibson paused long enough to hang the car microphone cord over the visor to avoid a citation from the parking meter patrols. When he caught up to her on the sidewalk, he asked, "Ever go inside the club when you worked in this division?"

She shook her head no. "I worked days. They didn't open until long after I was EOW (end of watch)."

The restaurant appeared to be closed to the public, but they could see several people inside who seemed to be getting the tables set up for a lunchtime crowd. They made their way to the glass-paned door. Gibson knocked, and when a young woman turned and looked his way, he held up his shield and mimed for her to let them in.

The woman opened the door and pointed out the owner. Gibson sauntered over with Donahue in tow while the two of them casually looked around.

“Are you Mike Bishop?” Gibson asked.

“I sure am, detective,” he said, extending his hand. ”You’re right on time.”

While he and Gibson shook hands, he flashed a broad smile at Donahue. “So, what can I do for you guys?”

Gibson squared his shoulders. “We’re looking into an old case, a murder; about six years ago. The victim was last seen leaving this location, although it was a nightclub at that time.”

Bishop gave him a knowing look. “The Carrie Ryson murder?”

“You remember it?” Gibson asked.

“Sure, I do. May 21, right? Changed everything in the Village.” He pointed to a table. “C’mon, let’s sit and I’ll get you some coffee.”

They took seats at a table by the window, one that hadn’t been set up yet, and while they waited for a waitress to bring them the coffees, Donahue gave Bishop a fast appraisal.

He was in his mid-fifties, big and muscular, the bouncer type, but a little soft in the belly, likely a product of age. His nose was flat, his chin was broad, and his brown eyes missed nothing. They were sharp and clear and never stopped moving. He appeared to be a man who could take care of himself.

The coffees showed up, and when the server wandered off, Gibson said, “So how is it you remember the case?”

“And the date?” added Donahue.

“Are you kidding me?” Bishop frowned. “That was the only time anything like that ever happened around here. How could I forget it? The cops were in here every night for a week, talking to everyone. It really killed our business.” His eyes looked from one to the other. “It was never the same after that.”

He glanced over at Donahue, and for a moment, she thought she saw him give her a wink.

Bishop continued, "I was told that the victim was the daughter of a cop, which is probably why they worked it so hard." His face clouded over. "You could tell they were pulling out all the stops. We got questioned over and over."

Donahue remembered what it was like back then. A cloud of depression hung over the Department, and everyone at the WLA station house had volunteered to work on the case.

Considering how thorough the initial investigators had been, she was starting to get the sense that it wasn't very likely that Bishop could, at this late date, be expected to give them anything new.

"Were you working at the club that night?" she asked.

"I was a bouncer back then. I bought the club from the previous owner four years later when it was no longer a popular hangout." He leaned forward in his chair. "You might remember we had a shooting here in the Village a few years ago. The streets were packed with tourists then, and a housewife, out for a walk with her kids, got shot in the head." He bit his upper lip and shook his head in disgust. "Some punk gang bangers taking potshots at their rivals. What a fucking waste!"

"I remember it," said Donahue. "It was awful."

Bishop snapped his fingers and shrugged. "Just like that, it wiped out the Village as a tourist destination. People stopped coming, and businesses closed, so I made the owner an offer, and he took it. Six months later, I opened this place." He glanced around. "More in keeping with the changing times, don't you think?"

Donahue nodded. "It's very nice. Is the food any good?"

Bishop laughed. "You should try the risotto and scallops. I've got a chef who's the greatest. Come back sometime, detective. I promise you won't regret it."

Was he coming on to her?

She almost laughed. "We'll see."

Gibson chose that moment to get things back on track. "What was the layout like on the night of the murder?"

Bishop rose to the occasion. He turned in his chair and pointed across the room. "We had a long bar over on the far wall, and a dance floor out in the center. Around the edges of the room were tables and chairs. It was pretty much a college beer bar. A DJ played music, and the kids drank and danced. Sometimes there was a live band. That was about it."

Donahue looked around and tried to visualize a bar full of college kids. "Did you know the victim personally?" she asked.

"Just to talk to her at the door, not much more. She came in here once or twice a week, usually with a girlfriend or two. She didn't drink much, but man, she sure loved to dance."

Gibson looked up from writing in his notebook. "Any guys she was partial to?"

Bishop shook his head. "Not that I noticed, but she was fending them off all the time. She was a good-looking girl, very flirty, but I never saw her leave with anyone. To be honest, she didn't strike me as the type."

"Did she have a boyfriend at the time?" Gibson asked.

Bishop gave that some thought. "One time she told me she did, but she never brought him around. Leastwise, I never saw her with anyone who fits that bill. So, did he really exist? I don't know." He looked over at Donahue and shrugged. "Lots of times college girls will say that they have one."

Donahue tried to conceal her smile. She'd done that herself in her wilder years, even putting on a ring once or twice.

Gibson leaned in. "Were there any guys you know of who were particularly interested in her? Maybe someone who might have carried a grudge just because she turned him down?"

Bishop laughed. "Hells, bells, detective. It was like I said. She was constantly fending off guys. But no one seemed obsessed or anything like that." His mood switched to somber. "I'll tell you what I told the officers back then. I don't believe there was any connection between her killing and the bar, and I still think that's the case."

Donahue leaned up. "Did you have a security camera set up inside or out in the parking lot?"

"Unfortunately, no, but I sure wish we did. Maybe it would have helped."

Gibson put away his notebook. "Well, thanks for your time, Mr. Bishop. We appreciate the coffee."

Bishop nodded. "It's Mike, and you're welcome." He turned to Donahue. "Come back and try the scallops. I'm not kidding, they're to die for."

They got to their feet, and the three of them shook hands.

"If you think of anything else—" Donahue said as she handed Bishop her card, "—just give us a call."

"I will."

As they were heading towards the door, Bishop said, "This is probably nothing, but I should probably mention it anyway."

Both detectives stopped in their tracks and spun around.

"There was a guy who used to come in here a lot before the murder, but he stopped coming around right after it happened." He ran a hand through his hair. "For that matter, a lot of people stopped coming by, particularly the women, especially after word got out about what happened. Anyway, the guy I'm talking about was always hitting on the better-looking girls, a real alpha male. He came in a couple of times a week, had his own posse, too, but after that night, he never came back."

Donahue said, "When you say *after that night,* do you mean he was in here the night she was killed?"

Bishop shook his head. "I don't remember if he was in here that night or not. As I say, he was in here a lot. But I do know for sure that after that night he dropped completely out of sight. I don't know his name, but I know the guy had money. That's why I remember him so well. He was Arab, I think, early twenties. Very short beard and mustache. Drove a red Ferrari and he flashed a big roll of green. Always paid cash for the cover and drinks, and the staff said he tipped big, too."

Gibson had once again taken out his notebook and was writing it all down.

"Do you remember his name?" Donahue asked.

Bishop shook his head. "Sorry, I don't."

"Anything else you can remember about the guy?" Gibson asked.

Bishop scratched at his chin. "One time he got a parking ticket when he left his car in the red zone outside. Even tore it up in front of the cop who wrote it. And when he got to the door where I was standing, I heard someone warn him not to piss off the cops." Bishop fixed his eyes on Gibson. "He was a real punk, detective. He just laughed. Said he worked for the government or something like that and the cops couldn't touch him."

Bishop shrugged as if he was aware that he'd just wasted their time.

"I know it's not much, probably just a load of crap. I mean, since when do government jobs pay a kid enough money to buy a Ferrari?"

Donahue smiled. "Everything helps, Mike. Let us know if you think of anything else."

"I will," he said.

Gibson shook his hand. "By the way, did you ever mention this guy to the detectives at or around the time of the crime?"

He shook his head. "I didn't think of it then, and as I said, I don't even know if the guy was in here or not that night."

When they climbed into their car, Gibson turned to Donahue and said, "It's a long shot, but this Arab guy might be worth tracking down."

Donahue agreed. "What if this guy was employed by a Middle Eastern country? Like at a consulate or an embassy or something like that? He might have had some kind of immunity, and maybe that's why he said he wasn't worried about the cops?"

"You're reading my mind," said Gibson. "But let's not get too excited. The guy would have no reason to show up at the club if the females stopped coming around. That would make most guys go elsewhere."

Donahue had to agree. It wasn't much, but at least it was a lead that no one had ever checked out before.

FIVE

Once they were back in the squad room at the PAB, Donahue began a computerized search of parking citations handed out in front of the *Club Darkness* for the three-month period that preceded the Ryson homicide. She soon discovered that parking citations were not maintained in computerized form until more than a year after Carrie Ann was killed. Frustrated, she took her concerns to Gibson and asked him if he thought the matter was still worth pursuing? He cogitated for a while, then told her he believed it was worth a shot. He suggested that she give a call to R&I (Records and Information), to see if she could locate the hard copies of the individual ticket books.

This turned out to be no easy task.

After speaking with several supervisors in various divisions, she was finally given a number to call for a little-known storage facility that was leased by the LAPD. A supervisor there advised her that they had row upon row of boxes full of ticket books that were labeled by division and year. He invited her to come over to the warehouse, and he promised he'd have his people find the box she was looking for. By now, it was well after lunchtime, and Donahue wanted to spend a little time on the DNA portion of the case, but because she'd missed her breakfast, she had to do something about getting a bite to eat.

She wandered out of the building and over to a nearby Japanese restaurant where she ordered the famous *B lunch* to go. Back at her desk, she wolfed it down; a bowl of *miso* soup, *teriyaki* chicken, lightly battered *tempura* veggies, and a bowl of white rice.

As she discarded the remnants of her lunch in the trash, she recalled that she had promised to give Zach a call. Reluctantly, for she had yet to decide how she felt about the way things were going between them, she picked up the receiver and punched in his number.

It was almost a relief when the call went to voicemail. She took a deep breath and waited for the chance to leave her message.

"Hi, Zach," she said. "It's me. I'm sorry I missed you." She paused for a moment and wondered what more she should say. At last, she added, "Last night was fun, but we still need to talk. I'll call you later tonight."

She hung up the phone. *That should buy me some time to think.*

With her hunger pangs now satiated, she reopened the Ryson file and began to read it meticulously. She paid particular attention to the reports from SID (the Scientific Investigation Division), which she carefully searched for anything that the original detectives on the case might have overlooked.

Two hours later, she got to her feet and stretched. She was ready to give Gibson a full report, but when she looked over at his desk, he was gone.

She scanned the squad room, checked the sign-out board, then spoke to a couple of detectives, but no one had seen him since lunch. Curious, she made her way to the Captain's office where she found Tom Elwood sitting behind his desk. His large form was bent over a stack of paperwork, so she knocked on the doorframe and waited for him to look up.

"What's up, Jen?" he said when he finally acknowledged her presence.

"Sorry to bother you, Captain. I was looking for Gibson."

Elwood leaned back in his chair. "I got a message that he's on his way over to Cedars-Sinai. Apparently, his wife was taken ill, and she was being transported by ambulance to the ER over there."

Donahue's face dropped with surprise. Her partner's wife, Claudette, was his true soul mate. It had to be hitting him hard.

"Why didn't someone tell me?" she asked.

"I thought you already knew."

She raced for the door, checked out a black and white from the motor pool, and made her way over to Cedars in record time.

When she got to the ER, she flashed her badge to get past the security at the intake counter, then made her way inside to the nurses' station where she recognized a friendly face from previous visits and quickly learned that Claudette was undergoing a series of tests. The nurse believed that Gibson was with her.

Donahue asked what was wrong, but she was told that she'd have to check with the family. She completely understood. The badge could only get her so far, and a patient's right to privacy trumped everything else.

She was guided back out to the waiting room where she found an empty seat among a sea of ill people and settled in to wait for Gibson to come out.

SIX

When he first arrived at the Emergency Room at Cedars, Ulysses Gibson found his wife lying in a treatment room; her skin was pale and clammy and she was frightened to death. Several nurses and a doctor were talking to her, and when she saw him at the door, she broke into tears of relief. She wiped at her eyes as Gibson walked over to the bed.

"Is this your husband?"

The question was asked by a white-coated doctor no older than Gibson's niece.

"I am," Gibson replied, coming to a stop next to the bed. Claudette held out her hand for him to take. He took it, leaned over, and gave her a kiss on the forehead.

"How are you feeling, honey?"

The doctor answered for her. "From what we can tell, she may have had a minor heart attack."

Gibson felt his stomach drop and his legs begin to buckle. He grabbed at the bedside railing to regain his balance. It took a few seconds, but he managed to slip into cop mode, a state of mind that shut down his emotions and enabled him to focus on what was being said.

The doctor continued, "I want to run her through a quick series of tests.

"What kind of tests?" Gibson asked.

"Well, I'd like to begin with an ECG, sometimes called an EKG. Basically, it's an electrocardiogram. It records the electrical activity of the heart, including the timing and duration of each electrical phase in her heartbeat."

"Will I need an operation?" Claudette asked.

The doctor gave her a reassuring smile. "This test is non-invasive, Mrs. Gibson. We will attach a few wires to little pads that go on the outside of your chest. This will help us to listen to your heart, and it will enable us to determine if a heart attack has occurred or if one is developing. It will monitor changes in your heart rhythm, and that helps us to know what is going on."

Claudette looked over at her husband. Her eyes were still wet with tears. When it came to important decisions, she had always deferred to him.

"Ulysses, what do you think?"

He squeezed her hand. "You need to do this, Claudie. It won't hurt, and I'll be right here with you."

"Okay, but I want my doctor to know what's going on. Will you talk to her first and see what she says?"

"Her doctor is Linda Chang," said Gibson.

"Dr. Chang?" The young doctor scratched his head. "I don't think I know her?"

"She's over at UCLA," Gibson replied. "I'll give her a call, but I don't think we should delay the ECG." He looked at his wife. "Take the test, baby. I'm sure Dr. Chang will say that's what you should do."

Claudette sniffled. "Okay, I'll do it."

Gibson nodded to the doctor and motioned with his head towards the doorway. Once the two of them were outside, Gibson extended his hand.

"Ulysses Gibson," he said by way of introduction.

The doctor shook it. "Peter Castor," he replied.

Gibson lowered his voice. "I got a call from a nurse who said that she was being brought over here by ambulance. Can you tell me what's going on?"

Castor crossed his arms and kept his voice down.

"She's complaining of chest pains and pain in her lower jaw. These are classic signs of a heart attack. We need to run an ECG to see where we're at so we can figure out what to do next."

A note of concern crept into Gibson's voice. "And if the ECG shows a heart attack?"

"Then I'd probably order up a CAT scan to see if we can pinpoint the damage, and I'd like to know what caused it, too." His eyes locked with Gibson's. "Does she have a history of heart problems?"

"High blood pressure, but she's been doing her best to keep it under control."

Castor put a hand on Gibson's arm. He'd heard enough.

"Then let's not waste any more time. I don't want to run the risk of her going into cardiac arrest while we're standing out here in the hallway."

Gibson nodded. "Do you mind if I stay by her side?"

"Not a problem," said Castor.

Gibson slowly followed him back into Claudette's room.

* * * *

Two hours later, a nurse came out to the waiting room and motioned to Donahue. "They just got back from the CAT scan. I know you're not immediate family, but Detective Gibson and his wife have given us permission to bring you in to see them."

"How's she doing?" Donahue asked.

"They'll have to tell you," said the nurse, "but I've been told that she's resting comfortably now."

Donahue followed the nurse into an examination room where Gibson was standing next to his wife, still holding her hand. Claudette was under a blanket, and apparently, she was very relaxed.

"Hi, Claudie," said Donahue. She walked over to the gurney bed. "How are you feeling?"

Claudette slowly shifted her eyes to Donahue.

"Oh my! Jennifer! You didn't need to come down here. My goodness! Such a fuss over nothing."

"It's not a bother," Donahue said. She put a hand on Claudette's shoulder and gave it a gentle squeeze. There was just the hint of a slur in Claudette's words. She was clearly under sedation, probably given to relax her for the CAT scan. Her eyes were closed more than they were open, and her breathing was shallow and even.

"How'd you find us?" Gibson asked.

"Elwood," Donahue replied."You should have given me a call," she scolded.

"I was preoccupied, but you're right. I'm sorry."

She reached over and put her hand on his arm.

When Claudette appeared to have fallen asleep, she whispered, "So, how's she doing?"

Gibson lowered his voice. "She's had a heart attack, a mild one. The doctor says there's damage to one of the chambers, but fortunately, it's minimal."

"But she'll be all right, won't she?" Donahue whispered.

"There's a partial blockage in one of her arteries. It looks like she's going to need a coronary bypass." He ran his free hand through his thinning hair and Donahue could tell that he was genuinely upset.

"How soon?" she asked. Gibson didn't answer right away, and to her way of thinking, he appeared to be in shock.

"Are you okay?" she asked.

"It happened right out of the blue. She was over in this end of town, shopping at the Beverly Center Mall. I was told that she collapsed, and mall security called the paramedics. It's gonna take me a little time to wrap my head around this."

For a moment, it looked to Donahue as if he was going to cry.

"They want to stabilize her first," he continued, "so it may be a day or two before she goes under the knife. They're going to keep her here until it's done."

"That means they'll move her upstairs," Donahue said as she caught his eye again. "Did they tell you who's going to be the surgeon?"

"A guy named Kruger, or something like that."

"I'll find out about him for you."

Gibson gave her a questioning look.

"Zach," she said. "He works here. Remember?"

"Oh, yeah. Thanks, Jen. That will help."

They stood there silently until Donahue began to feel like a third wheel.

"I'm going to get out of your hair," she told him, seeking a graceful way to be able to leave. "I'll let Elwood know where you'll be."

"The case—" he started.

"Don't worry about that. You take care of your wife. I'll watch the store."

Donahue left the ER and dialed Zach on her cell phone as soon as she was outside. Her call went to voicemail once again.

"Zach, it's me. I need you to do me a favor. My partner's wife was admitted to the ER at Cedars. Heart attack. She's going to have surgery from a doctor named

Kruger or something like that. Can you check him out for me and let me know if he's any good? We need to know right away. Thanks, honey, I'll talk to you later."

She hung up the phone, glanced at her watch, and knew she'd have to hustle if she was going to make it to her therapy appointment.

This was turning out to be one hell of a day.

SEVEN

Donahue took a seat on the overstuffed couch while Dr. Shari Bauer, her therapist, sat in a comfortable armchair just across from her. Bauer had her shoes off, feet tucked underneath her, and a notebook and pen in her lap.

The office was on the second floor of a three-story building in Beverly Hills, just to the south of Wilshire Boulevard. As offices go, it was small, but tastefully decorated with contemporary furniture and warm fabrics. Bauer lived nearby, just a few blocks away, in an expensive and well-maintained condominium, so to get a little needed daily exercise, she often walked to her office to meet with her patients.

Bauer was a therapist that Donahue had met on the very first case she'd ever worked for RHD. At the time, Donahue had been impressed with Bauer's skill as a therapist, her sincerity about her work, and most of all her integrity with the secrets of her patients. So a year or so after the trial, Donahue began to see the doctor on a professional basis to help her sort out the problems she always seemed to have whenever she tried to settle into a romantic relationship.

Bauer lifted a wayward strand of hair and tucked it behind her ear. Her hair was long and brown with touches of gray which she still liked to wear in a ponytail.

"So? What's new, Jen?" she said as she opened her notebook.

Donahue settled back in the cushions of the couch.

"My partner's wife had a mild heart attack today. I was over at the hospital before I came here."

Bauer looked up over the top of her reading glasses. Her piercing blue eyes were firmly fixed on Donahue's face.

"Would that be Detective Gibson's wife?"

Donahue nodded. "I watched how the two of them looked at each other and how inseparable they were, and I'm embarrassed to say that it made me jealous."

Bauer frowned. "Jealous? In what way?"

"That their relationship was so good." Donahue shrugged and took a deep breath. "Watching them together made me realize just how much I'm really missing from my life. And it suddenly hit me that if I were the one getting ready to undergo a major operation, there wouldn't be anyone special there to have my back."

"But you're still in a relationship with your doctor friend, right?"

"It's not the same. As I told you before, our schedules are so screwed up that all we seem to do these days is meet a few times a week for sex."

Bauer shifted her weight. It was sometimes surprising to her how blind even the smartest patients could be to what was really at the heart of the matter. Donahue was no exception. She was focused on the effect that her problem had on her relationships without any realization of what the problem actually was. It was time to help her to identify the real issue.

"You keep blaming this on your schedules, Jen, and while I'm sure that the two of you are really very busy, I can't help but wonder why you don't find some way to make more time for yourselves?"

"That's the problem in a nutshell," Donahue responded. "We're both busy all the time, and…"

Her voice trailed off as the proverbial light bulb suddenly went on.

"Oh, I see." Donahue began to nod slowly. "You're asking me to consider why making more time for Zach isn't a bigger priority for *me*?"

Bauer took a sip from a can of soda that she kept on the end table next to her chair. She did so intentionally to slow the conversation down. Donahue was now asking herself the right first question, and she wanted to give her time enough to reflect on what the answer might be.

"So?" said Bauer a few moments later. "Why isn't it a bigger priority with you?"

Donahue shrugged her shoulders, but Bauer had no intention of letting her off the hook.

"C'mon, Jennifer. When I asked you that question what was the first thing that popped into your mind?"

"Because I don't really care?"

"Is that what you really think?"

"No, it's not. I care for him…"

"But…?" Bauer asked.

"I don't know," Donahue replied weakly.

Bauer placed her hands together, fingertips touching. She was going to have to take a more direct approach.

"Let me try this in another way. From what you've told me about your relationship with Zach and a few of the others in your past, I get the sense that you need the drama of the chase to turn you on. But once you've got a man's attention, once he's interested in you, you seem to lose all interest in him, and eventually, you pull away." She locked eyes with Donahue and cocked her head. "Does that sound to you like what you've been doing?"

Donahue gave it a moment's consideration. "Maybe, but I'm not the only one. Zach doesn't seem to be doing his part to make our situation any better."

Bauer nodded slowly. She loved it when a patient worked it through, and Donahue was certainly bright enough to figure things out on her own.

"We're talking about you, Jen, not Zachary. But don't you think it might be possible that he's taking his clues from your withdrawal?"

That was it in a nutshell, and now that Bauer had called her out and put it out there for the world to see, Donahue had to face the truth that she might have been the one responsible for sabotaging most or all of her relationships.

Bauer waited patiently for Donahue to speak, but Donahue, for her part, pulled her feet up next to her on the couch and folded her arms across her chest.

The body language of withdrawal, thought Bauer. *She doesn't like going here.*

"I suppose he could be reacting to my behavior," Donahue finally admitted with some reservation. "But if that's the case, then why do I lose interest like that?"

"That's an excellent question, Jen. In a normal relationship, one party usually connects more quickly than the other. But over time, a certain amount of pulling back is the norm. That gives the second party time to catch up emotionally, and it's then that the relationship really begins to take off."

"So, are you saying that all I have to do is just let things play out?" Donahue asked.

"Of course not," Bauer replied.

From Donahue's history, gleaned piece by piece over months of previous appointments, Bauer was still puzzled as to the real reason for Donahue's inability to emotionally connect. There must have been something in her past, something that she wasn't yet feeling safe enough to reveal. But recognizing what trauma had initially caused her relationship problems wasn't always necessary for her to be able to get past it. A change in behavior could come about when a patient could correctly identify the reservations that the initial trauma had caused.

Bauer went over in her mind what she knew about Donahue's life history. She had been raised in the San Fernando Valley in a two parent home with an older brother. She'd been a good student all her life, and with a degree in Sociology at the age of twenty-two, she secured a teaching credential and then spent a year teaching grammar school students before being laid off due to budget cuts. She joined the police department right after the layoff, and after working Patrol, Community Relations, a two-year stint in Vice, and two years in Sex Crimes, she transferred to West LA Homicide where she quickly developed a reputation for thinking outside the box. On loan to RHD for about a year on a major case that didn't work out so well, she went back to Homicide in WLA until Gibson worked his connections to get her back downtown to RHD. She'd been there ever since, and couldn't think of a single reason why she'd ever consider giving it up.

Donahue was single, very attractive, and had lots of opportunities for serious relationships, but in spite of her popularity with men, she had never really experienced the process of courtship.

"So what's wrong with me, then? Why do I feel the way I do?"

Bauer exhaled slowly. "Look, Jen. I usually prefer to let my patient's figure out what's going on, but in all of our conversations, I've yet to discover exactly what has caused you to make the choices that you do. It's clear to me that you tend to jump into relationships too quickly, and often the focus of those relationships is all about the sex. You're afraid to connect emotionally. You're suspicious of a partner's true motives, and you seem unwilling to take a chance by letting yourself experience a genuine love as opposed to just sex."

"Wow!" said Donahue slowly. "You don't mince any words."

"You wanted to know what I thought," Bauer replied. She sat up straighter, putting her feet back down on the floor. "I think you do what you do because you're afraid that you're unworthy and will never be good enough."

Donahue felt tears welling up in her eyes. No one had ever said those kinds of things to her before this moment, and while it hurt to be the target of such criticism, it hurt even more when she realized that Bauer had just pegged her to a T.

"I'm not judging you, Jen," Bauer continued, "but your pullback in relationships is based on your own fears; fear that you're not good enough to deserve this man, and a fear that he'll discover that you're not as strong as you hold yourself out to be."

Donahue felt her tears run down her cheeks..

Almost there, thought Bauer. She softened her tone and pointed out, "Somewhere in your early life, something happened to make you feel less than worthy to be loved, and you've carried that low self-image into your dating relationships. Instead of accepting that the motives of the men you've become involved with might, in fact, be genuine—that they see the best in you, you do what, Jen? What do you do?"

Donahue, who was still silently crying, reached over and grabbed a handful of tissues from a box that was on an end table by the side of the couch.

"Think it through," said Bauer. "You're almost there."

For the longest time, Donahue didn't look up. Then, in a timid voice, she said, "I guess I run."

At last. Bauer smiled. *She's finally figured it out.*

"And why do you suppose you run, Jen?"

"Because I know that they can't really love me."

Bauer left her chair, came over, and gave her a hug before sitting down on the couch next to her.

"But that's where you're wrong. You're very lovable. You're accomplished, intelligent, beautiful and charming. And most decent men are looking for someone exactly like you."

"Then they're not looking very hard," said Donahue with a forced smile that broke through her tears. "Because here I am."

Bauer smiled but intended to stay on point.

"Subconsciously, you tend to seek out men that you sense will not be the kind to commit."

"I do?"

"Yes, you do. And why does that come as such a big surprise? You do it for your own self-protection."

Donahue fought to control her trembling.

She gets it, Bauer thought, then added, "All this time you've been setting yourself up for failure because subconsciously, you don't want to take the kind of emotional risk that real love always requires. And why? Because with risk can come failure, and that would mean that you might get hurt."

Donahue dabbed at her eyes with the tissue.

"Your problem is fixable, Jen. It may take some work, but I promise you, it's fixable."

Donahue looked off, unable to hold Bauer's glance.

"Look at me, Jen," and when she did, Bauer added, "You're not a hopeless case."

Donahue put on a brave face and tried to smile.

"Well, now that we know what's broken, what do I need to do to fix it?" she said.

Bauer smiled. "When you go home tonight, I want you to sit down and make a list of all the things that are good about you. Everything you can think of. When you come in here next time, we'll go over your list, and I guarantee that you'll be surprised by what you've left out."

Donahue sighed.

"And that's more than enough for today," Bauer said. "You look tired, Jen. Go home and get some rest."

Donahue shrugged. She picked up her purse and got to her feet. "I guess it's not going to be easy to face my demons, is it?"

Bauer reached out and touched her arm. "Most of the time, it's not, but this is a step in the right direction, and we'll be facing your problems together."

Donahue thanked her, then made her way to her car, and once she was back on the road, she gave a moment's thought to reflect on her pending homework assignment.

This is gonna be an awfully short list.

EIGHT

After a sleepless night, during which time she was preoccupied thinking about what Bauer had told her, Donahue decided to stop dwelling on her own problems in favor of those of her partner and the Ryson case. Like all experienced homicide detectives, she had learned to box up her personal feelings to be able to focus on her work, so she quickly made use of that ability to bury her own problems. She would deal with them later when she had more time.

She arrived at her desk at seven forty-five. The squad room was quiet, hardly anyone around, and there was no sign of Gibson—not that she had expected him to be anywhere but at the hospital—but she wanted to tell him that she had heard from Zach and that the word on Dr. Anton Kruger was excellent; that Claudette would be in good hands.

But when he hadn't appeared by eight, she placed a call to his cell which Gibson picked up right away.

"How's she doing?" Donahue asked.

"She had a good night." He sounded exhausted. "She's still asleep. I was just getting my first cup of coffee."

"Did you spend the night with her?"

"Uh, huh," he said with a yawn. "I caught a few winks in a chair."

"Did you get in touch with your daughters?" Gibson and Claudette had two, both of whom were married and living nearby.

"I did. They're gonna get their kids squared away at school then both of them are gonna come by."

"That's good! So listen, I heard from Zach. Dr. Kruger is a great surgeon. Zach checked with the people who count, and Kruger's reputation is well earned. The surgical nurses who work with him say he's one of the best they've ever seen. You've got nothing to worry about."

"That's a big relief," Gibson told her. "I'm sure Claudie will be glad to hear that."

They spoke for a few minutes longer with Gibson saying that he'd be coming in later in the day. Donahue advised him not to push it, that everything was covered, and when she hung up, she was convinced that Gibby was going to be MIA at the office for at least a couple of days.

She picked up her cup of Starbucks and the Ryson murder books, then made her way from the squad room to a small interview room just off the main exterior hallway.

Before settling in, she went back into the squad to see if Shari Thompson had shown up. She found her seated at her desk, pouring through a series of emails on her computer.

"Knock, knock?" she said, as she approached the cubicle.

"Who's there?" said Thomson, going along with the joke.

"Hatch!"

Thompson spun around in her chair and smiled.

"Hatch who?"

Donahue smiled back. "God bless you!"

"Oh my God, Jen! That's awful!"

"I know, but I thought it was one your youngest might appreciate."

"Yeah, right!" Thompson shook her head. "I'm afraid his taste in jokes is just a bit edgier?"

"Oh?" Donahue gave her a questioning look.

Thompson smiled. "I got a call to drop by his school yesterday. Apparently, he told a joke that got him in trouble."

"Really?"

Thompson nodded. "Knock, knock?" she said.

"Who's there?" replied Donahue.

"Nicholas."

"Nicholas who?"

"Nicholas girls should not climb trees."

Donahue, eyes wide and face frozen, finally got the joke and smiled. "That's actually pretty clever," she said.

"Tell that to his teacher."

Donahue pulled a chair from the adjacent cubicle which just happened to be her own, and after moving it into Thompson's, she quickly sat down.

"But it's not that bad," said Donahue, referring to the *Nicholas* joke.

"No one has a sense of humor anymore, Jen, especially school officials."

Thompson was a stunning looking blond, five-four, with curves in all the right places. Her great good looks were an asset at times, particularly when she and Donahue worked the streets when both were assigned to undercover vice.

She and Donahue were longtime friends. They'd spent time together as partners when Donahue did her two years in Sex Crimes. Thompson, who worked Vice before Sex Crimes, still held the standing record for the arrest of Johns who'd been naïve enough to think that a woman with her beauty would be turning tricks out on the streets.

The two women had worked several major cases together, including one which involved the Russian mafia. It turned out to be an experience that served to bond them together for life.

Thompson, who'd been on vacation for almost two weeks, leaned back in her chair and smiled.

"So how are you doin' Jen? Been slumming around again?"

"I'm here aren't I?" said Donahue. She smiled at Thompson. "So, how was your time off? Did you get out of town?"

"I wish. I took the boys to Disneyland, and I hit the spa a few times, but that's about it. How'd you handle things while I was gone?"

"I've been paired with Gibby on a cold case, but it won't be for long. It's pretty old, and we're not coming up with any hot leads. Oh, and before I forget, Gibby's wife has likely had a heart attack. She's going through a lot of tests and Gibby is with her."

"Oh, my God? Is there anything I can do to help?"

"Maybe drop by and check up on them. Claudette's over at Cedars."

"I'll go on by on my way home."

Donahue nodded. It was then that she noticed the small potted fern on top Thompson's filing cabinet. The fronds were brown and wilted, a sure sign that it had recently given up the ghost.

"Hold on," said Donahue. She got to her feet and went into her own cubicle where she located a long piece of crime scene tape.

"I want to report a killing," she said as she came back around the partition. She draped the tape around the plant.

Thompson looked up and an embarrassed smile crept over her face.

"Oh, that! My *Fergie the Fern* apparently had a bad week while I was gone."

"Babe, that's a cold case if I ever saw one. Your *Fergie's* been dead for at least a month. Don't you ever water it?"

"I guess I skipped a few waterings." And when Donahue rolled her eyes in disbelief, Thompson conceded, "Okay. Maybe I missed more than a few."

They laughed together, then the two of them got busy exchanging news and gossip about people they had worked with in the past.

Once the small talk was out of the way, Donahue got down to the purpose for her visit.

"The cold case I'm working on is Carrie Ann Ryson. Does the name ring a bell?"

Thompson shook her head. "Not exactly. Was it one of ours originally?"

"It's a homicide/rape. The victim was the daughter of Lieutenant Mike Ryson. It happened in Westwood, six years ago."

"Oh, yeah," she said slowly. "I remember it now. A strangulation case; West LA. right?"

"That's the one."

Donahue gave her a thumbnail sketch of the facts, and when she was finished, she said, "You got any suggestions on where we should begin?"

Thompson leaned forward. "I presume there were swabs and samples? What did they show?"

"There were traces of semen in the mouth and motile sperm in the vaginal vault. The guess is that he ejaculated pretty close to or during the killing. A DNA profile was put together by the lab, and when we first got the results, we ran them through the statewide system, but nothing has turned up so far."

It was the standard operating procedure to notify the submitting agency if a match turned up in the database, either from the ones already in the system at the time the initial search was conducted, or any new ones that were added at any time after that.

Thompson crossed one leg over the other. "So that just means our killer has still managed to fly below the radar. Did the victim have a boyfriend?"

"She did. He had an alibi and a different DNA profile, so he wasn't the one who left his calling card behind."

Thompson shrugged. "I'm fresh out of ideas, Jenny. From what I can tell, you've covered all the scientific bases."

Donahue sighed. "Okay, then on to Plan B. Have you run across any other homicides where the victim was found cuffed and strangled? I know it's a long shot, and a MO run at the time was negative, but you and I both know that there's always a case or two that manage to fall between the cracks."

Thompson thought it over. "Nothing right on point, but I do recall that there was one case out in the Valley, maybe ten years back. A DA I knew had the case. A guy filed a missing person report, claimed his girlfriend took off one day and never came back. Six months later he was picked up on a kidnap/rape. The detectives out in Van Nuys got him talking, and one thing led to another. He copped to his girlfriend's death. Said he strangled her accidentally. They were into that bullshit about her being choked to enhance the effects of orgasm." Thompson shook her head. "What a crock! Anyway, he panicked when she died and buried her beneath a warehouse floor where he was assigned to work as the caretaker. When they dug up the body, they got a surprise. Turns out her thumbs were still cuffed behind her back, and a necktie was knotted around her throat."

Donahue shrugged. "What a fuckin' sick world we live in."

"Oh? I don't know. The handcuffing part doesn't sound so bad, but getting strangled into unconsciousness to enhance an orgasm seems a teensy bit over the top to me."

"And this is coming from the mouth of a woman who has been known to say, *I'll try anything once; then I'll try it again a second time just to make sure?*"

"Guilty as charged," conceded Thompson, "but even I have my limits."

Donahue wasn't sure about that. Between the two of them, Thompson was the wild one, and she often shocked Donahue with stories from her days as a single. She was married now, with three young boys, but Shari and her husband were going through what appeared to be divorce by a thousand cuts. They had separated twice during the last twelve months, and Donahue was pretty sure from the way Thompson was acting recently—more attention to how she looked, and how she comported herself around men—that they were probably separated once again. And if that were the case, she would soon be adding more experiences to her storytelling repertoire.

"Well, thanks for the info about that other case, Shari, but it doesn't sound like what I'm really looking for."

"I would agree, but I'm just throwing it out there." She slowly reached for her coffee cup which was on the desk behind her. "Tell you what, though. The Captain's got me going to a meeting with reps from all of the divisional homicide units. If you like, I can ask around and see if anyone remembers any homicides more closely aligned with the one you told me about."

"I'd appreciate that," said Donahue. "As soon as I get some time, I'm going to run a MO check on non-homicide rapes. I'm gonna look for anything over the last six years where the victim got tied by one hand to the bed."

Thompson rolled her eyes. "You can bet you'll end up with more than a few. Tell you what, though. My schedule's light this morning. I can run it for you if you like? You meet me for lunch, and I'll have your results."

"Thanks, Shari. I'll owe you one." Donahue started to get to her feet.

"Don't thank me yet," said Thompson with a wink. "You've been here twenty minutes and I haven't heard a word about your love life."

Donahue smiled and shook her head. "Nothing to talk about."

Thompson laughed. "That's BS, and you know it. You've always got a guy in the wings. So spill it, sister. Are you still getting along with Doctor Zach?"

"Yeah," she said half-heartedly.

"Uh, oh! You don't sound like that's a good thing?"

"Long story," said Donahue. She was thinking about what Bauer had said to her and she was not about to dish to Thompson how bad it made her feel. She slowly backed her way out of the cubicle, but Thompson wasn't done with her cajoling.

"You need to remember, Jen, I live vicariously through singles like you."

Donahue lowered her voice to shift the subject quickly.

"Did you leave your wedding ring at home today?"

Thompson looked at her hand, then nodded. "He took off again a week ago."

Donahue nodded sympathetically. She was a little surprised that Thompson hadn't given her a call when it happened.

"It might be time for you to start talking with a lawyer. Then again, maybe you're better off right where you are."

When Thompson gave her a questioning look, Donahue added, "Obviously, you've forgotten how much it sucks to be dating."

Thompson smiled. "With three small boys and a husband who's never around, I've even forgotten how babies are made."

Donahue bit on her lower lip to smother a smile.

"Okay, kiddo. I'll see you for lunch, and we'll talk it all out over a glass or two of wine."

NINE

When she got back to her desk she found a note from the supervisor she'd spoken to at the Records and Information Division the day before. His people found the box of citations from West Los Angeles Division for the year of the murder, and he invited her to come by and go through them.

She checked in with Captain Elwood, her boss, filled him in on Gibson's whereabouts and Claudette's current condition, then drove over to the address for the warehouse.

It was another warm, sunny day in LA and she hated the idea of spending any time at all in a cold, dusty warehouse. She could only hope that the box of citations would be small and that she'd be in and out in record time.

But sadly, that was not to be.

Once at the check-in counter, she was presented with a large, cumbersome box full of bundles of citations. She sighed and her shoulders drooped. She now knew without a doubt that her morning was going to be entirely shot.

The supervisor was not about to let the full box go, so she had no choice but to open it there. She cut the tape, pulled open the cardboard, and gasped in surprise. There had to be ten thousand individual citations… *but* they seemed to be organized by month.

She located the month of the murder, a stack that was a good five inches thick, and decided that a hand search was going to be hopeless. It was then that she noted that the tickets were actually sub-grouped by reporting district—an interdivisional geographic breakdown done by the separate areas of patrol. She couldn't help but smile. From her time in patrol at WLA, she knew the number of the district she was looking for, so she took a seat at a nearby table and slowly opened the stack.

Perhaps this wouldn't be so bad after all?

Within a few minutes, she located the group that would have the citations from the area of patrol that included the address for the *Club Darkness*. The stack was only about one inch thick, a fact that made her smile with relief. She thumbed through it, looking first at the street locations, but then she decided that it might be faster to look at the make of the car—a Ferrari was what had been mentioned, but out of an abundance of caution, she intended to cull out all of the citations that she could find for any and all high-performance automobiles. This included Lamborghini's, Maserati's, Porsche's and Corvettes.

Twenty minutes later, frustrated and disappointed, she rolled her eyes. There were no citations for anything even close to a Ferrari handed out during the month of the murder.

Sure once again that she would be there all day, she opened her cell phone and placed a call to Thompson, explained her situation, and begged off the lunch date until later in the week. Then it was back to the box of citations where she recovered the stacks for the two months preceding the crime and began the process again.

Two hours later, after killing half an hour on change of scenery breaks—she tended to walk around when thoroughly bored—she found a citation for a red Ferrari with an address next door to the *Club Darkness.*

She smiled to herself. *This has to be it!*

She kept the citation separate from the others, and after reviewing the rest from the current stack, she returned all the others to the storage box. There was only the one, and she signed out for it before heading back to her office.

By the time she arrived at her desk, she was tired and in need of a good hot shower. It was just after three p.m., and she was starving for having skipped lunch. She debated with herself about whether or not she should just call it quits for the day and get something to eat?

Her stomach cast the deciding vote, so with her energy fading fast, she locked the citation in her desk and signed herself out on the board. This was a common practice among the members of RHD, a holdover from the past. If they were off to a particular location—like court or an interview—they would list it in large letters on the big board so that others in the squad who answered the phones would have some idea of where they could be reached.

Donahue wrote *EOW* (end-of-watch) next to her name. She'd already given the city eight straight hours, so she left the station and drove to a restaurant where she grabbed a meal-to-go.

* * * *

After picking up an order of orange chicken and fried rice from a Chinese takeout, she went directly home. She kicked off her shoes, poured a glass of Merlot, grabbed a quick shower, washed her hair, then slipped on a robe for comfort. She zapped the takeout dinner in the microwave, then settled on the couch in her living room. She wolfed the dinner down while she slowly sipped her second large glass of wine.

She hadn't heard from Gibson all day, so she called him on his cell, intending to leave a message, but to her surprise, he actually picked up.

"Hey there," she said. "How's she doing?"

"Hang on," he told her. She listened to what sounded like his footsteps, and she had the distinct impression that he was moving to where he could speak to her without his being overheard.

"Sorry about that," he finally said. "Claudie's resting, and I didn't want to disturb her." She heard him take a deep breath and she instantly knew that the news would not be good.

"She's got a buildup of plaque in her arteries, and one of them has narrowed where it leads into the heart. They're going to do a coronary bypass, Jen." His voice caught in his throat. "They're waiting for approval from our HMO. The doctor wants to do it tomorrow, so I guess that's where it stands."

Donahue leaned back on the couch. A coronary bypass was a no-nonsense, dangerous operation. *This was not good. Gibby must be at his wit's end.*

"Claudette is a strong woman, Gibby. She'll come through this okay, you'll see."

"I hope so." And then, in a rare moment of emotional candor, he added, "I don't know what I'd do without her?"

"Well, that's not something you need to worry about. Your wife is tough as nails. She'll be up and around in no time."

"I guess so," he said. "This doctor, Anton... I think his last name is *Kriegler...* or Kruger? That's it! Anton Kruger. Anyway, I like him. He said she's an excellent candidate for the surgery, so I guess we'll just have to wait and see."

Donahue had planned to give him a progress report on what she had done on the Ryson case but decided that this was not the right time to burden him with work. He clearly had enough on his mind.

"I thought I'd pop over tonight and say hello to you guys, that is if it's okay?

Can I bring you anything or something for Claudette?"

"We're fine, and I appreciate your offer to stop in, but it might be best to do it after the surgery. I think the girls are coming by tonight with our grandkids, so it's gonna be a little crazy."

"I understand, but you call me when she goes into surgery. I plan to hang with you in the waiting room."

She thought she could hear him smile.

"I'll call. I promise. And I'll tell Claudie that you sent her your prayers."

Donahue laughed. "That's exactly what I was going to tell you next. You beat me to it."

She heard him chuckle, "I wouldn't be the best Detective you ever studied under if I couldn't anticipate what you were going to say."

Once she hung up, she cleared away the remnants of her dinner, then placed a call to Zach. When he didn't answer, she left a message asking him to call.

She poured herself one last glass of Merlot, then moved into her bedroom and popped *Notting Hill,* into her DVD player. It was her favorite romantic comedy. She needed something to boost her spirits, and that was a movie that always gave her hope.

But five minutes later, wine still untouched and utterly exhausted, she closed her eyes and fell into a deep sleep.

TEN

Her alarm went off at five am.

Donahue pulled herself out of bed, quickly slipped on a Gortex running suit, slid her feet into a pair of cross-trainers, placed her iPod headset into her ears—and yes, she still used an iPod—then set off on a five-mile run through her neighborhood, a residential zone that abutted the Beverly Center Shopping Mall.

The air was clear and crisp, and the sky was free of clouds. It promised to be another warm and sunny day in the one-time desert basin of the city of Los Angeles.

As she eased into the rhythm of the run, she was grateful that she'd finally made the commitment to get back on an exercise schedule. Two weeks without running had added three pounds to her waistline, not to mention the havoc it wreaked to her sense of well-being.

For Donahue, running was her way to deal with stress, a ritual she'd embraced since her time in high school. It gave her the lift that she needed each day to face the harsh realities of a career that was poisoning her faith in her fellow man.

By mile three, her lungs were burning, and she made herself a promise that she'd cut way back on the occasional smokes that she used when highly stressed or out socializing. By mile five, she was gasping for air, and the promise of cutting back was sincerely replaced by a firm decision to stop...*right now*...cold turkey.

Back at her condo by six am, she showered, grabbed a breakfast of oatmeal, fruit, and two pieces of toast with jelly, then made her way downtown to her office, intent on getting to the heart of the citation mystery.

When she arrived at the squad room, she half expected to find a message on her machine from Gibson, but when she listened to what was there, there wasn't one, and it gave her just the barest twinge of relief. No news was good news, and she was therefore free to surmise that Claudette had enjoyed a restful night, for if she hadn't, Donahue was convinced that she would have heard something by now.

She unlocked her desk, slid her gun into the drawer, and pulled out the Ferrari citation. It had been issued to a model that was red in color for parking in a curbside red zone.

She sat down at her computer, logged into the DMV police website using her ID, then punched in the number of the license plate. A few seconds later, the information she was looking for popped up on the screen. The owner was listed as *Prestige Motoring, ltd.,* a corporation doing business out of the nearby city of Pasadena.

She then *googled* in the *Prestige* name, and came up with their address and telephone number. To save time, she called the business and let the phone ring until someone finally picked it up.

"Prestige Motoring," said a young female voice.

"Hi, there. This is Detective Donahue with the Los Angeles Police Department. I need to talk to someone about a car that you people leased to a person of interest about six years ago."

"Hold on," said the young girl, and a moment later, a male came on the line.

"This is Brett Harris. Can I help you?"

Donahue identified herself, gave him the license number, and told him she needed a name.

"I'm sorry, Detective, but you'll have to get a search warrant for those records."

"I will, Mr. Harris if you insist, but I'd like to save you some time. I'm working a homicide investigation, not a car theft or anything like that. We think it's possible that the person who leased that Ferrari from your company might have seen something that could help us catch the killer of a teenage girl. All I need from you is his name and a number where I can reach him. I can keep you completely out of it if that would make you feel any better?"

There was a hesitation on the other end of the line, so Donahue continued, "As I say, we're just trying to run down every possible lead. The dead girl was a college student and only nineteen."

Harris cleared his throat. "I've got two teenage daughters, Detective. I'll see what I've got. Hang on."

She smiled to herself while the call went on hold. Good thing good people still cared enough to help.

He was back on the line in under a minute.

"That particular Ferrari was leased to Prince Muhammad bin Abd al Aziz."

"Can you possibly spell that name for me?" she asked.

He laughed. "It's just like it sounds."

She smiled. "I can't even pronounce it."

He laughed again and then spelled it out.

"So Prince is his first name?" she asked.

"Nope. Apparently, that's his title," Harris told her. "It's my understanding that he was a member of the Royal Family of the House of Saud…as in…*the oil-rich nation of Saudi Arabia.*"

Donahue frowned. That opened up a whole new can of worms.

"Do you have an address or phone number for him on file?"

"I've got a number," Harris said, "but it's probably no good. He had the car for less than a year when we got a call to pick it up. We were told the family left the country. Not sure where they went. We sublet the car to someone else until the end of the lease."

Donahue thought it over. "Well, let me have that number anyway. I can always check with the phone company and see where they sent the final bill."

He read off the number.

"I hope that helps you out, detective. As I said, I've got two daughters. I don't know what I'd do if anything ever happened to either one of them. God bless you for the work you do."

Donahue was touched. "Thanks, Mr. Harris. I'll be in touch with you if we need anything else. And hey, thanks for making my job that much easier."

After she hung up, she ran the name of Prince Muhammad bin Abd al Aziz through the Department of Motor Vehicles, but she didn't get a hit.

Okay, so he didn't have a driver's license. Or, maybe what he had was an international one. So how in the world would I find that out?

She decided to try a different approach. She googled the Prince's name, but nothing popped up. She tried *Facebook* and *MySpace*, but the results were the same.

Frustrated, she got up from her desk and joined a few dozen cops and civilian employees who were grabbing a smoke just outside the front doors. And while she was technically true to her new commitment to go cold turkey, she refrained from lighting one up, but somehow managed to inhale enough second-hand smoke to satisfy her immediate craving.

Okay, she rationalized, so I'm quitting lukewarm turkey. It's still progress....

By the time she returned to her desk, she had an idea. She picked up the phone and called Gibby.

"Hey," she said. "Has she gone into surgery?"

"Not yet. We're still waiting. I've been told that the HMO is dragging their feet about giving us authorization for the procedure. I've called them myself twice, but they say it's under review." She heard him sigh. "It's really pissing me off, Jen. Her life is on the line, and all they seem to care about is how much it's going to cost."

"You think they'll approve it today?"

"Doesn't look like it, and the nurse tells me that Kruger is booked up pretty heavily with other surgeries, so if he shifts things around, it might still be a few days off."

She shook her head in disgust. The health care system was so broken. It made her angry and sick.

"Well, just hang in there, Gibby. I'm sure it won't be much longer."

"I hope you're right," he said.

She decided to bring up their case. It might help Gibson get his mind off the problems with the HMO.

"Have you got a second to talk business?" she asked.

"Yeah, sure. What's up?"

She filled him in on the traffic citation and what she'd learned, but she was up against a wall when it came to getting a photo of the Prince.

"So, I was wondering if you'd mind calling your buddy in Washington...you know, Don Flynn? Maybe he can get us a photo?" she said.

"Sure, I can call him. But he's your friend, too."

"I know, but I have the feeling that the last time I called him on the Russian case, I sort of used up his patience and goodwill."

"He's not that way, Jen, but sure, I'll give him a call. He'll want to know about Claudie and how she's doing. Can you give me the spelling of the Prince's name?"

She did.

"I'll call him right now and ask if he can get us a picture. And if so, I'll have him send it to you directly. Okay?"

"Perfect," she said. "Say 'hi' to Don and to Claudette for me."

"I will."

"And let me know if you need help with the HMO."

"Thanks for the offer, but you probably have no more clout than I do."

"Hey," she said, feigning hurt feelings. "I'm pretty good at yelling offensive insults to uncaring minions." She could hear him laughing until the line went dead.

She made her way to the Captain's office and gave him an update on the Gibson's situation and on the progress on the Ryson case. Elwood, who was himself an early riser, listened intently but could offer no suggestions as to what to do next.

Back at her cubicle, she checked the citation and suddenly had a thought. She located the name and the serial number of the officer who handed it out, and after spending twenty minutes on the line with a clerk in Personnel, she finally tracked him down to his current assignment at the substation at Venice where he worked patrol.

A call to the Venice Watch Commander's office landed her the cell phone number for Policeman Grade II, John Wesley Tate, who happened to be on the day watch schedule.

"John Tate," he said when he answered his cell phone. "Who's this?"

"Hey, John. We've never met, but I'm Jennifer Donahue. I'm a detective working out of RHD. Have you got a moment? I want to ask you about an old case from six years ago."

"Six years?" He laughed. "Take a shot, detective. I hope I can remember that far back."

"I know what you mean. Listen, this is a long shot, and I'm not even sure you're the one I'm looking for, but back on September 15 of that year, you issued a citation to a vehicle for parking in a red zone in front of a place called *Club*

Darkness—"

"A citation?" He started to laugh again. "*Jesus,* detective, no disrespect intended, but do you really expect me to remember a citation?"

"Normally, no, but this was for a red Ferrari, and as I understand it, the guy tore up the citation in front of you and—"

"Oh, yeah," he said slowly. "I do remember that incident. That guy was a real asshole. Go ahead. What's your question?"

"An asshole, huh?" Donahue smiled. "So what do you really think about him?"

Tate was silent, and she could instinctively tell that he was smiling.

"Not to mince words, he was a super asshole; an arrogant little prick, and a *pederast.* But other than that, he probably was a very nice guy."

"A pederast? Are you telling me this guy had sex with boys?"

"I guess that might be a slight overstatement," he said with a chuckle. "I just heard that word for the first time a few days ago, and this seemed like the perfect opportunity to use it as part of an insult."

Donahue laughed so loudly that other detectives in the squad room stopped what they were doing to see what was going on.

When she caught her breath, she said, "You're killing me, John. Why don't you just fill me in on what you remember about the incident?"

"There's not much to tell. I was just finishing up with a traffic stop, and this Ferrari pulls up and parks in the red zone. The guy got out in front of me and made his way towards the club. I called him back told him to move the car, but he turned his back on me and started talking to members of his posse. And when it became clear to me that he wasn't going to move the car, I wrote him a ticket, slipped it under his wiper, and called for a tow."

"Sounds reasonable," said Donahue.

"I intended to give the little prick an attitude adjustment by making him pay for the tow and the storage fees, but while I was on the horn to Central City tow, he walked back to his car, picked up the citation, and tore it up in front of me."

"Cocky little bastard," Donahue said. All cops were familiar with the type.

"By then I was pissed, so I detained him, asked for his license, and he produced a card, issued by the Government of Saudi Arabia. He told me I had no right to detain him, that he had diplomatic immunity, and when that checked out, he took his card back and went into the club."

"So he was the real deal?" she asked, unable to keep the surprise from her tone.

"Turns out he was. His father was the Saudi Ambassador to the US, and his *asshole son* was a legitimate consular employee. My Sergeant came out to the scene, made a few phone calls, then told me to drop it, so I had to let him go."

"Did your copy of the citation get submitted to the City Attorney?"

"It might have been, but as I said, there was no way to move it forward, and no one ever subpoenaed me to go to court on it."

"Well, thanks, John. I appreciate your time."

"Can you tell me what this is all about?" he asked.

"An old homicide, the Ryson case. You may even have worked on it at the time?"

"I sure did," he said. "We all got pressed into doing a neighborhood canvass. Several times in fact. So...*Wait a minute?* Are you telling me that little dirtbag had something to do with the murder?"

"Don't know. The Ryson girl was at the club the night she got killed. He used to hang out there, as you know, so we're just checking it out. Maybe he knows something that we could use?"

Tate smirked. "Well, good luck getting anything out of the guy. He's a real hard case. Have fun."

"You're probably right. So, thanks again for your input. I'll let you know if something turns up."

"Anything I can do to help, just let me know. That Ryson case still sticks in my craw."

"It does for all of us," she told him, and then she rang off.

* * * *

Donahue grabbed a lunch down the street from the PAB at a Japanese restaurant called *Aoi*. She ordered the B special—teriyaki chicken with stir-fry vegetables and a cup of hot tea for $5.25. Then it was back to the building with a stop outside for a quick smoke. She agonized, then rationalized, that one half a cigarette after lunch was not a real breach of her earlier vow to quit.

After all, wasn't a half a cigarette still progress?

After that, it was up to her office to once again pour through the Ryson file.

Most people thought the job of a detective meant solving your cases by going out on interviews. But really, the key to solving any case was information control, and that involved a great deal of reading. Once the facts were at your fingertips, a good detective could organize the data in such a way that what was important would stick out like a stop sign.

Donahue was a firm believer in that principle, so she carefully read and reread the Ryson file, took notes on the facts, and tried to put together a cogent timeline. But before she was finished, about three in the afternoon, she was suddenly interrupted by a call from Donald Flynn.

Flynn was the Assistant Director of the Secret Service. Years before, he'd done a stint in the LA Office as head of their Criminal Division. In that capacity, he had cases with the LAPD and members of the DA's Office. Lasting friendships had been formed, and it was not uncommon for those ties to lead to requests for assistance from each other that were usually and willingly followed through.

"So you and Gibby are working together again?" He said it with warmth.

"That's right, Don. It's nice to talk to you. I'm guessing Gibby gave you a call?"

"Please, Jen. You know he did, and for your information, you haven't overtaxed your welcome with me."

She laughed. "I knew I hadn't, but between us, I thought having Gibby call you might help him keep his mind occupied while he waits for Claudette to go into surgery."

"Ha! Remind me to never underestimate your way of seeing the bigger picture."

"You're too kind."

"He told me about Claudette." A somber note crept into Flynn's voice. "Can you do me a favor? I know he's got enough to worry about, but if you get any news about her, would you mind keeping me in the loop?"

"I'd be happy to," she said.

"Good, so now that we've got that out of the way, let's talk about Prince

Muhammad bin Abd al Aziz. Gibby was a little vague about where this guy fits into your investigation, so I was hoping you could tell me what's going on?"

Donahue opened her notebook, pulled out a pen, and started to doodle while she talked.

"The Prince was known to hang out at a club in Westwood Village around the time that a cop's daughter was last seen in there. A few hours after she left the club, she was murdered. We don't know for sure if he was in there that night, but if he was, we want to pick his brain and find out if he knows anything."

Flynn was silent for a moment. "Any indication that he might have been involved in your murder?"

Donahue was smart enough to know that the question was loaded. If she said yes, she could sense that a door might be shut. On the other hand, Flynn was a guy that Gibson completely trusted. She decided to go with honesty and see where it went.

"Not really, but the guy was a player, and the girl was in there a lot, so we can't rule him out. But at the moment, we have absolutely nothing to connect him to her. We're just fishing, so I hope that answers your question."

"It does," Flynn said, "and thanks for being honest." He seemed to take a moment to gather his thoughts. "The bad news is that the guy's got immunity. Six years ago his father was Ambassador to the United States. He's still in the ambassadorial service, and he's one of three prominent members of the Royal House of Saud who are in line for a shot at being the next King." He cleared his throat. "I'm sure you understand what that means. His kid had diplomatic immunity while he was on our soil, and if he was involved, while we might be able to take it up privately with the family through the Department of State, it might not be in the national interest to push it too far."

"Are we talking about oil?" she asked.

"Oil, our Middle Eastern alliance, national security, weapons contracts, on and on. I'm sure you get the picture."

Donahue sighed. She had hoped that this line of inquiry would be routine, but instead, it appeared that she had run into a giant buzz saw.

"I recognize the obstacles, Don, but at this point, all I want is a photo and a chance to ask him some questions. As I said, we've got nothing to connect him with the crime, but maybe he'll say something that could point us in the right direction."

"Did you try googling him to get a photo?" he asked.

"I did, but there were none. Apparently, he's pretty good at avoiding publicity."

Flynn finally relented. "Okay. It probably can't hurt. I've got a picture for you. I'll get it scanned and sent to your cellphone. And as for talking to him? Good luck! It's my understanding that he and his father are working at the Saudi embassy in Istanbul, Turkey. The old man is still an Ambassador there, and the kid still has the diplomatic family protection. And for what it's worth, my sources over at State are saying that he's a spoiled little royal with delusions of self-importance, so don't count on his giving you a whole lot of cooperation."

"I'll keep that in mind, Don. Thanks for your help. And for what it's worth, if we decide to go any further with this line of inquiry, I'll let you know."

"Fair enough."

She gave him her cell phone number and shortly after that, she rang off, not sure what her next step was going to be.

ELEVEN

It was back to reading the files and pouring over the case file details, but Donahue had a sinking feeling that she was getting nowhere fast. It seemed from the witness interviews that Carrie Ann Ryson was just what you'd want in a kid; grounded, responsible, and smart. Her friends all said that she was very well liked; a good student, a responsible drinker, and not the kind to engage in one-night-stands. She lived alone by choice and cared for her boyfriend, although she didn't really believe that he was *the one.* She was friendly when she went out partying, but not overly or suggestively flirty. To put it simply, she was just a nice girl who liked to have a little fun.

Pretty normal, thought Donahue. *A typical college age girl.*

On the night of the murder, she'd gone to the *Club Darkness* with two girlfriends; Mia Amoretti, a sorority sister, and Jenna Sue Corliss, a close friend from her Spanish class. They got to the club at eleven p.m., ordered a round of Bud Light's, then made their way to the dance floor where the three girls danced by themselves. Four or five songs later, according to Amoretti's statement, she and Jena Corliss left the dance floor while Carrie continued to dance. When asked if the victim had danced with a particular boy, both girls said that that they hadn't paid attention. They'd met up with a group of boys from school who were standing over by the bar. Both girls said that they lost track of Carrie until sometime later—at about one a.m.— when Carrie walked up and said that she was leaving. She gave both of her girlfriends a hug and said she'd see them around the next day.

"She wasn't drunk that I could tell," Amoretti had been quoted as saying, "and for sure she didn't leave with a guy."

Jena Corliss's statement offered a tantalizing clue. In it, she said, "She told me she had called for a cab, so I knew that she would get home safely."

Donahue put down the murder book and gently rubbed at her eyes. On the verge of getting a headache, she wondered, not for the first time, if she needed to get an eye exam?

She leaned back in her chair and closed her eyes. Thoughts were swirling around in her head and she needed to put things into perspective. It appeared to her that the victim's time in the club that night had not resulted in picking up a guy. Of course, it was possible that someone had been watching her, maybe even followed her home. He might have surprised her, then attacked and killed her. But it was just as likely that she was confronted by a total stranger: someone who saw her get out of the cab and followed her up to her door.

It was back to the interview section of the book where she located the statement from the cabbie. The detectives had tracked him down through the logbook of calls for service on that night. According to the cabbie—one Akil Mubarak, an Egyptian immigrant—she got into his cab at one-fifteen a.m., alone, and was driven directly to her apartment. The cabbie let her out on the street in front of her building, and *at her request*, he waited and watched until she made her way to the staircase which led to her front door. He didn't see anyone else around, and when asked about her level of sobriety, he stated that she wasn't really drunk, although she slurred a few words and appeared to be just a little bit high.

Now that was interesting. *Was she, in fact, intoxicated?And why ask the cabbie to wait? Was she worried about someone or something?*

That would be a question to discuss with her father. Perhaps, when she traveled alone at night, it was her custom to take extra precautions. If so, then she really was a very savvy girl.

The detectives reported that the cabbie had submitted a DNA sample and was cleared of involvement in the crime. Donahue sighed. The cabbie was a dead end lead, but at least that line of inquiry was solidly closed. She wondered if it might be worth interviewing Amoretti and Corliss again? A lot of time had gone by since the night of the murder, and perhaps they thought of something new, or heard of something helpful after the fact?

Probably not worth it, she thought, *but when it came to old cases, you just never knew for sure.*

She would have to mull that over in the back of her mind because as she thought about the citation, she wanted to determine if it ever went to warrant? If the ticket somehow made it to warrant, that might give her some leverage if she ever tracked him down for an interview.

She called the Court Clerk's Office in West Los Angeles, identified herself, and asked the employee on the other end of the line to run the citation number. She wanted to know if it was ever officially dismissed? It took a few minutes for the gum smacking girl to get her computer online, but once it was, she entered the citation number, then said, "What is it you want to know?"

Donahue sighed. "Can you tell me what happened to the citation?"

"It was dismissed."

Damn! No warrant.

"Is there a reason given?" she asked.

The clerk took a moment to read over the screen.

"The code given is the one for 'at the request of the People.' That would mean that the City Attorney requested the dismissal."

Donahue pondered whether or not to track down the Deputy City Attorney? She decided to do so since he or she might know something that never made it into any report.

"Is there anything else you need, detective?" The clerk sounded bored and ready to hang up.

"Yes, ma'am. Does it give the name of the City Attorney who handled the dismissal?"

The clerk paused for only a moment. "Mmm...Carla Grafton."

"Grafton? Okay. Thanks for your help."

Donahue hung up with the clerk then dialed the main number for the Office of the City Attorney. This time a more professional sounding receptionist informed her that Carla Grafton had left government service and gone into private practice more than three years ago. Donahue then called the Los Angeles County Bar Association and was given a current number for Grafton who was practicing from an office in the San Fernando Valley.

"Ms. Carla Grafton, please," she said when the phone was answered. She identified herself as a detective, and a few moments later, Carla Grafton picked up.

"Ms. Grafton," Donahue began, "I appreciate your taking my call. I wanted to ask you about a ticket you dismissed six years ago."

"Are you kidding me?" Grafton started to laugh. "I don't even remember the name of my husband back then."

Donahue chuckled. "I know this sounds strange, but this is one you might actually remember. It had to do with a claim of diplomatic immunity for the son of an Ambassador—"

"—from Saudi Arabia," said Grafton, finishing Donahue's sentence. "You know what? I do remember the case. It was the one and only time in my career when that issue came up."

Donahue smiled. She thought that might have been the case.

"Can you tell me the basis for the dismissal? I thought you had to be the Ambassador for immunity to apply?"

Grafton smirked. "At the time, so did I, but according to the Vienna Convention of 1963, a family member of a diplomatic agent is also given immunity from arrest and prosecution."

"That doesn't seem right. Why would the family members get a free ride?"

"Actually, it makes perfect sense. If the children of a diplomat could be arrested, pressure could be exerted on that diplomat in such a way that it might compromise his or her role as a representative of their country. The reason we agree to the terms of the Convention is to protect *our* diplomats in foreign countries, and in return, we are expected to honor the protections the Convention affords to *them*."

"And it covers everything?" Donahue asked.

"It sure does. From murder to weenie-wagging. Actually, if I remember correctly, while a traffic citation can be issued to a diplomatic agent, they can ignore it if they want to, and there's nothing we can do about it. And by the way, they *always* ignore the tickets."

Donahue could feel her sense of outrage growing by the minute. "So let me see if I understand this. If a diplomat or the family member of a diplomat commits a serious crime, like murder, there's nothing we can do about it? Nothing at all?"

Grafton considered the question.

"Actually, if something like that actually happened, we could request the country involved to drop the immunity, and sometimes they might. If they did, then we could prosecute. But generally, they don't. They may recall the person involved, or in rare cases, they might choose to prosecute that person in their own country, but that's about it."

"So, in this case, the citation that you handled, you simply dismissed it because it was not prosecutable?"

Grafton laughed. "Actually, I was going to send it to the Saudi Embassy in

Washington, home of the kid's father, along with a nasty letter about his behavior. It was going to be a demand letter for payment. But I got a personal call from the State Department ordering me to dump the citation forthwith, so I did."

"The State Department?" Donahue's voice betrayed her surprise. "Why would they be involved?"

Grafton lowered her voice to a conspiratorial whisper. "I asked that very same question, detective, but I never got an answer."

Donahue ran a hand through her hair. It didn't make sense that the State Department would concern itself with a traffic ticket. *What kind of juice did this kid really have?*

Donahue pressed her further. "Any idea who this person was who called you from the State Department?"

"Actually, I do remember his name. It just popped into my head. He had this really deep voice, like Darth Vader, or should I say, like James Earl Jones. He said,*'This is Allen Rendleford, and I'm the Under Secretary of State…'*"

Grafton then chortled.

"La-de-da da," she said. "Like I was supposed to immediately drop to my knees and give him a hummer. The guy was a pompous ass."

Donahue laughed. She knew the type. Perhaps this guy Rendleford was still with the government? It might be worth the effort to track him down.

She leaned back in her chair. "Well, let me thank you, Ms. Grafton. You've given me a lot of information, and I really appreciate it. Thanks again."

* * * *

Her phone began to ring, and when Donahue glanced at the caller ID, she discovered to her surprise that it was Dr. Zach.

"Hey, babe," she said. "Long time no see."

"Jen?" His voice had taken on an ominous tone. "You might want to get over to Cedars right away."

She felt her heart begin to race while an icy hand squeezed at the base of her stomach. "Why? What's wrong?"

"It's your partner's wife. She's had another cardiac incident. She's doing okay for the moment, they've got it under control, but I ran into Kruger a few minutes ago, and he was rushing off to scrub in for the procedure."

Her free hand went to her forehead. "Where's Gibby?"

"He was with her in her room, but they may kick him out when they prep her for surgery."

"I'm on my way." She got to her feet. "Thanks, Zach. Will you be around?"

"I've got a few patients that I have to see, but I can meet you after that—if you want me to?"

"I do," she said.

His voice softened. "Call me when you get here."

"I will."

She made her way to the Captain's office, let him know what was going on, then ran down the stairs to the parking lot. She wanted a cigarette in the worst way but found a way to resist the urge.

Remember how you felt after your morning run?

It was to become her newest mantra.

TWELVE

At Cedars-Sinai Hospital in West LA, Donahue made her way to the ground floor information desk where she was given directions to Claudette Gibson's sixth-floor room. She quickly found it without difficulty, but when she arrived, she discovered that the room was empty. A trip to the nearby nurses' station revealed that Claudette had already been taken into surgery, so she was directed to a waiting room two floors down where she found Ulysses Gibson sitting on a couch and staring blankly at a soundless TV set that was running an MSNBC news report.

Jacket off, hat pushed back off his forehead, and with his tie undone at the neck, he was not his usual, impeccably dressed self.

"Hey, partner," she said. She entered the otherwise unoccupied room, sat down on the couch next to him, and placed her hand on his forearm.

"How are you doing?" she asked.

His smile was distant. "I'm not the one having the surgery."

"She'll be fine, Gibby." She tried to muscle a smile. "Zach says her surgeon is one of the best."

Gibson massaged at the stubble on his chin. "Speaking of doctor Zach, he popped in here a couple of times. He was looking for you."

"I'll track him down later. In the meantime, what happened? I thought she was doing okay?"

"She started having chest pains, then trouble breathing. I ran out and yelled for a nurse, and the next thing I know they were calling a code." He rubbed at his bloodshot eyes. "She never went unconscious, but the doctor showed up a few minutes later and they increased her dose of blood thinners." He swallowed hard. "Once she was stabilized, he said he was going to review the scans again, but in the meantime he wanted her to be prepped for surgery."

"Jesus! You guys must have been terrified?"

"I didn't understand everything he was trying to tell me, but he said that they're going to open her chest, take several veins from her legs, and then graft them onto her coronary arteries in such a way as to bypass the blockages." His voice grew shaky and he started to tear up. "I think he said they're going to have to stop her heart to do it."

Donahue knew how scared he was. Claudette was everything to him, and this was undoubtedly a very serious operation. She rubbed his arm and tried to instill confidence.

"She'll be on a heart-lung machine," she told him. "It's called 'Off-Pump Coronary Artery Bypass Surgery." They do it all the time." She smiled. "I learned about that from Zach. Anyway, thank God she was here when it happened."

Gibson chewed at his lower lip. "I know, but I can't help but worry."

"And I would be worried if you weren't worried," she told him.

He gave her a half smile. "Your boy, Dr. Zach, calmed Claudie right down. Then Kruger came back and told us that the main blood vessels leading in and out of her heart were most likely clogged with plaque. He said a bunch of other stuff, and a lot of it didn't really stick. But I heard him say *triple bypass,* and *he needed to do it now,* so we signed the surgical forms and off she went."

"Have you called your daughters?"

"They're on their way in."

Donahue set her purse on the floor in front of her and leaned back on the couch. "I'll stick around here, too. How long did they think the surgery would take?"

"He wasn't really sure. If there were no complications, he thought maybe six or seven hours."

"Okay. It's going to be a long wait." Donahue looked around the room, then spotted a coffee maker on a credenza set in front of a floor to ceiling window. "They've got coffee," she said, getting to her feet. "Can I get you a cup?"

"Naw, I've had too much already."

Donahue found a clean styrofoam cup, and once it was full, she returned to the couch.

"What have you been up to?" he asked.

"We can talk shop another time. You've got other things to think about."

She took a sip of the coffee.

One of his eyebrows went up. "I'd rather keep my mind off the surgery. Have you been working the case?"

She spent the next twenty minutes filling him in on the details of her investigation and her most recent efforts to track down the Prince.

When she was finished, he said, "You've put a lot of time in on a lead that might be going nowhere." He lifted his gaze to meet hers. "Particularly if this guy can never even be prosecuted."

"Weren't you the one who once told me that our job is to solve it and gather the evidence, and leave the decision to prosecute to the DA?"

Gibson smiled. "Well, if I said that, it must be right. I just wish I could be helping you out."

"You're needed here, Gibby. I'll cover for you while you get your wife through this, and if something breaks, I'll let you know."

"Thanks, Jen." He took a deep breath, then exhaled slowly. He was trying not to tear up. "So what's your next move?" he finally managed to say.

"I thought about it on the way over, and once I get the photo from Flynn, I thought I'd go back to the club and show it to Bishop. I want to make sure we're talking about the same guy. Assuming it is, maybe I can track down the girls that Carrie Ann was with that night. I want to see if they remember him or if he was even there when her killing occurred?"

Gibson nodded, then added, "Show it to the cop who wrote the citation, too. We don't want to leave any loose ends."

"Good idea. Anything else?"

Gibson gave it some thought. "Run it past her father, too. Maybe he'll recognize the guy."

"He seemed pretty sure that his daughter wasn't seeing anyone but her boyfriend."

"I know, but you can never tell. It's worth a shot."

A knock on the doorframe caused them both to turn around. Standing in the doorway was Zachary Hunter.

"Am I disturbing you guys?"

He nodded a greeting towards Gibson, then took in Donahue with an even, white smile.

"Not at all, doctor," said Gibson as he got to his feet. "Please, come in."

Hunter entered the room and walked over to Donahue. She remained seated, so he leaned in and kissed her on the mouth. As he pulled back, she looked up at him and smiled. He held her gaze for a moment, then glanced over at Gibson.

"I put a call into the surgical suite. Everything's going well. She's comfortably sedated, and her vital signs are steady. So far, no problems at all."

Gibson felt an overwhelming sense of relief.

"Doc, I want you to know how much I appreciate your taking the time to help me out. I...*ah*..."

His voice had filled with emotion before it trailed off.

"That's quite all right," Hunter told him.

Gibson looked at the two of them and could sense an underlying tension.

"I think I'll take a little walk and stretch my legs." Gibson got to his feet, nodded to the doctor, then made his way from the room.

As soon as he was gone, Hunter took a seat on the couch next to Donahue.

"How are you doing?" he asked.

"I'm okay," she said, but her tone of voice betrayed a deep sadness. She looked up at his face and held his glance.

"Actually, I'm not. I don't know where this is going with us, Zach? It seems like we're both so damn busy that there's never enough time for just us."

"You could always switch to a different division," he said calmly.

"No, I can't." Her pent up resentment now bubbled to the surface. "You want me to give up my career? Why is that fair? Just because I'm the little woman?"

"I'm not saying that," he told her.

"It sure sounds like it," she replied. She shook her head. "I can't do that Zach, and you know it. I've worked too hard to get where I am, and it's wrong for you to expect me to give it all up just like that. I'd be miserable, and I'm sure you don't want that."

"I can't change what I do, Jen," he said with a sigh. "I'm a surgeon. I'm always on call. You knew that when we started up."

"No one is asking you to change," she replied.

"*Well, it sure sounds like it*," he said, parroting her earlier response.

Donahue sensed he was mocking her, and her expression quickly showed her disdain.

Hunter realized at that moment that he'd gone too far.

"Okay. This might not be the time or the place to go through this. Maybe all we can do for the moment is keep it the way it is. It's not what either of us wants, but maybe it's all we can have for now."

They sat there in silence, neither one looking at the other. Finally, Hunter glanced at his watch and stood up.

"I've got to go. I've got a surgery scheduled in fifteen minutes, so I need to scrub up."

He leaned over and placed a hand on her shoulder. "At least think about what I said, about keeping things status quo."

He stood in front of her, but when she made no effort to answer, he turned on his heels and walked out of the room.

THIRTEEN

Seven hours later, Dr. Anton Kruger made his way into the waiting room. Gibson was the first one to spot him, and he immediately got to his feet. Donahue and Gibson's two daughters and both of his sons-in-law were quick to follow suit.

"She's doing fine," Kruger said to Gibson. He then shifted his glance to the group at large. "Sit down everyone. I know you're probably tired of sitting, but I've been on my feet for a long time, and since I'm going to sit, then you should, too."

Gibson introduced the group to Kruger and they quickly took their seats.

Kruger set his lanky frame down on the arm of a nearby couch. Still dressed in his surgical greens, he removed his paper slip-on hat to reveal a head full of neatly cut, dark gray hair.

"The surgery was very successful. There were no complications. We did the triple bypass, and she's resting comfortably in the ICU. She'll be there for the rest of the night, primarily because of her age, but there's a full-time nurse assigned to her care, so I see no need to rush her off to a regular room."

Gibson cleared his throat. "How long will she be in the hospital?"

"I would like to keep her here for about a week. She's going to be uncomfortable, so she'll be on pain meds for a day or two, and then we'll slowly start to taper them off."

He looked over at the daughters. "Your mom is one tough cookie. Before the surgery, she told me that I'd better make sure that she pulls through the procedure or she won't be making me a batch of her famous lemon cupcakes."

Everyone laughed.

"That sounds like her," said Gibson. He was feeling much relieved and was actually smiling.

"Will she be on a special diet or anything like that?" asked one of the daughters.

"Before she's released, we'll go all through that, but the short answer is *yes*.

Apparently, she's had high cholesterol readings for years, so we'll put her on medications and try to monitor pretty closely what she eats."

Kruger looked over at Gibson. "How are your cholesterol levels?"

"A little high."

Kruger nodded. "Then the diet we put her on will probably benefit you as well."

He turned to the daughters. "Because both of your parents have high cholesterol, I want you ladies to get in and get checked. There's a lot we can do to head off problems if we get you on a healthy regimen while you're still young."

Both girls nodded.

"I'll see that we all get checked out," Gibson told him. "When can we see her?"

Kruger checked his watch. "Considering that she's going to be in there all night, let's give her another hour or so for us to assess her condition. After that, she won't be awake, but if you and your daughters want to go up to the ICU and take a quick peek, I'll allow it, but only for a couple of minutes. She needs to get her rest."

Kruger got to his feet. "I'll be by to check on her tomorrow morning, so if there aren't any more questions, I need to get to work on my post-surgery notes."

They shook hands and Kruger left. Everyone was smiling. The relief was palpable.

"Well, I think I'm going to take off," said Donahue. "Give her my love, will you Gibby?"

"Of course." He walked over and gave her a hug, something he rarely did, and Donahue hugged him back.

"You don't need to come in tomorrow," she said. "You take care of Claudette, and I'll cover the fort."

He nodded.

She said goodnight to Gibson's family and made her way out to her car.

Zachary was down in the ER on an auto crash case and couldn't be disturbed, so after picking up a salad on the way home, she took a quick shower, wolfed the dinner down, then jumped into bed with a self-help book.

Ten minutes later, she turned off the light and fell into a fitful sleep.

FOURTEEN

The next morning, after a five-mile run through the pre-dawn peacefulness of her neighborhood, followed by a long, hot shower, Donahue treated herself to a chilled grapefruit half, an egg white omelet, and a piece of rye toast before driving to the squad room at the PAB where she poured herself a cup of very black coffee before heading to her desk. She checked out her emails and found one sent to her by Don Flynn, the Assistant Director of the Secret Service.

Underneath the heading, there was a typed note from Flynn that said: *It's a copy of his passport photo. It's the only one we had on file.*

She opened the attachment and found a photo of Prince Muhammad bin Abd al Aziz. He had strong features, a five-day growth of full beard, and was wearing a red and white *ghutra* head scarf, which was securely held on his head by an *igal*, the black, rope-like cord that holds the *ghutra* in place. She decided that he was attractive enough to turn a girl's head, and she revisited the thought that perhaps her victim had met this man and had willingly invited him back to her home.

She returned to her desk and noted that there was a message slip lying next to her phone. It said that Shari Thompson was running late and that she would be in as soon as she could.

Donahue began her plan for the day by developing a list of people to contact, and she was just getting ready to start a computerized search for Carrie Ryson's two girlfriends when her telephone began to ring. Thinking it was probably Thompson, she answered the phone with a question.

"Rough night last night?"

There was a momentary pause, then, "Is this Detective Donahue?"

A deep male voice?

Oops...

"Yes, this is Donahue. Can I help you?"

"You certainly can." The voice became less than cordial. "My name is Allen

Rendleford, and I understand that you've been making inquiries about Prince Muhammad bin Abd al Aziz?"

Donahue's eyebrows went up. *Allen Rendleford? Wasn't that the name that Carla Grafton had given her?*

She needed to be sure.

"And who might you be, Mr. Rendleford?" she asked.

"I'm with the Department of State, and what I want to know is whether or not your inquiries have anything to do with that old rape case allegation against the Prince? Because if it does, I'm wondering why you people would be resurrecting that case for any reason, given the fact that the matter was resolved years ago?"

It was him!

Rendleford the A-hole!

But wait a minute? Did he say "that old rape case allegation?"

What the hell is he talking about?

She knew that the Prince was never considered a suspect in the Ryson murder case, so what does this guy mean when he says that the matter was resolved years ago?

But rather than fly off the handle at the man's perceived self-importance, she took a deep breath and counted to three.

"Mr. Rendleford, with all due respect, I don't know you from Adam, so I'm not about to discuss anything with you that I might or might not be doing until I can verify your identity and your government affiliation."

Rendleford provided her with the main telephone number in Washington for the Department of State, and he advised her to call the public switchboard there and to ask for him.

"I will await your immediate callback," he said before hanging up.

She stared at the receiver in her hand. Her first instinct was to ignore his demand for a callback, but then, her curiosity about *an old rape case* involving the Prince had her completely intrigued. So she called telephone information in Washington DC and requested the main number for the Department of State. The number provided by the operator was a match for the one that Rendleford had given her, so she placed a call to State, asked for Rendleford by name, and after two rings, he was once again on the line.

"This is Detective Donahue," she said when he identified himself. "What can I do for you, Mr. Rendleford?"

"It has come to my attention that you've been making inquiries about Prince Muhammad bin Abd al Aziz." This time he appeared to be a bit more circumspect.

"That's correct," she said, wondering how he'd gotten wind of her investigation? "I was attempting to locate a photograph of him."

Rendleford's voice took on a conspiratorial tone. "You know, of course, he had diplomatic immunity when that rape allegation first surfaced. His arrest record has since been expunged, and as far as I know, the so-called victim has moved on with her life."

It suddenly hit her like a ton of bricks. *Rendleford was talking about a different rape, not the rape and murder of Carrie Ann Ryson!*

She sat bolt upright. Should she let him know that she was looking at this guy for a different case? If not, how could she go about pulling the details of the old rape case out of this guy, especially since he seemed clearly intent on burying the past?

"Can I ask you, Mr. Rendleford, were you the representative of the Department of State at the time of the allegation?"

"I was," he replied. "And I thought we had an understanding with you people that the issue was resolved. The Prince had diplomatic immunity at the time of the incident, and there's no way he can be subject to prosecution."

"That's my understanding as well," she said. She tried to think fast, then hit on an idea.

"It's probably fortuitous that you called," she told him. "My department got an inquiry from the Royal family. Apparently, some property belonging to the Prince was taken into evidence at the time of the incident, and the family would like to have it returned. Unfortunately, everyone who worked on the case at this end has either retired or moved on, so I don't have a case number to determine the status of that property." She took a deep breath and crossed her fingers. "By any chance, do you have the LA number handy so that I can check it out for them?"

"Of course I don't," he said, and she sensed that a note of cautious suspicion had entered his voice. "If what you're saying is true, it doesn't explain why you were seeking the Prince's picture?"

She laughed; but it sounded forced, even to her.

"Oh, that! Well, I figured we'd need to have a photo to have some way to identify him if he came in to retrieve his property. But that was before I learned that he's now out of the country and that someone else will probably come in to claim it for him."

She knew it sounded lame, but it was the best she could come up with on such short notice.

"What property do you still have in evidence?" Rendleford asked.

He sounded really suspicious.

"The inquiry was about a wallet and its contents," she said. It sounded the most plausible thing she could think of to say. "But until I can find the case number, I can't begin to track down the evidence reports to see if we still have it or if it might have been destroyed?"

Get back on the offensive, she told herself. Get some info from him.

"Understand, Mr. Rendleford, I'm only doing this as a courtesy to the family. I don't plan to follow protocol and force the Prince to come in personally to claim his property."

Would that do it?

"I really don't have the number," he finally said.

She countered, "Well, maybe if you had the date of the incident? That would help a great deal."

She could hear him shuffling through papers.

He was going for it!

"My records show that he was arrested on June third." He then provided her with the year.

She quickly did the calculations. Six and a half years ago? That was five months before the Ryson homicide.

"How about the date of the rape?" she asked. If the Prince's record was expunged, it might be easier to track it down through the date of the assault.

He once again shuffled the papers. "June first," came the reply.

"And the victim's name?"

She was going for broke now, and while she might be able to track it down on the basis of the information she already had, the victim's identity would make it a piece of cake.

"Rudinova," he said after a while, "but that's all I remember." There was a long pause, followed by, "Look, detective, this matter dies here and now. Go ahead and do your best to locate that wallet, but after that, you're to drop this case, and under no circumstances is it to surface again for any reason. And in the future, if you have any questions regarding the Prince, you'll direct them to me. His family is significant to the welfare of this country, and any misguided inquiries by you or one of your colleagues could seriously jeopardize this nation's foreign policy, not to mention our economy. Do I make myself clear on this?"

Her instinct was to tell him to stick his attempt to intimidate her up his narcissistic ass, but she held her temper in check. She had what she needed to move her case forward, so for the time being, she would forgo the satisfaction of telling him off so as not to interfere with her investigation.

"Look, Mr. Rendleford, I'm just doing my job and trying to help his family while they navigate the system. I doubt that you'll be hearing from me on anything else related to this guy."

"I hope not, but just to make sure, I'll be contacting your Chief to let him know that we expect this matter to be put to rest once and for all."

It took all she had to control her temper.

"Do what you like, Mr. Rendleford, and have a nice day."

When he abruptly hung up his phone, she said aloud,

"And *fuck you*, too."

* * * *

For the next five minutes, Donahue seethed. She wasn't used to being threatened, especially by a pompous bureaucrat who thought his word was law. But it was worth putting up with his attitude because Rendleford had inadvertently given her a lead, one that might be of real significance. The Prince was somehow involved in a rape case, and that was cogent to her investigation. It was something she definitely intended to look into in spite of Rendleford's threat.

Shari Thompson walked in and went straight to her desk in the cubicle that adjoined Donahue's. She was standing there, taking off her jacket and getting ready for the start of the workday when Donahue became aware of her presence.

"Hey, Shari. Got a minute?"

Thompson looked over. "Sure. Slide on over and give me a moment to get settled."

Donahue dragged her chair over from her own cubicle and sat down while Thompson removed her weapon and placed it in her desk.

"Is this about the Ryson case?" Thompson asked, sitting down.

Donahue nodded. "I was wondering if you had any luck tracking down any other rape homicides where the victim was cuffed or tied by her hands to the bed?"

"I did a five-year M.O. run, both before and after the date of your homicide. No hits."

Donahue pursed her lips. "How about just rapes where the victim was tied down? Any luck there?"

"I found two. Both of them were solved and resulted in convictions, but they both occurred before your homicide case, and both suspects were already in custody when the Ryson girl was killed."

Donahue let that sink in, then told Thompson what Rendleford had said. Thompson frowned. "But I ran your suspects name through the computer and he never came up as a named suspect in any case?"

"Rendleford said his record was expunged. Could that have happened?"

Thompson gave it some thought. "It's possible."

"So how would we find out?"

"If his arrest got pulled from our data banks, I guess I'd probably have to check with the former Supervisors of the Sex Crimes Units to see if anyone still remembers the case? Any idea when this crime went down?"

"Rendleford said it was five months before my murder case." She consulted her notes. "Sometime around December of 2009. The woman's name was Rudinova."

She looked up at Thompson who asked, "First or last name?"

"I don't know, but it sounds like a surname to me."

"It should be enough," said Thompson who turned on her computer and started to type.

Three minutes later, she had the victim's name.

"Alyssia Rudinova," she said to Donahue, "and here's the LA number that was assigned to the case." Thompson looked up from the screen. "You got a few moments?"

Donahue smiled. "For this? Of course!"

"Good! Let's take a walk down to Records and see what we can find?"

The two women went down to the basement floor and spoke with a clerk at the Records counter. There they confirmed their suspicions that the hard copies of the reports would have long since been sent to storage. They would have to fill out a request form, and once the records they sought were located, they would get a call from the storage location to come and pick them up.

Thompson filled out the form, then the two of them returned to Thompson's cubicle.

"I think Maria Alvarez might have been the Officer in Charge of Sex Crimes when this incident went down," said Thompson. "She's now a Lieutenant out in West Valley. Let me give her a call. Maybe she remembers the case?"

Thompson dialed the West Valley number, then looked over at Donahue and smiled. "After all, it's not often that we get a Prince as a named suspect."

It took several minutes, but Alvarez finally came to the phone.

"Hey, Shari," she said. "What can I do for you?"

Thompson explained their situation. "We've put in a request for the records, but it could take days, so I thought maybe you might have heard of the case we're looking for back then when I think you were in charge? And if so, I wanted to pick your brain."

"I remember it well," Alvarez said. "It was the one and only time I ever had to deal with a diplomatic immunity situation."

Thompson gave a thumbs-up to Donahue, then said, "Can I put you on speaker, Maria? I've got Jen Donahue here. She's the one who's looking into the case."

The call went to speaker, and Donahue asked. "Thanks for taking our call, Lieutenant. Can you tell me anything about the case?"

Alvarez cleared her throat. "Well, first off, you're wasting your time looking for the records. They're not in storage. The files were pulled and turned over to the Feds."

"Can they do that?" Donahue asked.

"They can, and they did."

"Was this on national security grounds?"

"I'm pretty sure that's what they claimed, but let me tell you what I can." Alvarez took a deep breath. "The victim was a working girl, a clerk in a flower shop, I think. She met your guy at her business, and he asked her out. He took her to the Beverly Hills Hotel, the Polo Lounge, and bought her a rum and coke. After the drink, he wanted to show her the view from his three million dollar penthouse condo on Wilshire Blvd, so she got in his car and on the way to his place she began to feel dizzy. She thinks he put something in her drink because the next thing she remembers is waking up in his bed."

"She was drugged?" Donahue asked.

"Probably, but we never did know for sure. She didn't tell anyone in law enforcement about this until two weeks after it happened. So if he did spike her drink, it had long since passed out of her system. Anyway, she woke up a few times with him on top of her, but she claims that she kept passing out.

"The next morning, when she woke up in his bed, he was already up and gone. She said she was sick and still dizzy. She went to the bathroom and noticed dried semen on her belly. And apparently, she'd been sodomized because she felt pain in the area of her anus. She located her clothes and discovered a hundred dollar bill tucked into her thong. Nice touch, huh?"

"Really classy," said Donahue.

"Anyway, she called herself a cab and went home. Eventually, she filed a complaint at the WLA station, and we ended up with the case because of the guy's connection to the Saudi Ambassador."

"Did you talk to the suspect?" Donahue asked.

"We did. He made no effort to hide out. We found him at his condo. He told us that drugs were *not* involved and that the acts between them were completely consensual. He said he left her the money to help her get home because she was still sleeping and he couldn't wait around."

Donahue's shoulders slumped. "That doesn't sound like a prosecutable case."

"No. It sure wasn't." Alvarez was momentarily silent. "The victim told me that she had a laceration to her right wrist. It had healed pretty much when I met with her, but you could still tell that she'd been bound up in some way during the assault."

Both Donahue and Thompson exchanged a glance, and Thompson mouthed, *No shit?*

"Was she tied to the headboard?" Donahue asked.

"Possibly," Alvarez replied. "I don't remember for sure. I'd have to check the reports."

Check the reports?

Donahue and Thompson exchanged another surprised glance, and Thompson leaned forward and said, "But I thought they were all turned over to the Feds?"

Alvarez lowered her voice.

"*Oops?* Did I forget to turn over my working copy? Oh my goodness! I'm such a naughty girl."

Thompson and Donahue both smiled.

"Perhaps one or both of you ladies might like to drive out here tomorrow?" said the Lieutenant. "By then, I might be able to locate what you're looking for."

"What time would you like me there?" Donahue asked.

"Anytime before eleven. I've got a staff meeting after that."

"I'll be there first thing," Donahue said, then added, "By the way, did you ever have any personal dealings with a guy named Rendleford from the Department of State?"

"Is he a friend of yours?" Alvarez asked cautiously.

"Not in this lifetime," Donahue replied.

Alvarez sniffed. "Pardon my French, but he's a flaming asshole. He came down on us like a bolt of lightning. He actually called the Chief, and the very next day we were ordered to bury the case."

Donahue glanced over at Thompson, then said to Alvarez, "I should tell you that I just spoke to the guy this morning." She described the way she'd misled him into thinking that the Saudi's just wanted the Prince's property back.

Alvarez chuckled. "We managed to get a photo of the guy before his lawyers showed up and put a stop to the booking. Hell, we never even got his wallet out of his pants."

"I was winging it," Donahue said. "It was all I could think of to throw him off track." She paused for a moment. "Anyway, he said he was going to call our

Chief this morning, so you might want to rethink your willingness to resurrect that old report of yours?"

"Just keep it to yourself," Alvarez said. "I'm not worried about any repercussions. Besides, I suspect our current Chief has learned over time that it doesn't pay to mindlessly kowtow to the Feds. You come out here tomorrow and I'll give you the reports."

"Fair enough. Thanks, Lieutenant."

Alvarez hung up the phone and Thompson nodded to Donahue.

"You've got a pretty good lead there, Jen. Let me know if there's anything else I can do?"

"Thanks, Shari. With Gibby off for a while, maybe the Captain will let us get back to our usual pairing? I'll talk to him when I can, but in the meantime, I'll keep you in the loop."

FIFTEEN

After a filling lunch at a nearby cafe, consisting of a grilled cheese sandwich, an apple, and a diet coke, Donahue made her way back to the squad room where she was surprised to see Gibson sitting at his desk. He was focused on a conversation on the telephone, so she sat down in her cubicle and waited for him to finish.

"How's she doing?" she asked when he hung up the receiver.

Gibson gave her a broad smile. "She's doing fine, Jen. A little cranky, and very sore, but fine."

Donahue raised her arms in a V for victory salute.

"Oh, man! I was so worried about her, Gibby. Thank God!"

She stood up, walked over, and gave him a hug.

A flush appeared on his dark skin, but the smile remained on his face.

"Thank you for being there, Jen. It meant a lot to us."

"Don't be silly." She slowly pulled back. "You guys are just like family."

Gibson nodded. He appreciated the height of that compliment. He leaned back in his chair and cleared his throat.

"Well, now that we've got that out of the way, why don't you bring me up to speed on the case?"

Donahue grinned. "I thought you'd never ask."

She returned to her desk, pulled out the case files, then rolled her chair over to where he was seated. She laid out the blue case notebooks and opened one up to the log sheets where she had written her summary of what she had learned.

She spent the next thirty minutes bringing him up to speed on the investigation, including the phone call from Rendleford, his intent to call the Chief, and the prior rape allegation that had swirled around the Prince. When she was finished, she passed him the photo she'd received from Don Flynn.

Gibson picked it up and studied it before putting it back in the file. He looked over at Donahue.

"So, he said he was gonna call the Chief?"

Donahue nodded.

"Well, I'll talk to the Captain about that, but there's no way we're gonna walk away from this case."

"My sentiments exactly!"

Gibson picked up a cup of coffee that he'd been nursing through her recitation and took a sip.

"So where do you want to start with this?" he said as he put the cup back on the desktop.

"It's time to track down the girls who were with our victim that night. Their names are Amoretti and Corliss. I want to know if they know our boy, and if so, did they ever see him hanging out with Carrie Ann?"

Gibson pointed towards the case file.

"Did the Coroner's report on the Ryson girl indicate whether or not they ever did a toxicological screen?"

"They did, but it was for the usual stuff, like cocaine, heroin, pot, and meth. All negative. But the lab never checked for GHB, Rohypnol, or the other date rape drugs. I'm sure they've got samples of her blood on file, and if so, then maybe we can get them to re-run the screen?"

"You realize that stuff leaves the blood pretty quickly?"

"I know, but *if* she was killed while she was still under the influence, and *if* they took the sample within a reasonable time, and *if* they preserved it properly, I'm hoping *if* it's there, it will still show up."

Gibson fixed his eyes on hers, and his were twinkling.

"That's a lot of ifs, Jen. I'm proud of you. You've really moved this case along. Nice job!"

"I'm learning," she told him, but she savored the compliment.

"Okay, you check out the lab angle while I bring the Captain up to speed on where we're at. After that, I'll help you hunt down the witnesses."

"Ha! By the time you and the Captain get through telling war stories and kibitzing, I'll have tracked them both down by myself."

Gibson smiled as he got to his feet.

Donahue kept her eyes on his.

"I'm glad you're back," she said, "and I'm glad that Claudette is doing so well."

He flashed her one of his trademarked, bright smiles.

"Me, too."

* * * *

Two hours later, Captain Tom Elwood walked into the squad room and asked Gibson and Donahue to join him in his office. When they were seated, he said to Gibson, "I appreciated the heads-up on your case. I just finished a meeting with the Chief, and it's always nice to know in advance what he wants to see me about."

Neither Gibson nor Donahue spoke. Both were waiting to learn the results of the meeting.

Elwood leaned back in his chair and steepled his fingers together.

"As you suspected, the Chief got a call from Rendleford." He started to laugh. "And I gotta to tell you, the Chief was not a happy man. Rendleford ordered him to keep the wraps on that old rape allegation, claiming it was an issue related to national security." Elwood shook his head. "You'll be happy to know that the Chief doesn't take kindly to being threatened. But after the call was over, he gave it some thought, and he told me to tell you that since it's not prosecutable, he doesn't want any mention of it in the press. In fact, he doesn't want it to get out at all."

Donahue started to object. "But we're not—"

Elwood held up his hand. "Let me finish."

Donahue pursed her lips and nodded silently.

"*However...*the Chief says you're to go full bore on the homicide *and let the chips fall where they may.*"

Gibson and Donahue both smiled.

"So, tell me something, Jen?" Elwood leaned back again and put his feet up on his desk. "What did the lab say?"

"Well, they told me there are at least three possible drugs that he might have used. GHB, the first, is an odorless and tasteless drug that stays in the system for eight to ten hours. It can be a syrupy concoction, but it also comes in a powder form. It depresses the central nervous system, and when given with alcohol, it can take effect within ten to fifteen minutes. The victim is usually unconscious for three to four hours, and in low doses, inhibitions are reduced which can lead to a sense of euphoria followed by drowsiness and sleep. And afterward, there's no memory."

"What's the risk of death by mixing the drug with alcohol?" Elwood asked.

"It can easily cause death."

Elwood shook his head. "What else did they say?"

"The other major drug used for date rape attacks is Rohypnol. It's a benzodiazepine. It's ten times as powerful as Valium and comes in the form of a pill. It dissolves in beverages and intensifies the effects of alcohol. An amnesic state is produced within ten minutes and can last up to eight hours." She shrugged her shoulders. "Once ingested, the victim doesn't stand a chance."

"How long does it stay in the system?" Gibson asked.

"If a blood sample is taken within four hours, it's detectable. But the best method of detection is from a urine sample. GHB will show up in the urine for eight to ten hours, and Rohypnol for up to sixty."

Elwood looked from one to the other. "I don't suppose there's a urine sample?"

Donahue shook her head. "No, and we're not sure the blood was taken within four hours, but they're going to run the screen anyway and we'll see what we get."

Elwood ran a hand across his forehead. "And if she was drugged?"

Donahue shrugged. "There's probably no way to trace it back to him, but if she was drugged, it would seem to match the MO that was used with the earlier rape victim."

Elwood nodded his understanding. "Bottom line here is that it doesn't matter if he drugged her or not. It's death by strangulation, not an overdose. Right?"

Donahue nodded.

"Do we even know if he and the victim were together that night? Or, for that matter, at any other time?"

"We're working on that," she replied.

Elwood studied the two of them, then directed his comments to Donahue.

"Jen, I want you on point on this case. I want Gibby to be free to take care of his home situation. And if you need any assistance, get Shari to help you out."

"That's not necessary," Gibson interjected.

"Yes, it is." Elwood's tone was firm. "If something changed with Claudette's situation, you need to be with her."

He locked eyes with Gibson, took his feet off the desk, and sat up straight.

"Look, Gibby, her welfare is more important to all of us then a cold case that looks like it can never be filed. And besides, from what I can tell, Jen has got the case under control, even if she has managed to piss off the Federal government."

Gibson and Donahue laughed, and whatever tension had been building rapidly dissipated.

"So, are we clear on this?" Elwood asked.

Gibson nodded.

"Jen?"

"Yes, sir."

"Good." Elwood got to his feet which signaled that the meeting was over.

Back in the squad room, Gibson said, "Did you track down the two young ladies?"

"Sure did. I thought we could go out and see 'em tomorrow morning."

"Sounds like a plan. I'm gonna get out of here. I've got something cooking at home."

"Got a hot date?" Donahue asked with a smile.

Gibson smiled. "If you must know, I've hired a nutritionist. She's coming over to the house tonight to give the girls and me a lesson on how to prepare meals that will be low in cholesterol."

"What a great idea!" Donahue smiled broadly. "You'll be right on top of things when Claudette comes home."

"I sure hope so. I don't usually do the cooking, so this is gonna be really interesting."

Donahue reached out and touched him on the arm. "You'll do fine. I've got the interviews all set up, so meet me here tomorrow morning, around eight?"

"You got it." He packed up his things, waved goodbye, and left the squad room.

Donahue sat down at her desk. It had been a long day, and she felt the need for a cigarette. The thought of smoking surprised her until she realized she was feeling very anxious about Zachary.

One way or another, she needed to get their situation resolved. The uncertainty was weighing heavily on her mind, and while she hated the idea of a confrontation, she knew she needed to deal with it quickly for the sake of both of them.

She took a deep breath and reached for the phone.

"Hi," she said when he answered. "Did I catch you at a bad time?"

"I just finished a big case. Good outcome." He sounded upbeat. "So, what's up?"

"I just wanted to say *hi* and find out if we're going to get together tonight?"

"Sure. Your place or mine?"

She paused for a moment. "Maybe we could meet for dinner. I think we need to talk."

"If that's what you want. You up for sushi?"

"Sushi's fine," she said. "Our usual spot?"

"Can you think of any place better?"

She smiled. "About seven?"

"I'll make the reservation. See you then."

She hung up the phone and sighed. She needed some time to think. There was so much riding on this meeting tonight, and she still didn't know what she was going to say.

Hell! For that matter, I still don't know what I want.

SIXTEEN

Donahue finished the last bite of the *Crème Brulee* they were sharing before wiping her lips with a linen napkin. She looked across the table at Zach Hunter. He had pushed his chair back and was studying her with the kind of intensity that he usually reserved for his patients.

"Did you like the desert?" she asked.

"Yeah," he said as he stifled a yawn. "It was great."

They'd gone to dinner at their favorite Sushi restaurant, then back to her apartment for wine and dessert.

They were seated in chairs on a balcony that overlooked the building's courtyard one floor below. The warm Santa Ana condition—the name given to the winds that blew in from the eastern desert—kept the evening shirt-sleeve comfortable, while candlelight on the table and soft music from an iPhone that played through the living room speakers completed the mood she had wanted to set.

She slid back her chair and began to clear the dishes.

"Leave those," he said. "That can wait."

She sat back down and watched as he poured more wine into their glasses.

"To us," he said, raising his glass.

She lifted her glass and took a sip. This was the moment that she dreaded, the moment they'd been headed for all evening long. It was time to have…*the talk*.

"Why don't you just say what you want to say and get this started?" he said. "I'm a big boy. I can take it."

She looked down at her plate. Zach was right, of course, and he was reading her like a book.

"I've been doing a lot of thinking, Zach, about us and where this seems to be going." Her shoulders drooped. "Oh, God! Why is this so difficult to talk about?"

He waited for her to gather her thoughts, and finally, she did.

"I want more than what we've got, Zach. At best, I only get to see you once or twice in a week, and—"

"But I've told—"

She held up her hand. "Wait a minute. I need you to hear me out."

He stopped talking and folded his arms across his chest.

"I've tried to make this work, Zach. I know how important your career is. I get that. It's demanding and time-consuming, and there's nothing I can do about that. But I know you, too, and you think we can keep going on like this until I give up my job."

"I never asked you to do that," he said.

"You want me to be a housewife, to be home and available at your beck and call. And I know you think your career is more important than mine." She took a deep breath. "But I can't give it up, Zach. I love what I do. And it's important to me. It's what I've worked for ever since I came on the job."

"Then don't give it up." He leaned forward in his chair. "I don't see any reason why things can't go on the way they are right now? We both have our work, and when we're not working, we have a little time with each other. What's wrong with that?"

She closed her eyes and shook her head, then sighed.

"That's exactly the problem, Zach. The only time we seem to have for each other is when we get together for dinner and a roll in the hay." She locked her eyes onto his. "That's not enough for me, honey. I need more. It makes me feel cheap and—"

"And what?" he asked. "Used? C'mon, Jen. Is that what you're trying to say?"

"I don't know what I'm trying to say, but it just doesn't feel right."

"Look, I know this situation isn't perfect, but it's what we've got. I want more time with you, too, baby, and the fact that we make love whenever we do get together is because we *don't* get enough time for each other in between. But I'm not using you, Jen. I'm in love with you, and frankly, at the moment, I don't see a solution to our time crunch. I can't do anything about my schedule, just as you can't do much about yours." He reached over the table and touched her on the arm. "Our reality is this: if we do end up getting married, you'll be the one who'll be carrying the babies. So doesn't it make sense to consider your current career as the one that's temporary—at least it would be—as opposed to mine?"

Her eyes narrowed. "So, if I understand your position, Zach, you're saying that I should be the one to put my career on hold to enable us to spend more time together, on the possibility that you *might* someday propose marriage, which *might* lead to our having a house full of kids?" She held his glance. "Is that what you're saying?"

"Yes…I mean *no*…at least not the way you're saying it." He ran a hand through his hair. "You know, you're starting to sound like a lawyer."

He reached out and took her hand.

"What I'm saying is that I love you, and I don't see any reason why things can't stay this way until we're ready to take the next step."

She pulled her hand away.

"Except, if *I'm* not happy with the current situation, then *I'm* the one who has to make the change… not *you*."

He raised his voice. "Only because one day you'll be the one who will be putting your career on hold, and if having a better mesh to our schedules *now* is so important to you, then a different assignment at your department might give us more time together?"

She shook her head. "I'm not ready to give up my work in homicide, Zach, not for a future that seems so full of *mights*."

An uncomfortable silence settled in between them.

He finally got to his feet, dropped his napkin on the table, then stepped around the table and kissed her on the cheek.

"You need to decide what's most important to you, Jen. Your career or our relationship?"

He turned and started for the door.

"Where are you going?" she asked.

"I'm going back to my place." He turned around to face her. "If you look at this objectively, you'll see that you're not being realistic. The guy you seem to want is someone who will be at *your* beck and call; someone who'll be there no matter how crazy your schedule gets. Well, I'm not in a position to be that guy, and I never will be. I'm sure there are a few guys like that whose schedule could work with yours, but they'd probably be homeless and unemployed."

He lowered his chin, held her glance, and knew right away that he'd gone too far.

"I'm sorry," he said. "A bad attempt at humor. Let me know when you decide what you want?"

And with that, he was gone.

Donahue stared at his back as he closed the front door. She slowly got up, stacked the dirty dishes, carried them over to the sink, and mechanically scraped them off.

Tears appeared at the corners of her eyes. *This wasn't the way it was supposed to go?*

Or was it?

SEVENTEEN

In the morning, after a breakfast of coffee and a blueberry muffin—a guilty treat to assuage the misery she was feeling over the way things had gone the night before with Zachary—Donahue signed out for herself and Gibson on the board in the squad room. She then made her way down to the underground parking lot where he was waiting for her in an unmarked car.

As the senior officer of their team, he was given the privilege of a take-home vehicle, so it often fell to her to sign them both out while he moved the car closer to the elevator.

"We all set?" he asked as she shut her door and belted herself in.

"Aren't we always?" she replied.

"Oh? Are we cranky this morning?"

"Just drive." He watched as she put on her sunglasses, then he put the car into gear and drove away from the building.

"Dr. Zach?" he asked, offhandedly.

Her silence let him know he was right.

He fiddled with the air conditioner. "Okay. You can talk with me about it when you're good and ready."

She glanced over in his direction. "You're certainly Mr. Nosey this morning."

"Just concerned." A small smile worked its way across his face. "I don't like it when you're preoccupied. It distracts you from your work."

"This? From you?" Donahue rolled her eyes. "What's the old adage? People who live in glass houses…."

Gibson steered his way into a lane change.

"You're right about that, and I stand chastised." He looked over at her. "So? What's got your panties in a twist?"

In spite of herself, she smiled. "What I'm going through is nothing compared to your situation. So don't worry, it won't affect my work."

He shifted his weight in the seat. From their past conversations, he had already divined the nature of her problem. It was one that affected most cops. Police work was hard on relationships, and their particular division, RHD, had the worst relationship break-up rate of all.

"For what it's worth, I've always put my work in Homicide before everything else," he said. "It was something I was proud of, too. It took a little time, but eventually, my wife got used to it."

She watched him intently.

"But as great as I thought that was, now that she's ill, I'd give anything to get that time without her back." He paused for a moment, and when he spoke again, his voice was shaking. "To me, this whole medical problem of hers has put my job in perspective. *It's just a job.* And the only thing that matters is how much time you get to spend with the person you love."

Donahue didn't speak. Instead, she turned her head forward and stared out the windshield. He took that as a sign that she was giving some thought to what he had said.

A minute or so later, he asked, "Do you want to take the lead when we talk to this gal… Jena Corliss?"

"I'll be happy to."

Her cell phone rang, and she glanced at the caller ID. The number that popped up was for the LAPD Serology lab.

"This is Donahue," she said.

"Detective Donahue? Hi. This is Eddie Gault in Serology. Have you got a second?"

Donahue smiled. In the true meaning of the phrase *science nerd*, Gault was the poster boy. Short, balding, and severely overweight, he seemed to have little or no life beyond the lab. She'd come to know him reasonably well over the last several years, and during that time she reached the conclusion that his only serious interests outside the job were golf—poorly played if you listened to his stories—and fast food, which seemed to be the only thing he ate. And with Gault there was also just a tiny complication—he seemed to have a crush *on her.*

Donahue softened her voice. "I've got all the time in the world for you, Eddie." She looked over at Gibson and mouthed *Eddie Gault.*

Gibson smiled. He knew about the crush.

"I'm gonna put you on speaker-phone, Eddie. I'm in the field with Gibson." She pushed the button. "Okay, Eddie. What's up?"

Gault nervously cleared his throat. "I, um... managed to locate the blood sample from the Ryson case, and before I get started, I just wanted to make sure that I know what it is you're looking for?"

"Can you check for Rohypnol or GHB? The victim might have been drugged before she was killed."

"Um..." Gault cleared his throat again. "I can try, but a lot is going to depend on how long she was dead before the sample was taken. And even then, it's possible that it won't show up."

"I know it's a long shot, Eddie, but we have to check out everything."

He paused for a moment, as though he was struggling to find a way to keep the conversation going. He finally said, "I'll do my best. I've got nine other cases ahead of yours, and all of them are rushes, so it may take a while before I can get to yours."

She looked over at Gibson and rolled her eyes. "Whenever you have time, Eddie. Ours is not a rush."

He was silent again, and then, as if encouraged, he said, "The fact that you're not screaming at me to have it for you yesterday makes me want to push you to the top of the list."

Gibson shook his head and smiled. It was all he could do not to laugh out loud.

"You're a sweetheart, Eddie," said Donahue, smiling, "but I'm really not in a rush. Just do it when you can."

"Okay," he said. "Thanks. I will."

The line went dead, and Gibson laughed. "That boy has got it bad."

Donahue slapped him playfully on the arm. "I think it's cute."

The rest of the drive was conducted in relative silence while both of them gathered their thoughts about the pending interviews.

Gibson pulled up in front of a flower shop where Jena Corliss was working as the assistant manager. When they entered the store, she came from the back and greeted them cautiously.

"Let's go next door to talk," she suggested. They left the store in the hands of an assistant and settled at a booth in a nearby cafe where Gibson ordered coffees that arrived in a flash.

Donahue took the lead. “As I mentioned when I called you, Jena, we’re re-interviewing everyone in the case, hoping we can learn something new that might send us off in the right direction.”

An attractive brunette with emerald green eyes, Corliss nodded her understanding.

Donahue folded her hands together on the table. “So why don’t you start by telling us what you remember about that night?”

Corliss pursed her lips in thought. “Okay, on the night it happened, Mia and I left the sorority house and caught a ride over to Carrie’s apartment with Suzy Wilson, another girl from my sorority house. Suzy dropped us off about ten p.m. Carrie was still studying, so while she started to get dressed, Mia and I fixed ourselves a couple of screwdrivers; you know, just to take the edge off.”

“Did Carrie have one too?” Donahue asked.

Corliss shook her head. “She didn’t want to take a chance. She had an exam the next day.”

Donahue nodded.

“I think Mia and I each had two drinks,” Corliss added, “then the three of us all walked to the Village and went to the club. When we got there, the place was pretty full, so we started to dance, and the party was on.”

“Were you dancing with any particular guys?” Donahue asked.

Corliss shook her head. “It wasn’t like that. I mean, some people were coupling up, but almost everyone out there was on their own. Anyway, after about thirty minutes, Mia and I saw a guy that we knew. We left the dance floor and joined him. He and his buddies bought us some drinks, so we hung out with them at the bar.”

“Where was Carrie during this time?” Gibson asked.

“Still dancing, I guess.”

“You didn’t see her?”

“You mean was I keeping tabs on her? The answer is no.” Corliss blew gently on her coffee to cool it before she took a sip. “I knew she was okay in the club, so it wasn’t really necessary.”

“You were underage,” Gibson said. “Did that pose a problem with you getting served?"

Corliss smiled. "We all had phony ID's. Carrie never used hers to buy a drink because her dad was a cop and she didn't want to risk getting caught. But if someone handed her a drink, well, she'd take it. I mean, she wasn't a prude or anything like that."

"Did you see anyone give her a drink that night?" Donahue asked.

"No, she stayed on the dance floor most of the night." She thought for a moment. "I did see her once. She was dancing alone with one hand on a post." Corliss smiled. "It was as if she was dancing in a trance and the post was her partner." She took another sip of her coffee. "That girl had some *sexy* moves."

Donahue shifted in her seat. "So how did the rest of the evening go?"

Corliss shrugged. "Well, Mia and I danced a few times. I danced with different guys, some I knew and some I didn't." She shrugged. "The few times I did notice Carrie, she was dancing alone or with different guys, no one guy in particular. In fact, her normal routine, if you could call it that, was to dance with a guy one time and then move on." She shifted her glance from Donahue to Gibson. "She had a boyfriend that she cared about, so she wasn't really interested in picking up guys."

"Did a lot of guys hit on her?" Gibson asked.

"All the time. Carrie was always brushing them off."

"Did she flirt a lot?" Donahue asked.

Corliss held her glance. "Sure, but she never went off with anyone, at least, not that I know about. As I said, she had a steady boyfriend, so I'm pretty sure she was getting what she needed with him."

"Did you have a lot to drink that night?" Gibson asked.

"Not that much." Corliss studied him carefully. "I didn't have a final for another few days, so I wasn't really that concerned." She was silent for a moment. "I guess I had a buzz going on, but you know, I wasn't hammered."

Donahue reached for the sugar and added another packet to her coffee.

"So when was the last time you saw Carrie?" Donahue asked.

Corliss closed her eyes for a moment, clearly troubled by the memory.

"When she came over to say she was going home. I guess it was about one a.m. Mia tried to talk her into staying for a while, but she said she had her final and she needed to get some sleep. I told her that she shouldn't walk alone, and she said she wouldn't." She looked from Donahue to Gibson. "She said she'd take a cab, so we hugged goodnight, and she walked out the door."

Corliss looked down at the table then up again at Donahue. "I keep thinking back to that night, you know, wondering if I could have done something differently?"

Donahue let the silence between them hang for a moment, then said, "I've got a photograph that I want you to look at." She pulled out a manila folder and removed a blowup photo of Prince Muhammad bin Abd al Aziz. She placed it on the table between them. "Do you recognize this guy?"

Corliss frowned. "Is this the guy who did it?"

Donahue shook her head. "I just want to know if you've ever seen him before?"

Corliss picked up the photo and studied it for a while.

"You know, I think I do remember this guy. He wasn't wearing the head scarf thingy, but this is him. I don't really know him too well, but I saw him at the club a few times." She raised her eyes and caught Donahue's. "I don't think he was there that night, but I'd seen him before. He was always with a couple of guys. And I remember that the three of them always wore black, like they were mysterious or something like that. He used to hit on everyone, a real *dog.* If you were anywhere close to him, he would offer to buy you a drink."

"Did he ever buy you one?" Donahue asked.

"Once," she said, "but he wasn't my type, too forward and too pushy. Besides, I didn't like his two friends. They didn't seem friendly to me."

"Did you ever see this guy leave with any girls?" Gibson asked.

"Once in a while."

"What did he talk about when you spoke with him?" Donahue asked.

Corliss shook her head. "I have no idea. All I remember are my impressions, and as I said, he wasn't my type." She cocked her head towards Gibson. "Maybe Mia can tell you more about him. I know she talked with him at least a couple of times."

Donahue put the photo back into the folder. "Anything else you can tell us about him or about that night?"

Corliss shrugged. "Nothing about him." She sighed. "I just wish I'd done something to keep her at the club. Maybe it might have made a difference."

Donahue put her hand on Corliss's arm. "It's very unlikely that it would have changed anything, so don't beat yourself up. What happened is not your fault. Carrie Ann was the victim of a predator, and killings from guys like that are almost impossible to prevent."

They walked her back to her flower shop, and Donahue gave her a business card and asked her to call if she remembered anything else.

Back in the car, Donahue said, "I was hoping she'd tell us he was there that night."

Gibson gave her a nod. "Let's see what Mia has to say?"

EIGHTEEN

By the time they made it back downtown, the sun was high and shining brightly in a cloudless sky. Gibson had initially struggled with their air conditioning unit, but the flow of air coming in was still less than adequate. In frustration, he pounded on the dash a few times, but it didn't make any difference.

"Just once I wish this thing would work on days when the temperature gets over eighty-five."

Donahue merely let him rant. A lot of what was coming out was a reaction to the stress he'd been under with his wife's heart attack.

Forty-five minutes later, they arrived at the Wells Fargo Private Client Banking Offices in downtown LA. They made their way to the upper floors where they were asked to wait in a comfortable lobby until a well-dressed blond in a business suit guided them inside to a window office where the three of them took seats at a table to the side of her desk.

Donahue took in the room. It was beautifully furnished in lustrous dark woods with an oversized desk, a conference table, and a stunning view of the city. She could clearly see the Pacific ocean, almost twenty miles to the West, and beyond that, twenty-six miles off the coastline, the Island of Santa Catalina.

"A billion dollar view," she whispered to Gibson.

Considering that Amoretti had only been an undergraduate six years ago, it appeared that she had done quite well for herself since her time at UCLA.

On the wall behind the desk were two framed hunting prints along with a business degree from UCLA and a graduate degree in banking from the Marshall School of Business at USC.

"I see you went to USC," Donahue said as she gestured towards the sheepskins on the wall. "It must make it tough for you when the Bruins play the Trojans in sports?"

Amoretti smiled. "Actually, no matter who loses, I always celebrate with the winner."

Donahue noticed the wedding ring, and with minimal prodding, she learned that Mia met her husband three summers ago while both were working on their graduate degrees.

"He works as a television producer," she added.

Donahue brought the conversation around to the night of the Ryson murder, and she had her recount what happened as best as she could. Her story matched that of Jena Corliss with one crucial exception. She remembered the Prince from the night in question.

"Yeah, I know him," she said as she stared at the picture. "Or, rather, I did know him back then."

"Tell me about him," Donahue said.

"He was a player. His come on was to buy you a drink. I usually refused, but a lot of others didn't." She looked over at Donahue and smiled. "He claimed he had a Ferrari and he tried several times to get me to go for a ride with him."

"And did you?" Gibson asked.

"No way!" Amoretti folded her arms across her chest. "Getting involved with a guy like that would be a total waste of time. Besides, he was an Arab…or something like that, and from everything I've been told about Middle-Eastern men, they treat their women like property—" She locked her eyes on Gibson, "—and I'm nobody's property."

Gibson smiled.

Donahue prodded. "But you're sure he was there that night?"

"Yeah, I saw him there. He came in pretty close to closing time."

"Was Carrie Ann still there when he arrived?"

Amoretti gave that some thought. "Yeah, I think she was." She flashed a half-hearted smile. "It's been a long time, you know?"

"Did Carrie Ann know him or speak to him that night?"

"I think she spoke to him once or twice, but I don't know if she did that night." She looked over at Donahue. "He had a preference for blonds, so I'm sure she had his interest."

In Donahue's mind that explained why the Prince had shown more interest in Mia then he had in Jena who was a brunette.

"So where did you see him at the club that night?" Donahue asked.

Amoretti racked her brain to remember. "I think I saw him up by the bar for a while and maybe once or twice on the dance floor."

Donahue was having trouble containing her excitement. "Was Carrie Ann out there while he was on the dance floor?"

"Maybe." Then she gave it more thought. "Change that to probably. She was out there most of the evening."

"How about when she left the club? Was he still there?"

Mia shook her head. "I don't know. I do know that Carrie Ann was alone when she left, but I don't remember if he was still there or not?"

The rest of the interview produced nothing they could work with, so an hour later, when they were finished, the two detectives made their way to their car.

Donahue felt energized from what they'd learned in the interview, and she turned to Gibson when they got in the car.

"We're closing in on him, Gibby. I'm thinking that he followed her home and took her when she entered her apartment."

Gibson nodded. "That would shoot down your GHB theory."

"Maybe so, maybe not, but it doesn't much matter. The important thing here is that we've put the Prince in the club on the night that she was killed." She rubbed her hands together. "It's looking good, Gib. All we need now is a break."

Gibson cocked a brow. "We've made progress, Jen, but we're still a long way from wrapping this up. After all, we've still got nothing to connect him with the crime."

"I know, and I won't exclude any other theory that comes along, but the deeper we get into this, the better he's starting to look to me."

NINETEEN

Gibson parked their car in the lot at the West Valley Police Station, and the two of them entered through the back door. The squad room was quiet, with most of the detectives out doing interviews in the field or making appearances in hearings held at the Van Nuys courthouse. After getting directions from a blue suit who was buying a cup of coffee from a vending machine, they made their way through the hallways to the office of Lieutenant Maria Alvarez.

She was seated at her desk, working on the schedule for the Patrol Division, when she noticed them standing in the doorway.

"Right on time," she said. She ushered them in and offered them seats.

When Donahue introduced Gibson, Alvarez reminded him that they had met a few years before at the annual RHD Christmas Party.

"I was a redhead then," she said with a smile.

"That's right!" Gibson slowly smiled. "Now I remember. You had a hat on with blinking Christmas lights—"

"Please," she said while shaking her head, "don't remind me."

They laughed while Alvarez pulled a file out of her desk. "Here it is," she said. "I trust you'll forget where you got it?"

She passed a plain manilla folder full of police reports across her desk and into the hands of Donahue.

"We will."

Donahue placed the folder in her lap.

Alvarez said, "I went through the file last night. I've already told you what I remember about what happened to her, but when we went out and picked him up, that's when things got interesting fast."

"How so?" Gibson asked.

"He asserted his claim of diplomatic immunity. We checked it out with the US Attorney's office, and they said that we had to let him go. Then the State

Department got involved. They demanded that we turn over all of our reports. Ostensibly, the Feds were going to try and have him recalled and prosecuted in his own country, but it didn't go down that way."

Donahue's face clouded over. "What happened?"

Alvarez lowered her voice. "A couple of weeks later, I called the State Department official who was handling the case. It was the same guy you spoke to, Rendleford, a genuine, first class ass wipe. Anyway, he told me the victim refused to go forward with the case, so the matter was dropped. But apparently, he didn't take too kindly to the idea that I might still be showing some interest in the case, so he placed a call to our Chief, and through the chain of command, I got word to drop it...*no ifs, and or buts.*"

Donahue shook her head in disbelief. She could sympathize with Alvarez's obvious frustration over the incident. It was one thing to have your suspect catch a pass on the case, but when your own department didn't back you up for doing your job...?

That really sucked.

Donahue leaned forward and said, "You were going to check the reports to see if your victim was bound in any way during the attack?"

"She was. When I saw her for the first time, she had a nearly healed cut mark around her right wrist. I asked her about it, and she said that when she woke up that morning in his bed, she saw a piece of plastic string in the bed beside her. I guess that it was the remnants of a *Flexicuff.* I think he cut it off her wrist when he finished having sex."

Donahue exchanged glances with her partner, then refocused her eyes on the Lieutenant.

"I don't suppose there's any way that we can reach her?"

Alvarez smiled. "I ran her name through our search program this morning and discovered that she's a fully credentialed teacher. She works at a middle school in Santa Monica, teaching math. The address and other info you need are on a sheet inside the cover of the file *that you didn't get from me.*"

Donahue gave her a wink, then she and Gibson thanked her and got to their feet.

"If there's any way to take the guy down," Alvarez said, "please do it."

TWENTY

Back in the car, Donahue used her cell phone to call the Wintergreen Progressive School in the city of Santa Monica. From the Assistant Vice Principal, she learned that Alissa Rudinova would be taking her lunch break at noon.

Donahue looked at her watch. They had less than forty minutes to get there. "We better hurry," she said.

Gibson put the pedal to the floor and they flew down the freeway and over the hill from the Valley, switching freeways twice until they made it to Santa Monica. They pulled up at the school with five minutes to spare, and Donahue led the way into the building.

The Wintergreen school was one of several private schools nestled in a commercial/residential area just north of Pico Boulevard. The school was non-denominational, but catered primarily to wealthy west-siders.

Spread out over five meticulously landscaped acres, the campus consisted of a dozen or so single-story, ultra-modern classrooms. There were meditation courtyards, tranquil water features, and a sports field that looked as though it belonged to a major university.

"Will you look at this place?" Gibson couldn't believe his eyes. "It sure is a far cry from the grammar school that I went to," he groused.

Donahue glanced over and smiled. "We may not have gone to schools like this, but we certainly didn't have to pay a year's salary for a single year of grammar school education."

They stopped at the attendance office, got directions to *Mrs. Rudinova's* classroom, and waited outside the doorway until the last of the students had filed out on their way to the schoolyard and the swanky outdoor food pavilion. They spotted her through the glass window in the door. She was seated behind her desk, reading over a stack of papers.

Gibson entered the classroom. "Mrs. Rudinova?" he said softly.

She looked up. "Yes?"

"I'm Detective Gibson." He held out his LAPD identification card. "This is my partner, Detective Donahue. Can we talk to you for a few minutes?"

"Of course," she said.

As she stood up and came out from behind her desk, Donahue noted that she was tall and thin, with legs that any woman would kill for. She was dressed conservatively in a knee-length dress. Her shoulder length blond hair was stylishly cut and worked very well with her narrow face.

If she was surprised by their visit, she didn't show it.

"What's this all about?" she asked.

Gibson smiled politely. "We'd like to talk to you for a few minutes about the incident that you were involved in a few years back when you were the victim of an attack."

Donahue noticed a slight crack in Rudinova's otherwise stoic façade.

"There's nothing to talk about," she said. Her accent was thick but completely understandable. "It's done and over with."

"In one sense it is, but we'd like to know more about Muhammad bin Abd al Aziz. We're looking at him for other stuff."

Rudinova shook her head. "I don't—"

At that moment, an older, well-dressed woman with gray hair pulled back and worn tight to her skull strode purposefully into the room.

"Good day to you, detectives. I'm Adelia Stern, the Assistant Vice Principal. Is everything all right?"

Her eyes narrowed, then shifted as she focused on her teacher.

"Alyssia?"

Alyssia Rudinova nodded and smiled wanly.

"Everything's fine, Mrs. Stern. These Detectives want to talk with me about some property that was taken from my residence."

The Vice Principal looked concerned. "You were burglarized? Oh my goodness! When was this?"

Rudinova responded slowly. "It was a while back, Mrs. Stern."

Donahue assessed the situation and correctly deduced that Rudinova did not want the subject matter of the prior incident disclosed to the Vice Principal. She could hardly blame her. People tended to gossip, and something like this would get around quickly.

She caught Rudinova's pleading glance and said, "Why don't we take a walk off campus so that you can get something to eat while we finish up our inquiries about the recovered property?"

Rudinova looked greatly relieved. She opened a drawer and pulled out her purse. "I know a great little place just down the street," she said.

They left Mrs. Stern standing in the classroom and made their way off campus.

"She's very curious," Rudinova said, once they were a block away from the school. "And she's a—how do you say—a gossip?"

Donahue smiled. "We've got people like that in my office, too."

Rudinova led them to a place called the *Vanilla Bake Shop* on nearby Wilshire Boulevard.

"I know this place," said Donahue. "But they don't serve lunch here."

"I'm not eating lunch today," said Rudinova. "But they've got great coffee."

Inside, Gibson bought a box of assorted *cupcake babies* and three steaming cups of freshly brewed coffee. They took seats at one of the tables, and both Donahue and Gibson began to devour the cupcakes. Rudinova took one but didn't take a bite.

"These make a great lunch," Gibson said. "I'm going to have to tell my wife about this place."

"Your nutritionist will have a cow," Donahue replied with just a hint of a smile.

Gibson laughed. "I won't be telling her if you won't," he said before he took a third little cupcake and popped it into his mouth.

Donahue finished hers and directed her attention to Rudinova.

"Thanks for agreeing to talk with us," she said.

"I don't really want to." Rudinova took a sip of her coffee and wiped her mouth with a napkin. "The truth is, I don't even like to think about it."

"I completely understand, and just so you know, we wouldn't even be here if it wasn't really important."

Rudinova's eyes swept back and forth between the two detectives. She was apparently waiting for Donahue to say more, but Donahue didn't oblige. Instead, she started off with small talk, designed to put her at ease.

"The Vice Principal referred to you as *Mrs.*, and I notice that you're wearing a wedding band. Congratulations!"

Rudinova grinned. "My married name is now Silverberg, but I continue to use Rudinova for my career. My husband, William, is an attorney. We have two amazing children…"

Her smile quickly vanished as she suddenly switched gears.

"I have never told my husband about that incident. I don't want him to ever find out."

Donahue held her glance. "You have nothing to fear about that from us. We're conducting a completely separate investigation."

When Gibson nodded in agreement, Rudinova noticeably relaxed.

"I told the detectives everything the first time, so I don't know what I can say that would be any different?"

Donahue leaned forward. "Can I call you Alyssia?"

"My friends call me Andi."

Donahue opened a manila folder and removed a photograph of Muhammad bin Abd al Aziz. "Andi, do you recognize this man?" she asked.

Rudinova took the photo and her hand began to shake.

"He's the one who attacked me. My God! I never thought I'd see his face again." She started to tear up.

Donahue placed her hand on Andi's arm in a gesture of support and took the photograph back.

"It's okay," she said. "We understand." She slid the photograph over to Gibson who returned it to the envelope.

When Donahue asked her about her first meeting with Aziz, Andi gave the same story that she had years before. When she got to the part about the drink at the hotel, she said, "I ordered a vodka martini, and he had one of his bodyguards bring it over from the bar."

"The waiter didn't bring it?" Gibson asked.

She shook her head. "When we sat down, he asked me what I wanted, then sent one of his bodyguards to get it."

Donahue shot Gibson a look. In all probability, the bodyguard had been the one to spike the drink. Since he wouldn't have been able to claim immunity, he should have been charged with the crime.

"I took a few sips of the drink and felt pretty drunk. He laughed at me and teased me saying he thought all Russian women could hold their alcohol."

"Where were his bodyguards while you were drinking with him?" Donahue said.

"They sat at a table nearby."

Gibson leaned forward. "Do you remember leaving the hotel?"

She shook her head. "I woke up once, and he was on top of me, but that's all I remember until the next morning."

"What do you remember when you woke up?" Donahue asked.

Rudinova sniffled. "I was in a bed, in what they told me was his apartment or condo, I guess. There was a piece of plastic in the bed, something he had used to tie my hands together."

"Were both of your hands tied?" Donahue asked.

"I don't know. I guess I thought so at the time, but only one of my wrists was actually cut." She looked down at her hands, then held up the right one. "It was this one, and if you look closely, you can still see the mark on my wrist."

Donahue took her hand. She could just make out the smallest hint of a linear scar on the back of her wrist.

"Is it possible that only this hand was tied to the bed?"

Rudinova thought about it for a moment.

"I guess so. I don't really remember much about what happened."

"And you were sexually assaulted?" Donahue asked softly.

Rudinova nodded and hung her head.

Donahue thumbed through some of the reports she'd brought along from the Ryson file. Among them was a photo of the plastic *Flexicuff* that was used to tie Carrie Ann to her bed.

She put the photograph on the table in front of Rudinova.

"Does this look like the plastic object that you saw in the bed?"

Andrea picked up the photograph and studied it carefully.

"Yeah, this looks like it."

Donahue nodded. She picked up the photograph and put it back in her file.

"I can't think of anything else to ask you, Andi." She looked over at her partner.

Gibson prompted, "Did you want to go into the actions of the Feds?"

"Oh, yeah!" Donahue shifted her glance back to Rudinova.

"I understand from the detective who handled your case that the Feds were going to have you testify in some kind of a proceeding to have Aziz recalled and prosecuted by his own country, but that you refused. Can we ask you why?"

Rudinova shook her head. "I don't want to talk about it."

"Why not?" Gibson scratched his head. "Did Aziz or someone in his group threaten you?"

She didn't speak.

Donahue waited, then said, "You don't have to tell us if you don't want to. As you know, we couldn't prosecute him back then for what he did to you, and we still can't. But what you've told us today will help us with our current investigation."

Rudinova gave her a puzzled look. "Did he do this to someone else?"

"We think so."

Rudinova closed her eyes and shook her head.

The two detectives got to their feet.

"Wait," she said.

They sat back down.

"I wanted to testify against him but that man wouldn't let me do it."

Donahue held her glance. "What man?"

"His name was Rundle…or something like that. He said he worked with the Department of State."

Donahue attempted to hide her surprise. "Was his name Rendleford?"

"That's right! That's his name."

Gibson leaned forward. "What do you mean he wouldn't let you testify?"

Rudinova's eyes narrowed.

"He brought me into an office in his building and told me in private that if I continued to cooperate with law enforcement, and if I testified against that man, he would see to it that my green card would be revoked, and he would put me on the first plane back to Moscow."

Donahue was stunned. She looked over at Gibson for guidance, but he too appeared to be mystified.

Rudinova hung her head. "I told the attorneys that I didn't want to cooperate and that was the end of it."

Donahue's surprise turned to anger. *Why would the State Department, in the form of this man Rendleford, want to let the suspect get away with this crime?*

One way or another, she planned to find out.

TWENTY-ONE

When they walked into the RHD squad room, one of the two detectives who was seated in a nearby cubicle looked up.

"Hey, guys," he said. "Where've you been? You missed the training day."

Donahue looked over. The detective who was speaking was George Tanner, a big, hulking man who shaved his head completely as a way to effectively deal with the loss of his hair on top.

She looked over at Gibson who gave her a shrug.

"We've been out in the field," she said to Tanner. "What training are you talking about? I didn't have anything on my calendar."

"Last minute," he said. "FBI was here to talk to Sex Crimes, and the Captain thought it would be a good idea for us to sit in." He looked over at the other seated detective. "Q and I were the only ones here, so we drew the short straw."

She put her purse down on her desk and said, "Well, Lord knows you can always use a little training, Tanner. Did you learn anything?"

"The speaker was a psychologist with big, curly hair. He had it slicked down when he started, but as the morning went on and it dried out, it began to grow bigger and bigger." Using his hands, he held them up above his head and pantomimed a giant circle.

"And that's what you got out of the session?" Donahue rolled her eyes. "Tanner, you're hopeless."

Tanner shook his head. The color had drained from his face.

"There was also a movie," he said. "The subject was *bestiality*. They showed us a video that some wing-nut made while he had carnal knowledge with a pig."

"Oh, geez," said Gibson who rolled his eyes and settled into his chair. "You've got to be kidding me?"

Tanner sighed, "I wish I was. I don't think I'll ever be able to look at a piece of bacon in quite the same way."

Quan, his partner, laughed while Donahue scrunched up her nose.

"I'm really sorry we missed that," she said to Tanner, "but when they show one with an elephant, I'll be there for sure."

Tanner sat up straighter. "They have one with an elephant? Oh, man! I've gotta see that!"

Donahue rolled her eyes and shook her head. She consulted her *Rolodex*, wrote down a phone number, then walked it over and handed it to Tanner.

"Tanner, you need to get professional help. Call this number, anytime, night or day."

Tanner looked at the number. "A psychiatrist? Very funny, Donahue."

Quan and Gibson both laughed.

Donahue turned to Gibson, then whispered, "Remind me to download and frame a picture of Porky Pig. I'll inscribe it "To Tanner, thanks for the memories," and we can leave it on his desk right next to his computer."

Gibson laughed again. "You're dangerous, Jen."

She smiled tightly, but her thoughts had already drifted to the Ryson investigation while a flash of anger quickly changed her mood.

Gibson slid his chair next to hers and looked at her over the top of his reading glasses.

"You okay? You look upset."

"I am." She folded her arms across her chest. "Where does that bastard at the State Department get off threatening that girl with deportation?"

"Politics," he said with a shrug, but he was also similarly incensed.

"You mean *bullshit*, don't you?" She took a deep breath and tried to calm down. "What's with our government anyway? Protecting a rapist like that. I've got a good mind to hang a case on that guy for extortion."

Gibson snorted and shook his head.

"What?" She said more sharply than intended.

"Rendleford is not our problem. We've got to stay focused on the Saudi."

Donahue was silent for a moment. Then said, "You're right, and I'm sorry I went off like that, but I'm not through with that guy, not by a long shot."

"Well, in the meantime, while you're contemplating your revenge, where do you want to go with our case?"

"I'm thinking we should get a DNA sample from the Prince?"

Gibson thought it over. "We could get a search warrant, I guess, but it won't do us any good as long as he's out of our jurisdiction."

"I know." She glanced over at the Captain's office. "Let's talk to the boss and see if he'll give us the okay for a trip?"

"Perhaps we should find out where he is before we present this to Tom?"

Donahue smiled. "I think Don Flynn said that he and his father are in Istanbul, Turkey. You wanna check with him again and make sure?"

Gibson nodded. He went back to his desk and placed a call to Flynn, who called him back thirty minutes later.

"I checked with the State Department," Flynn said. "Aziz is still in Istanbul. His father is the Ambassador there, so the kid is still protected by the provisions of the Vienna Convention."

"Were you able to trace his movements after he left the LA jurisdiction?" Gibson asked.

Flynn was quiet for a moment, and Gibson could hear the rustling of papers.

"I wrote it down somewhere," Flynn said. "Ah! Here it is. He left LA in July of 2010."

Two months after the Ryson homicide.

Gibson quickly wrote that down.

"He was in Saudi Arabia for the next ten months," said Flynn, "then joined his father in London. He worked as an Attache in the Saudi consulate until a little more than a year ago when he joined his father in Istanbul." Flynn paused for a moment. "Either he's on a very short leash with his father or the old man is grooming him for a life in the diplomatic service."

"Probably both," Gibson added.

Flynn shuffled his papers. "My source also said there was an allegation of misconduct initially lodged against the kid but that the records indicate it was later withdrawn."

Gibson's ears perked up. *Was there something more to this guy's background?*

"Any idea what was in the allegation?" Gibson asked.

"No idea," Flynn replied. "My source didn't have any details, but I can tell you that it was filed during his last six months in the States."

Gibson nodded to himself. It was probably the Rudinova rape allegation. That would make perfect sense.

There was a moment of silence between them before Flynn said, "I've given you what you asked for, Gibby, so how about filling me in on what's going on?"

"Well, to begin with, the allegation of misconduct was a rape by drugging. Jen and I are working on an unsolved rape homicide that bears a lot of similarities to the earlier rape."

"You do understand that the immunity issue is going to stop you cold?" said Flynn.

"I know, but Jen and I are getting paid to determine if he's our boy. After that, if the government chooses to let him go, there's nothing we can do about it."

After careful consideration, Flynn said, "I'd have to look into it, but if I remember correctly, I think his home country can choose to prosecute him if they want to?"

"That was tried on the earlier rape case," Flynn said, "but we just found out that the victim was threatened by a State Department employee with deportation if she went forward with the case." He let his words sink in. "Politics trumping over justice."

The silence on the line caused Gibson to ask, "You still there?"

Flynn said, "I was just thinking...I called the State Department this morning to get your information. I hope I haven't stirred things up enough to cause you any problems?"

"It's okay," Gibson replied. "We're just doing our job."

"I don't know, Gibby." There was a cautionary note to Flynn's tone. "Washington's a funny place. These guys—particularly in this administration—well, they like to play hardball. And if they decide you're not playing by *their* rules, they can cause you all kinds of grief."

Gibson pursed his lips. "Let 'em try."

"Gibby, I'm not just talking about our people. The Saudi's play for keeps, too."

"Thanks for the warning, Don, but we've got it covered."

Flynn took a deep breath. "So where are you going with this? What's your next step?"

"We're going to see if we can get a DNA sample. That will either make or break our investigation."

"Well, let me know if you need more help."

"Thanks, Don. We'll stay in touch."

"You do that...and Gibby?"

"Yeah?"

"Watch your back."

TWENTY-TWO

Gibson passed on the information he had received from Flynn to Donahue who had wisely spent her time getting coffees for both of them while he was on the phone. When Gibson finished his recitation of facts, he mentioned to her Flynn's warning.

"You think we're biting off more than we should?" she asked as she took a seat at her desk.

"That's never stopped us before."

He stood up, removed his coat, hung it on a nearby coat rack, adjusted his suspenders with his thumbs, then eased back into his chair.

Her eyes found his. "Good. Then we're still on the same page with this?"

"That we are." There was a noticeable smile in his tone of voice. Nothing got him more focused on the task at hand than a suggestion that there might be those who didn't really want him to do his job.

Donahue took a quick sip of her coffee, then made a few notations in her notebook.

"The way I see it," she said looking up, "he left the country right after the Ryson murder. Maybe it was planned that way, or perhaps it was just coincidental. Who knows? But once he left our fair city, I think we can assume there were no more victims within our jurisdiction."

Gibson nodded. "I see where you're going with this. We should be looking for other victims in London and Istanbul."

"Precisely."

She rolled her chair closer to his and spoke in a conspiratorial whisper.

"What do you say we poke around a bit and see what he's been up to since he left LA?"

"I've got no problem with that. But…" His voice trailed off as he stretched out his chin.

Donahue was puzzled. “Your point?”

“Once we put his name out there, it looks like we’re going to stir up some folks in the State Department. Our necks will be sticking way out there, Jen, so before we get ahead of ourselves, I think it would be a good idea to make sure that we’ve covered our butts.”

“So, we run it by the Captain?”

Gibson stuck his thumb up in the air.

“Higher? The Chief?”

Gibson nodded.

“But what if he stops us before we get started?”

“That’s a real possibility.” He rubbed at his nose, then adjusted his reading glasses. “Our suspect is bulletproof, Jen, and unless I’m reading this wrong, the Chief is liable to hit us with… ‘If he can’t take a fall, no matter what you uncover, then why should we waste our time and money?’”

“That can be answered two ways, Gibby.” Donahue’s voice had taken on an edge. “Maybe Aziz didn’t kill her. In that case, we have an obligation to get his DNA, clear his name, and get our investigation back on track.”

“But you don’t think for a moment that he’s innocent,” Gibson said.

“That’s true. I think there’s a good chance he’s the one.”

“So, enlighten me as to your second point?”

Donahue softened her tone. “Look, we might not be able to put this bastard in jail, but at least we can see it through and maybe give Carrie Ann’s father a measure of closure. You’ve seen that guy and what her murder has done to his life. He deserves to know the name of the man who killed his daughter.”

Gibson shrugged. “I can’t disagree with you on that, but all I’m saying is we better be ready to go to the mat because no one wants to spend money on a case that we know can never be filed.”

Donahue bit her lower lip as she worked to keep her temper in check.

“I’ll tell you what. You set it up so that I can be the one to talk to the Chief, and I’ll remind him that it’s *our job* to find out who did this first, and it’s the DA’s to tell us that we haven’t got a case.”

She folded her arms across her chest and held his glance, daring him to find fault with her logic.

"You'd say that to his face?" Gibson teased. He could barely contain his smile.

"Do you doubt it?"

He held up his hands in surrender. "Nope, not for a nano-sec." He stood up and started to pace. "Okay," he finally said. "If we go to the Chief now with what we've got, he'll tell us to go pound sand. I just don't see him authorizing the money we would need to chase this guy down for a DNA sample...leastwise, not on the strength of *only* our suspicions. On the other hand, if we could turn up another victim of some kind in the UK, then maybe we could get *the Cousins* to come on board and share with us the costs of going forward?"

"You think we could get the Brits to buy in?"

"I don't know, but in the end, it may be our only way to nail this little bastard or rule him out."

Donahue seemed sold. "I've got an acquaintance who works at New Scotland Yard," she said as she thumbed through her *Rolodex*. "He's a Detective Inspector I once met at a terrorism conference. I might still have his number somewhere, and if so, I could give him a call and see what he has to say about who we can talk to?"

"Well, in that case, as long as we're gonna poke a stick into this beehive, we might as well go all the way." Gibson sat down on the corner of his desk. "Let's check our boy out with Interpol. I don't know exactly how they're set up, or what kind of information they've got on file, but while working in London, I'm thinking that he could just as easily have spent his weekends somewhere on the Continent. We could ask them to run our suspect's travel info and see what kind of data they've got?"

Donahue nodded. "Make's sense to me."

She found the telephone number she was looking for and held it up to show Gibson.

"Detective Inspector Mark Grayson." She laid the card down on her desk. "Okay. I'll give him a call while you make the inquiry with Interpol."

* * * *

"Mark? It's Jennifer Donahue, LAPD. We met in Los Angeles, back in fourteen at the Conference on International Terrorism."

There was a time lag on the connection, and even though it was only a few seconds, his silence was enough to make her think that he might not remember her at all.

"Detective Donahue," he finally said. "Sure, I remember you. A striking blond with a smile that could bring a man to his knees. How are you?"

Donahue laughed to herself. Mark Grayson was at least twenty years her senior. Tall and distinguished, he had a full head of gray hair, a narrow face, and the kind of good looks and personality that were known to tempt married and single women alike.

While in Los Angeles to lecture to law enforcement personnel on the structure of terrorist cells and their recruiting techniques, they'd met at the pastry table during one of the numerous breaks, and while he'd done his best to convince her to join him for dinner, she'd put the kibosh on his attempted pursuit, but let him take her to lunch instead.

He'd been charming and informative, and by the time the meal was over, he had offered to be her guide if she ever made it to London. Now, after hearing his voice, it had her wishing that she'd made an effort to follow through with his invitation.

"So, Mark, are you still in the anti-terrorism business?"

Grayson chuckled. "I'm getting too old to learn anything new."

"That'll be the day."

They exchanged small talk for a while, then Grayson put things back on track.

"So, tell me, Jennifer, to what do I owe the honor of this inquiry?"

She filled him in on the details of her investigation and asked him to help her connect with someone whose specialty was handling rape cases.

Grayson took his time to respond.

"I'm sure you appreciate the sensitive nature of your investigation. Our own relationship with the Saudis is also rather delicate, so if you have no real objection, I'd prefer to make the inquiries myself rather than bring in someone else and risk losing control of what I see, at this point, as a *very confidential* and *very preliminary* investigation."

Donahue knew she could trust him to do a thorough job, so she accepted his offer and gave him more details about Aziz's MO; specifically, his propensity to cuff his victim to the bedpost using only one of her hands.

"I'll see what I can find out," he said. "Any chance you'll be popping over the pond?"

"Not sure. Hope so, but I'll have to let you know."

As she hung up the phone, she glanced over at Gibson who was also just finishing his call. His brow was furrowed and a look of disappointment was etched across his face.

"Any luck with Interpol?" she asked.

"They came up dry. No arrests, no wants."

Donahue frowned. "What about cases with our boy's MO?"

"They don't track that kind of information. The guy on the line told me that they only deal with identified subjects. He said we'd have to check with individual countries if we want a search done for unsolved cases."

They sat quietly before Donahue said, "While I'm thinking about it, we should probably track down the two detectives who worked on this case the first time. We might want to get their take on things before we go much further?"

Gibson opened up one of the notebooks. "While I track them down, why don't you see if you can scrounge up the physical evidence for this case? I'm sure there's nothing that's going to jump out, but we should give it a shot just the same."

She picked up the phone, made a few calls, and arranged for the evidence to be pulled for them and made available the following morning.

"They'll have it for us at nine a.m.," she said when she got off the phone.

Gibson nodded. He was still on the phone, doing his best to track down the investigating officers.

She studied his face, and for the first time, she noticed the toll that Claudette's illness was taking. Clearly, he hadn't been sleeping too well, not with the constant worrying about his wife. But it was more than that. Overnight, he appeared to have aged significantly. Dark circles had appeared just under his eyes and small patches of stubble that he'd missed with his morning shave now marred his normally fastidious appearance. His shoulders seemed rounded instead of thrown back, and as she mulled it over, he was moving around at a snail's pace, as if struggling to find the energy just to do the simplest tasks.

In the face of such overwhelming worry, she wondered how much longer she could realistically expect him to continue working on the case.

He was still on the line, apparently on hold, when she said, "I can finish up that call for you." She held her hand out for the receiver. "Why don't you get out of here and take a little break?"

He waved her off, spoke to someone, then promptly rang off.

"We can meet both of them tomorrow morning at eleven, over at Hollywood station."

Donahue nodded. She got to her feet, looked at her watch, then stretched. Perhaps, if she called it quits, he too would get the message.

"I guess that's all we can do for today." She gave him a knowing look. "I'm burned out, used up, and calling it quits." She pulled her purse from her lower desk drawer. "You heading over to the hospital tonight?"

Gibson nodded. "Claudie is starting to complain about the food, so I guess that's a good sign." He smiled wanly. "She's pushing them to let her go home."

Donahue thought about him as Claudette's primary caregiver. He would willingly handle the role, but he would worry surely about his competence in a medical emergency, and that would eventually take an even greater toll.

She walked over to his desk and put a hand on his shoulder.

"Are you going to get a nurse or someone to help at the house when she comes home?"

"It's not covered by our HMO, so if I do, it's going to be only part-time, probably during the days when I'm down here."

"How about your girls?" Donahue knew his daughters were close to their mom. They both would volunteer, of that she was certain.

"They're planning to drop by during the days, but at night, it's yours truly, and to be perfectly honest, I'm scared to death."

"You'll do fine. Just don't hover over her like an old bumblebee. Your wife is a very strong woman, Gibby, and I doubt that she'd take too kindly to you being an old fussbudget."

Gibson laughed, and Donahue warmed to the old, familiar smile.

"Just don't let them push her out of Cedars too soon," she cautioned. "Zach says the HMO's are famous for that."

"I'll keep that in mind." He put on his hat, pulled it rakishly over one eye, and headed for the door.

"Thanks, Jen," he said over his shoulder. And then he was gone.

She walked back to her desk and packed up her things while her eyes soaked in her surroundings. Several detectives were still seated at their desks, writing reports and answering phones. In the background, like white noise, other telephones were ringing, their callers now relegated to answering machines.

In the corner of the room, at a borrowed desk, a retired DA, who now worked as a volunteer, was sifting through an unsolved murder file. He was searching for clues that others might have missed; just one more victim of the demons that frequently haunted the souls of those who worked on homicides for far too long.

She walked out of the squad room, acutely aware of the toll that the job was exacting from her spiritual being.

What am I doing to my life?

It was time to go for a very long run.

TWENTY-THREE

Depending on the season, night time in downtown Washington DC could be the very essence of beauty and tranquility—as when it was covered in two feet of snow. The rest of the year, it was more of a breeding tank for the irrational violence that seemed to afflict those born to poverty and struggling with hopelessness, an all too prevalent occurrence on hot summer nights.

It was nine p.m. on a muggy, sweltering evening, and Allen Rendleford was still at his desk. He was staring out his window, acutely aware of the fact that the beauty of the city lights set against the night horizon concealed an undercurrent of malevolence just four floors below.

He rarely stayed at the office this late, but the energy crisis, reflected in the escalating cost of gasoline, had become a worldwide problem. And while he could offer no solutions to the economic catastrophe that it engendered, it was his job to stay on top of the political machinations that could subtly affect the market and keep the prices moving up.

Today had been one of those awful days. Rebels had struck at a tanker farm in eastern Nigeria causing severe damage to a critical refinery. Production would be halted for months. And to make matters worse, futures traders had driven the cost of a barrel of oil to a new record high. The public was both angry and confused, and the oil-producing nations, while paying lip service to the rest of the worlds' concerns, were secretly laughing behind the backs of the consuming countries, as their untapped supplies of underground crude grew more and more valuable with each passing day.

He caught his reflection in the plate glass window and momentarily balked. He looked thin and haggard, not the picture of health he used to be. His years of working at this stupid job had taken their toll. And while he was sure that he would soon seek new employment in the private sector, his party and the President were so out of favor that a loss in November was all but assured. He would miss the power that came with his appointment as Assistant Under Secretary of State for Political Affairs; a position he had hoped would be a springboard to a higher and more powerful office.

He wasn't worried about his future. There were many in the energy field who owed him big favors, and he had no qualms about calling them due. The consulting jobs would come, and that was fine with him. As the only son of an oil and gas explorer from the fields of west Texas, he did not want for money. The trust fund set up by his family was more than he could ever use.

No, it was the loss of his identity as a senior government official, the surrendering of his insider power, and the recognition that he was going to be just another ordinary citizen that was going to bother him the most, and in truth, he just wasn't ready for that.

Harvard educated in the early 1970's, followed by a combat stint in Viet Nam as a Second Lieutenant in the United States Army where he was twice decorated for bravery, he knew the meaning of sacrifice and all that it entailed. After his tour in the military was over, he worked for years in the private sector, clawing his way up to the top of the corporate ladder for giants like Aramco and Phillips Petroleum. But the accolades he received for his hard work and his dedication left him feeling hollow and ultimately unfulfilled.

He wanted more out of life, and while he never said so vocally, there resided at the fringe of his conscious thoughts the absolute belief that he was a man of destiny; one whose sole purpose in life was to change the path of the world for the better. That was why he'd taken this Presidential appointment; why he'd worked so hard and so loyally for the current administration; and why he buried his conscience and had done so many personally repugnant things—all in the name of God and country; all for the privilege of putting his personal mark on the nation's first long-term energy plan.

He was part of a group that tried to start thinking about the future; ten, twenty, even fifty years out. Getting by in the present just wasn't good enough. A carefully crafted strategy would have to be employed to get the American public to a state of energy independence. In the long term, synthetic fuels, electricity, and conservation would be the keys to a successful future, but during the transition, reliance on America's middle-Eastern allies and their petroleum production was a necessary evil; one which had to be nurtured and watched over so as not to disrupt the flow. And, of course, any long-range strategy meant that thought had to be given to who would be the successor to the throne of the House of Saud, the royal family of Saudi Arabia.

This had been Rendleford's particular contribution to the overall strategy. Early on in the administration, he had been the one to identify Prince Bandar bin

Abd al Aziz as the leading candidate and the likely inheritor to the throne. And he was also the one who'd spent the better part of the last seven years helping to strengthen America's ties to the Prince. It was a plan that showed all the earmarks of future fruition, one that should go a long way towards establishing Rendleford's personal reputation as a forward-thinking tactician, a visionary, and a genius in a world beset by mediocre thinking. But all of this could vanish in a single heartbeat if care wasn't taken to keep the name of Prince Bandar bin Abd al Aziz from being dragged through the mud by a scandal involving his son that was not of Bandar's own making.

The call from Interpol had come in thirty minutes ago, and it had taken that long for Allen Rendleford to begin to get control of his temper. All of his work, all of his planning, now put into jeopardy...all because of Muhammad, Prince Bandar's punk-ass son, who liked to drug unsuspecting girls for sex...and a cop or two who weren't content to leave things well enough alone.

The officer he'd spoken to was Belgian; a man who knew his job; a man who did what he was told.

"You asked to be notified if any inquiries were made concerning Prince Muhammad bin Abd al Aziz?"

"That's right," Rendleford replied, suspecting what was coming as he rubbed his right temple in dismay.

"We received an inquiry at 16:04 your time." His accented English was heavy but understandable. "It came from a Detective Gibson of the Los Angeles Police Department." There was a momentary pause, and Rendleford waited while the man thought through the translation. "He was seeking information on your subject relating to any holds or warrants for crimes of any kind."

"What did you tell him?" Rendleford asked. He could feel his blood pressure rising.

"I did not personally take his call. Another officer did."

Rendleford sighed. "What did the other officer tell him?"

"He was advised that there were no wants or warrants on file," the man replied.

"And were there?" Rendleford asked.

"No, sir. None that we are aware of."

Rendleford took a deep breath and felt himself calming down. If there were no new allegations, then perhaps this potential mess might just go away on its own.

"Did he say anything about the subject? Ask any questions? Give any indication of why he was making the inquiry in the first place?"

The Belgian said, "I was told that his primary inquiry was related to sexual offenses, but I do not have additional details."

Rendleford leaned forward and picked up a pen. "Did this Detective Gibson leave a telephone number?"

"Yes, sir, he did." The officer gave him the number, then rang off the line.

Rendleford had given the matter a lot of thought before deciding what course of action should be taken. Those cops were on to something, and if they weren't, they were bringing up old news that could still cause the kind of embarrassment that might lead to a weakening of the Prince's political position. Either way, it had to be stopped. There was no way he could allow any spurious allegations to make their way to the press. In fact, if certain people in the administration even thought that there was a chance that the boat could possibly be rocked, they'd be hunting for heads, and his own was one that would be served up on a silver platter.

Nope, there was no way that that was going to happen. The kid's father was sacrosanct, and it had to remain that way.

He picked up his phone and placed a call to a familiar number at the Department of Homeland Security.

"Alberto Hernandez," said a voice when the line was picked up.

"Alberto, I need a favor."

"Personal, or on the clock?" said Hernandez.

"This is business." Rendleford leaned back in his chair. "I need you to set up some wiretaps. It's a matter of national security. I have the work number for a Detective Gibson of the Los Angeles Police Department. I'd like his calls to be monitored, and those of another detective named Jennifer Donahue. I spoke to her several days ago." He searched his desk and looked unsuccessfully for the piece of scratch paper that had her number. "I don't seem to have her number at this moment, but I'm guessing that she probably works in the same unit as this guy Gibson. Anyway, I'll need both of their numbers monitored, as well as their personal cell phones when you track them down."

Hernandez was silent for a moment. "You want taps placed on the work and personal telephones of two police Detectives?"

"That's correct, Alberto. It's a matter relating to national security. How long will it take?"

"Is this a FISA situation?"

What Hernandez was referring to was the Foreign Intelligence Surveillance Court which was a US federal court established and authorized under the Foreign Intelligence Surveillance Act of 1978, to oversee requests for surveillance warrants against spies inside the United States.

"It's not a FISA," he answered. "It's strictly domestic; no spies involved."

"Well, if I'm going to write an affidavit, I'll need to know what it's all about?"

Rendleford scratched his head. Maybe he hadn't quite thought this through? He would have to come up with some possible offense being committed by the two detectives to have sufficient probable cause to obtain the warrant, and since he had no authority to write the warrant himself, he had to rely on Hernandez who was a law enforcement official with the power to investigate the situation.

"Look, Alberto. I'm really up against it. I don't want an affidavit out there. Is there any way we can do this off the books?"

"Oh, man, I don't know?" said Hernandez. "In the current environment, that could be trouble for both of us."

It was clear to Rendleford that Hernandez wasn't wild about doing this off the books. He couldn't fault the man. It would put both of them at risk of a criminal indictment.

"Okay, Alberto. Let me tell you what I've got, and you tell me the best way to go forward."

He told Hernandez about the years ago allegation lodged against the Prince, and that the two detectives were apparently reopening the investigation in spite of the fact that it was closed down back in 2012 by order of the Department of State.

"Look, I already spoke to Detective Donahue and told her that the previous allegations were bogus, and on top of that, even if true, they were not prosecutable because the Prince had diplomatic immunity. But it looks like Detective Gibson is intent on reopening the investigation, and we can't allow that to happen. We're in delicate negotiations with the House of Saud over a number of issues, not the least of which is their cooperation with our efforts in Iraq and Yemen. Rumors of criminal behavior on the part of the Prince's son could severely damage our relationship with the Kingdom, and it could change the future line of succession to the throne, and that would conflict with our national interest."

Hernandez seemed to be giving it some thought.

"I know some guys," he finally said. "They'll work off the books. but if you discover something, it can't be used as evidence."

Rendleford smiled. "Thanks, Alberto. I owe you one."

"I'll get back to you when things are in place," said Hernandez, "but we never had this conversation, Allen."

"Trust me on this one, Alberto. This is one of those situations that doesn't fit in the mold, but the potential impact on our international relations could be devastating."

"Oh, I trust you, Allen, but if this goes south, you're on your own."

"Fair enough, Alberto. Just get it set up as fast as you can."

TWENTY-FOUR

The next morning, Donahue arrived at the squad room and found Gibson sitting at his desk, his jacket off, reading the sports section of the Los Angeles Times. She stared at him with undisguised surprise. She'd never seen him reading a newspaper, much less when on duty and seated at his desk.

"What's up?" she said as she set down her purse.

"Nothing," he replied. "I just got here a little early, that's all."

Donahue smiled. With his wife still stuck in the hospital, she could only surmise that Gibson was lonely and rattling around in his empty home.

"Get any sleep?" she asked.

He smiled and folded up the newspaper. "I got a few hours."

"Good. You ready to go?"

"Where are we headed?"

"I thought we could start at Records and take a look at the physical evidence."

Gibson checked his watch. "Will we have time before our meeting in Hollywood?"

"Should be no problem."

They made their way to the Records Unit, logged in, and were presented with a single, large, cardboard box that the night shift had already pulled for their inspection. They each donned a pair of latex gloves, and Gibson produced a knife to cut the seals on the box. The items booked in at the time of the homicide were contained in individually sealed packages that they examined one at a time. Many of the items had no relevance to the case, but at the time they were taken into custody, little was known about the facts or the cause of death. Hence, the philosophy, *take it all and sort everything out later.*

As they moved through the list of items, several became the focus of their attention.

Donahue opened a package labeled *blouse*. White, with a small collar and short sleeves, she carefully unwrapped it, noting that the evidence report indicated that it had been found on the carpeted floor, five feet from the bed.

"Look at this," she said as she laid it out flat. "Two of the buttons are missing."

Gibson leaned over and took a look. "Anything in the report about loose buttons being found?"

Donahue scanned the two pages listing the items booked in from the crime scene.

"Here it is," she said. "Items 53 and 54. Taken from the floor next to the bed." She looked up from the page. "This would tend to negate any claim that she went willingly to bed with this guy."

"Not necessarily," Gibson responded. "When passion takes over, clothes can get in the way."

"You speaking from first-hand knowledge?" she teased.

He snorted a laugh.

She went back to examining the blouse. "Check out the label, Gibby. This blouse is *designer*."

Gibson's brows went up, and his eyes narrowed.

"So?"

"So, she didn't strike me as particularly well off, and this blouse would have cost her quite a bit." She gave him a knowing smile. "So, I'm just saying, it's not likely that any young girl would sacrifice a really expensive designer blouse just for the sake of passion."

Gibson smiled. "You speaking from first-hand knowledge?"

Donahue smiled, a twinkle in her eye. "Of course." She rewrapped the blouse and put it back into its envelope.

In the meantime, Gibson located the package labeled *Flexicuff* and carefully opened it up. He knew from the reports that the plastic strip had been locked very tightly around the Ryson girl's right wrist. To get her body out of the apartment, the coroner's investigator at the scene had clipped it off her wrist on the side that was directly opposite from the locking mechanism.

"There's print dust here," he said. "Obviously, they ended up with nothing."

"At least they tried," Donahue added. "Can you read off the serial number for me? I want to make sure that it was copied down correctly in the evidence report."

She was aware of a robbery case where two numbers in the batch sequence printed on the flexible cuffs had been transposed. It was months later when someone discovered the error; months that had delayed a connection between the cuffs and the robber who had brought them to the crime scene.

Gibson put on his reading glasses and one at a time, he read off the numbers.

"They match," Donahue said, dejectedly. "There goes another possible lead."

Gibson laughed. "It's just a batch number, Jen, and unless the entire batch was sent to the same dealer outlet, it could have come from any number of possible stores."

"I know," she replied, "but a girl can hope, can't she?"

They went through the rest of the items; jeans, panties, low heeled sandals, a small gold cross on a chain, a stuffed teddy-bear, and a picture of the victim with two high school aged girlfriends. But there was nothing of major significance to the case that initially might have been overlooked.

They rewrapped the items, then spent some time going through the pictures in the homicide book. They wanted to establish in their minds where the items had been found in relation to other pieces of evidence at the scene. When they were finished, they placed everything back in the box and turned it back in.

On the way to their car, Donahue thought about the photo of the victim and her friends. So young, so naïve, and so utterly guileless; a horrible crime like this could happen without warning to anyone, and in this case, it had.

It just wasn't fair.

Don't make it personal, she cautioned herself, but it was hard not to. Objectively, she needed to think of the victim as an object—a theoretical person—and not as a once living human being. To get too close to the tragedy itself would mean that she would end up taking on the pain and sorrow felt by everyone else concerned. That pitfall could cause her to think with her emotions and not with an open mind.

At the car, Gibson said, "Well that was a big bust." He started the engine.

"Oh, I don't know." Donahue buckled her seatbelt. "The torn blouse and the Flexicuff are still in existence, and that's a start."

Gibson laughed. The Records Section was famous for losing track of booked evidence, especially when a case was more than a few years old. Many of the earliest cases were missing selected evidentiary items due to carelessness in handling, and in the case of famous, celebrity victims, the actual theft of an object as a *souvenir.*

His partner was right again. The booked evidence still in existence was clearly a decent start.

"Did you happen to notice what wasn't there?" Donahue asked.

"Enlighten me," he replied.

"No picture of her boyfriend, no letters, and no diary. I'm beginning to think that Carrie Ann was a bit of a loner."

"Now that you mention it, you're right. My daughters' rooms were always full of photographs and stuff like that." He looked over at Donahue. "What do you suppose that means?"

Donahue shrugged. "Loners tend to give off a particular vibe. Maybe our boy picked up on it?"

Gibson glanced over in her direction. "More vulnerable?"

Donahue nodded. "Easier prey."

TWENTY-FIVE

When they pulled up at the Hollywood Station, Gibson found a parking spot in the lot behind the building and the two of them entered through a back door that was labeled "Employees Only."

Once inside, they made their way to the Watch Commander's Office. It was there that they found the two guys they were looking for: Tommy Salerno, now the Hollywood Watch Commander—who was seated behind his desk—and Archie Morse, his former partner, now a retired detective. The two men were busy discussing old times, and Gibson, who personally knew them both, introduced them to Jennifer Donahue.

Salerno, a broad-shouldered man in full uniform shook her hand and asked, "Have you guys got time for an early lunch?"

Gibson glanced over at Donahue who nodded in the affirmative.

"Sure," said Gibson. "Why not?"

The four of them walked to a small Thai restaurant on nearby Sunset Boulevard where they took a table towards the back and ordered the daily special. Once they were settled in, Salerno said, "So you're looking into the Ryson case?"

"That's right," Donahue replied.

"It's a tough one," Morse added. He was a massive man with large forearms, a flat forehead, and a buzz cut reminiscent of his time spent in the Marines. He was dressed in slacks and a short sleeve button down shirt, and proudly sported a tattoo on his forearm of an American eagle that was losing its crispness due to the passage of time.

"We've gone over everything in the books," Donahue said. "Is there anything we should know that wasn't written down?"

The question, by itself, might seem insulting if asked by anyone outside the department, but all homicide cops were careful not to express their opinions about a case in writing, so the two detectives knew precisely what she was looking for.

Morse looked over at Salerno, who tacitly nodded. "Have you met Ryson's father?"

"We have," Donahue said.

"A major pain in the ass," Salerno told them. His smiled tightened, and he shook his head. "He called all the time, asking for daily progress reports. Hell… Arch and I even had to tell him to back off a couple of times."

"More than a couple," Morse said. He took a sip from his glass of ice water.

Salerno nodded, then continued.

"He was working Vice at the time. Even went undercover in that club the girl was at on the evening she was killed…the *Darkness* or something like that?"

"*Club Darkness*," Morse corrected.

"That's it," Salerno said with a nod. "Anyway, he was hanging out in there almost every night for a couple of months, hitting up all the patrons for information."

"He mentioned that to us," Donahue said. "But I take it he got nowhere?"

"Never told us if he did," Salerno replied.

Donahue noticed that Salerno sat ramrod straight in his chair. His eyes, pale blue, were watchful, and when he spoke, his voice carried the air of authority of one used to expressing opinions that were beyond being challenged.

The conversation went on hold when the waitress walked up with their food. Once she was gone and everyone started eating, Donahue asked, "I presume you cleared him?"

Salerno looked up as though the question was a personal affront, but she held his glance and waited for a reply.

He swallowed what was in his mouth. Then, "Of course we did. He was at home with his wife. Besides, the DNA we took from the victim wasn't his."

"Just wanted to make sure," she said, still holding his stare. "There was no mention of that in the file?"

"Maybe that report got misplaced," said Morse whose tone let her know that he was being facetious.

Salerno added, "Back then, we figured there was no reason to put it down in the file once we knew he was in the clear." Then, as further justification for what they had omitted, he said, "Why let the defense think we even gave the father a look?"

Donahue accepted the reasoning behind the decision. If a suspect were ever apprehended, the defense would be searching high and low for a fall guy, and it was not beyond the realm of possibility that they might try to pin the killing directly on Carrie Ann's father.

And as for the DNA, while the investigators believed that the killing occurred as part and parcel of the act of sex, a less scrupulous defense team might try to claim that the daughter must have had consensual sex with their client earlier that same evening, and that her father found out, become enraged, and murdered his own daughter. They could allege that tying the victim's hand to the bedpost had been a ploy to focus suspicion away from the father and onto the person that his daughter had been with.

A winning strategy? Not likely, as most juries would see right through it. But Salerno knew what he was talking about. It would only take one juror to foul up a verdict, and the mere fact that they'd even spent time looking at the father might cause an unsophisticated juror to believe that there was more to the case than they were being told.

"Holding stuff out like that wouldn't work, today," said Gibson. "These days we have to log in everything we do."

"I know," said Salerno. "Times have changed, and if we had to do it again, we would've put it in the report."

"I'm sure we did," said Morse, with a wink. "As I said before, that page must've been misplaced."

Donahue nodded. It was a small transgression, given when it occurred, but things like that had a way of blowing up later.

"We saw him in there one night," Morse told them. "You remember that, Tommy?"

Salerno nodded.

"He was seated at the bar, looking like the typical barfly." Morse laughed, and when he did, his whole body shook. "I didn't even recognize him at first. Hell, the guy can do wonders with makeup. But it was the eyes that gave him away. Intense! That's the only way to describe them. They took in everything and missed nothing."

"Too bad he didn't come up with a lead," Gibson said. He had finished his food and was wiping his lips with his napkin.

"Yeah," Salerno added. "It's a shame. We could've used something to work with."

Donahue sat back in her chair. "Anything else that didn't make it to the book?"

Salerno shook his head. "Nope, that's it. We were under the gun on that case, so we put everything down that we had. We just didn't catch any breaks."

"We worked it hard, too," Morse added. "The girl was a nice kid. She didn't deserve what happened."

"Any theories?" Gibson asked.

Salerno gave that some thought. It was apparent to Gibson that he was holding back.

"What?" Donahue asked. She too had picked up on his reluctance to answer the question.

Salerno smiled tightly. "Yeah, we have a theory. We think she picked up someone at the club."

"Or arranged to meet someone at her place," Morse interjected. "See, there was no sign of a break in, no evidence of a struggle. It might have been a case of rough sex..."

His voice trailed off as Donahue thought about the implications. It was indeed possible that the girl had consented to have sex with someone that night, and it wasn't unheard of that bondage—or even limited strangulation—might be utterly consensual between those involved. Could the death have been accidental? She chided herself for not considering that possibility on her own.

"How about drugging?" she asked.

"We did a toxicological screen," Salerno said. "It was negative for hard drugs."

"What about GHB or Rohypnol?" Donahue asked.

"We talked it over," Morse said, "but we ruled it out. When she left the club she was doing fine, and the cabby said that she had no apparent problems, so we ruled it out."

"Why?" Salerno asked. His expression grew stern. "You come up with something that we don't know?"

"Not really." Donahue wasn't willing to share their lead with anyone at the present time. "Just thinking out loud."

"You might still be able to check the blood sample," said Salerno, "but I don't know for sure if that stuff would have cleared her system before the blood sample was taken? Hell, I don't know if it would even show up after all this time?"

"We're already checking that out," Donahue conceded. "Just dotting our I's and crossing our T's."

Salerno seemed satisfied with the answer.

"You know, I was never completely convinced by the alibi that her boyfriend gave. I know he was studying with his friends, but a crime like this, the way it went down, I just couldn't shake the feeling that he might have been involved."

"But the DNA cleared him," Donahue said.

"Yeah," Salerno replied. "Somebody else put it to her, but what if the boyfriend came by that night and saw what was going on? He could have waited until the other guy left, confronted her, killed her where she was in bed or even staged the scene."

"It's possible," Gibson replied, "but not likely. Not based upon what we know about the girl."

"You think?" Salerno laughed. "Why is it that everyone believes that nice girls don't have their kinky side?" He looked over at Donahue. "Did you ever work sex crimes?"

"As a matter of fact, I did," she replied.

"Then you know the old cliché...you can't judge a book by its cover."

Donahue nodded. It was true. When it came to sexual activity, no one could possibly know what goes on in anyone's private life. In fact, Americans might seem like prudes in public, but in private, they tended to be as wild and uninhibited as any other culture.

Salerno swallowed a bite of food, followed by a gulp of coca-cola. "And besides," he said when his mouth was empty, "crimes like this, more often than not, involve the boyfriend or a husband."

Morse interjected, "Tony's feelings have been honed by years of experience, and I've got to tell you, when it comes to gut instincts, Tony has got a perfect record." He smirked when he mouthed, "*He's always wrong.*"

Donahue laughed, then made the decision to probe a little further.

"Tell me something, Lieutenant. Did the name of Muhammad bin Abd al Aziz ever come up in your investigation?"

Salerno leaned forward and stared. "You got something?"

"Not really," she replied.

"Then why are you asking?" Morse said.

It was out of the bag now, so she really had no choice.

"The guy was a known player who hung out sometimes at the club. He may have seen something, we just don't know." It wasn't the whole truth, but at least it was less than a bald face lie.

Salerno was the first to respond. "Never heard that name before. What is he, an Arab?"

"A Saudi," she added, "but we've got nothing to connect him to the crime, and I mean nothing." She shrugged. "Just trying to look at all possible angles."

She wasn't sure they were buying it, but if they weren't, at least they were professional enough to keep their skepticism to themselves.

Salerno looked at his watch. "Well, I've got to get back for a meeting." He turned to Gibson. "A cop's daughter is family. We owe her old man to see it through, so let me know if there's anything at all I can do to help you out?"

"Ditto," Morse added.

He wiped his mouth, got to his feet with the others, then lowered his voice and said, "If you do find the guy that did it, don't hesitate. Put him in the ground."

TWENTY-SIX

Back at her desk in Parker Center, Donahue made a number of telephone calls until she located the manufacturer of the *Flexicuffs*, and once she had one of the executives on the line, she gave him the serial number from the Ryson case evidence and asked him to track it down.

She looked up. Gibson was watching her. She covered the mouthpiece and said, "Just double checking." And after she was told that they'd have to call back, she hung up the phone and walked over to Gibson's desk.

"I just saw the Captain go into his office. I think it's time for us to fill him in."

She led the way with Gibson in tow, and soon they were seated in front of Elwood's desk.

"So where are we now on this case?" the Captain asked.

Donahue filled him in on the interviews with Salerno and Morse, the calls to London and Interpol, the torn blouse belonging to their victim, and the call to the dealer of the Flexicuffs.

Elwood listened intently, then said, "Old news. There's nothing new to work with."

"I'm not finished," she said, a bit miffed that he wasn't waiting for the end of her presentation.

"*Well, pardon me.*" He showed her no quarter. "I thought you were done."

She launched into a recitation of their interview with Andi Rudinova, the similarities with the M.O. used in their crime, and her revelation that Rendleford, at the Department of State, had used extortive tactics to pressure Andi Rudinova to keep quiet about her attack.

"That's mildly interesting," Elwood said, "but from what I can tell, it's not really germane to your investigation."

Donahue looked over at Gibson and frowned. This was not going the way she had hoped.

She told Elwood about the interview with Mia Amoretti and her belief that

Aziz had been in the club on the night that Carrie Ryson was killed.

On hearing that, Elwood sat up straighter. "Did she place him with our victim?"

Donahue checked her notes.

"She saw him out on the dance floor, and Carrie was out there at the time, but she doesn't know if the two of them hooked up."

Elwood shrugged. "Close, but no cigar."

"Look," she said, "it's tenuous, I know, but I think we've got enough to justify getting a sample of his DNA."

"You'll never get a warrant with that," Elwood said.

"I know," she replied, then smiled sweetly. "I was hoping to convince you to send Gibby and me to Istanbul so that we could pick up a sample without anyone being the wiser."

Elwood laughed and turned to Gibson. "Are you in on this, too?"

"Jen's right," Gibson said with a shrug. "Look, Boss, we may not be able to prosecute this guy, but we should at least do our best to find out if he's our killer."

Elwood sat back, gave it some thought, then folded his arms across his chest.

Not a good sign.

"I don't think I can sell it to the Chief," he told them. "Your suspect's connection with the victim, at best, is tenuous, and a trip like that would be costly. And even if you did get a DNA sample, and even if it matched the DNA that was left at the crime scene, that *shit-bird* Aziz still has immunity." He shook his head. "Nope, I don't see the Chief untying the purse strings for a trip to clear a case that can never be filed."

Donahue leaned back and softened her voice.

"The victim was nineteen and the daughter of one of our own. We owe it to her father to see this through. And, the rank and file expect us to work it forever if need be. Everyone keeps reminding me we're talking about family—"

Elwood closed his eyes briefly. "Okay. You're right. It's worth a try. I'll let you know what the Chief has to say."

Back at her desk, Donahue got a call from the manufacturer of the Flexicuffs.

"The cuffs you're interested in were part of a bigger lot of one thousand, and it turns out that the entire run with that particular serial number was sold to a single gun store in Los Angeles."

That was good news. At least all the cuffs with the same batch number were distributed out of a single retail store.

"Can you give me the name of the gun store?" Donahue asked. She reached for a pen and a piece of paper.

"Heston Gun Shop." He gave her an address on Slauson Avenue.

Donahue thanked him and hung up.

The Heston Gun Shop was a well-known store in the South-central end of the city. The volume of sales at that location was high, and not surprisingly, many of the guns legally purchased were used in street crimes.

She looked up the phone number, called the store, and waited for the manager to come on the line.

"This is Howard Jackson," he said.

"Mr. Jackson, this is Detective Donahue, LAPD." She went on to tell him about the batch of Flexicuffs and their interest in the names of whoever were the buyers.

"We wouldn't have that information," Jackson said. "We don't track that type of purchase."

Donahue was surprised. "You mean anyone can buy a pair of Flexicuffs, and there's no way to track their identity?"

"They could buy a hundred pairs and we wouldn't care," Jackson told her. "See, there's no law against owning Flexicuffs, so we're not required to keep track of the people who purchase them."

Donahue thought that over. Perhaps there was another way to connect her suspect to the store.

"If I give you the name of someone, could you check your records and see if he ever made a purchase of anything at your store?"

"I might be able to," Jackson replied. She could tell by his tone that he was growing tired of the questions and the work it might take to provide her with an answer.

"I'd really appreciate it if you can do this for me," she said.

Jackson grunted. "And if I didn't, I suppose you'd be serving me with a subpoena or a search warrant?"

Donahue smiled. "Something like that."

She gave him the full name of Aziz and Jackson put her on hold. Ten minutes later, he was back on the line.

"I ran his name through our customer database, but it didn't pop up."

"So he didn't buy the cuffs at your store?" she said, more to herself than to Jackson.

"I didn't say that," he replied. "Look, anyone could have bought those cuffs for him. Like I say, owning them isn't a crime, and if an order is paid for with cash, we don't bother to take down names."

Donahue realized that Aziz could have sent in one of his bodyguards to purchase them, or for that matter, anyone else. And if they didn't use a credit card, they were screwed.

"Well, thanks for your time," she said. "If I come up with any other names, I'll —"

But Jackson hung up the phone before she was finished.

Asshole! She turned to Gibson. "Well, that was a great big goose egg."

Gibson slid his chair back. "Let's go next door and get a beer. We've earned it."

Donahue checked her watch. It was close enough to quitting time, so she made up her mind.

"You gonna buy?"

They walked down the street to a bar at a nearby hotel; an after-work hangout where cops liked to gather. A few greetings were exchanged before they took a table near the back. Gibson ordered a beer while Donahue settled for an apple martini.

The first round was consumed while they discussed Claudette's condition and how Gibson planned to cope with her after-discharge care. He was anxious about how it would go but seemed less worried than he'd been several days ago. When the second round came, Donahue opened up about her situation with Dr. Zach.

"I just don't see how it's going to work out," she told him. "You can't build a relationship when both people are working all the time."

Gibson took a sip of his beer. "Far be it from me to give advice—"

"But you will anyway," she interjected, lifting the glass to her lips.

Gibson smiled. "But I will anyway." His eyes locked with hers. "I've spent a lot of time this past week going over my life and how I've lived it."

"And?" she said when he failed to continue.

"And, I really screwed up. Claudette's illness has opened my eyes." He leaned forward, elbows on the table, chin rested in one palm. "This job, as addictive as it is, means nothing compared with the times I've spent with my wife. And if I were to lose her now, everything I've done on this job would count for nothing. I should have spent more time with her, No, that's wrong. I should have *made* more time for her, because in the end, when it's all over, it's the time with her that I'm going to miss and not this thankless job."

"That's so sweet," Donahue said. "But shouldn't you be telling this to her?"

"I plan to," he replied, "but I'm trying to make a point here." He studied her face for a long time. "Are you in love with the guy?"

She took her time before answering. "I don't really know."

"Does he make you happy?"

Donahue gave him a nervous laugh. "What is this, Gibby? Twenty questions?"

"Does he?"

She sighed. "I guess."

"I guess doesn't sound very convincing, Jen."

"I know."

"Look. If you really love Zach, then you do what you need to do to make it work." He put his lips on the beer bottle and finished it off.

"But we both have our careers to think about, and—"

Gibson interrupted her. "If you love him, don't be afraid to let this job go."

Donahue closed her eyes. She was feeling the two drinks and starting to worry that she might say more than she intended.

"But I love this job."

Gibson laughed. "You've got it ass-backward. When it's real, you should be saying 'I love him, and I *enjoy* this job.' There's a world of difference."

But Donahue was thinking that just the opposite was true. She loved the job and *enjoyed* her time with Zach.

Maybe her confusion stemmed from the fact that she was consciously trying to make something work that her unconscious mind knew wasn't right.

Gibson waived his hand, and when a waitress appeared, he ordered another beer. Donahue begged off a third martini.

"Just remember this," he said when the waitress had gone. "In the end, it's only the relationship that counts and not the number of cases you solve."

"Words from the wise," she joked.

"Words from a slow learner," he corrected.

Gibson's third beer arrived, and with a flourish, he took a first swallow.

"By the way, Jen, you did a good job in Tom's office. You played the family card at just the right moment. You really had me convinced."

Donahue frowned. "I wasn't playing a card. I was serious."

"Hold on." Gibson raised his hands in surrender. "I know you were serious. I was giving you a compliment on the timing of your remark, and I'd be willing to bet that Tom plays it the same way when he takes your request to the Chief."

Donahue smiled. "I hope you're right. We need to clear this case up."

"We will, but in the meantime, we'd better figure out an alternative plan for getting a DNA sample, just in case I'm wrong about the way this is going to go."

Donahue had been thinking about that for several days, but there really was no easy solution.

"Short of convincing a Turkish cop to follow him around waiting for him to spit on the sidewalk, I'm fresh out of ideas."

"I'll work on it," Gibson said. He looked over at her glass and pointed. "You ready for another?"

"Not a chance." She gathered up her purse. "I'm already over my limit." She slowly got to her feet. "Thanks for the advice, Gibby. I'll give it some thought."

"You do that," he replied.

TWENTY-SEVEN

In the morning, after a three-mile run through her neighborhood, a bowl of instant oatmeal and an organic banana, Donahue arrived at the squad room where she found a little sticky note placed on her desktop phone. A message taken by someone on the night watch team advised her that Detective Inspector Grayson of New Scotland Yard had tried to reach her during the night and wanted her to call him back as soon as practical.

She dialed his number and was moderately surprised when he actually answered the phone. She checked her watch. London was eight hours ahead of Los Angeles time.

"You're still in your office? Very impressive," she said.

He laughed. "Actually, I was headed out the door. We just finished rounding up a cell of Bulgarian nationalists. Nothing spectacular, in fact, rather a third rate bunch if you ask me, but the whole operation was very time-consuming."

"Bulgarian nationalists?" She smiled into the phone. "You've got some awfully exotic criminal groups in your town."

"You don't know the half of it," he replied. "And speaking of strange, we did a search of all solved and unsolved rape cases while Prince Aziz was a guest in our country and nothing popped up."

Donahue cursed under her breath. It had been a long shot, of course, but she had banked on the fact that they'd come up with something they could use.

"Well, thanks for trying," she said. "I appreciate—"

"Hold on," he said quickly, "I'm not done. We also did a check of all our solved and unsolved homicides that involved an act of rape, and we found two cases where our victims were both young women; blond, in their early twenties, and both were secured by one wrist to their beds."

Donahue rocked forward in her chair. "You're kidding!" Her excitement was palpable. "Any chance it could be him?"

"We have DNA from semen left at both crime scenes, and they were a match, which means that the same man had intercourse with both of our victims. But just like you, we don't have a DNA sample from Aziz on file, so we can't say for sure that it's his."

"So, we're in the same boat?" Donahue asked.

"It would appear so."

Donahue's mind was reeling. Now that it looked like there might be additional victims, the British government could be expected to cooperate with her investigation, and the more people she could enlist to her cause, the greater the likelihood that others could be convinced to also come on board.

She had what she thought was a brilliant idea.

"Any chance you can send us a copy of the genetic sequencing from your DNA? I'd like to have our people run a comparison with the DNA from our crime scene. I think the first step is to make sure that the same guy was the perpetrator in all three of the cases."

"I was thinking the very same thing," Grayson said with a chuckle. "What is it that the kids like to say.... *you show me yours first, then I'll show you mine...?"*

"I thought it was *lady's first*."

Grayson laughed. "Perhaps there's room for a compromise."

"Simultaneous emails? I can send ours off to you in a couple of minutes?"

"Fair enough." He put his hand over the receiver for a moment, and Donahue could detect a muffled conversation. When he came back on the line he said, "We can send you ours in about twenty minutes."

"That's great!"

Grayson added, "In the meantime, we'll keep checking with our hospitals and dental clinics to see if Aziz had any procedures while he was here. If he did, hopefully, there are blood or tissue samples still lying around on a shelf somewhere."

They exchanged email addresses, then ended the call.

Donahue located the Ryson sequencing report and sent it off to Grayson. When Grayson's two pages of similar results were received, Donahue got on the phone to the crime lab and arranged for a technician to receive Grayson's reports and to compare them with the sequencing from the Ryson case.

When the lab tech agreed to standby, she emailed him what he needed, then paused for a moment to contemplate what to do next.

Gibson walked in, a smile on his face.

"What's up?" Donahue asked. The improvement in his demeanor was a pleasant surprise.

"Claudette's getting released tomorrow," he said. He took off his hat, laid it on his desk, then removed his coat and hung it on a nearby rack.

She leaned back in her chair and smiled. "Congratulations! You all set with things at home?"

"I think I'm on top of it." He sat down in his chair and turned to face her. "An RN from the insurance company called and said she's going to be our case monitor. She's arranging for a wheelchair and a physical therapist, so it's starting to look pretty good."

Donahue knew the stress he'd been under all week long and what a relief this turn of events must be.

"I'm really happy for you guys," she said.

He noticed that the smile on her face didn't fade away. "What are you grinning about?"

She held up the printed out email reports from London.

"My contact at Scotland Yard came through for us. They found two unsolved rape-murders connected together by DNA. Both victims were cuffed to their beds. I've got our lab looking at the sequencing report, but it looks to my inexperienced eye that it's gonna be a match."

Gibson smiled. "So whoever did ours did theirs?"

"Looks like it."

Gibson grinned. "Well, I'll be damned. Have you told the Captain?"

"Not yet. I was waiting for you to come in."

"Let's go talk to him now. This changes everything."

Donahue's phone rang. She picked it up, had a short conversation, then gave the thumbs up to Gibson.

"It's a match," she said as she hung up the phone. Her eyes were twinkling. "The crime lab guys want to see the rough test data before they say anything in court, but it's crystal clear…the same guy killed all three, and I'd be willing to bet my firstborn that the guy we're looking for is gonna be Prince Aziz."

"Your first born, huh?" Gibson smirked. "Is there something you want to tell me?"

"It's a figure of speech, you bozo." She got to her feet, unable to sit, but not sure what she ought to do next.

Gibson looked at his watch.

"I'll tell you what. I'll go in and tell the Captain, you get on the horn and tell your guy in London that we're looking for the same guy. After that, we'll see what happens."

Donahue returned to her desk and dialed in Grayson's number. This would be a call she was happy to make.

TWENTY-EIGHT

Four hours later, Donahue, Gibson, and Captain Tom Elwood were summoned to the office of the Chief of Police.

Chief Damian Brennon, a transplanted New Yorker who previously served as Police Commissioner of the NYPD, had recently taken over as Chief in Los Angeles at the request of the Police Commission. It was his stated goal to bring the department into compliance with a Federal Court consent decree that had been issued to oversee the activities of the Department. To accomplish this mandate, Chief Brennon replaced many top police officials. In his short time in office, he had already set up a check and balance system to oversee the training and conduct of officers assigned to the field, and he worked hard to cement relations with the various leaders of the city's ethnic minorities, all in an effort to improve the level and quality of officer service.

And surprisingly enough, it was working. Morale on the department had improved substantially, and community leaders were less critical of the department overall when the now rare, but unavoidable, problems occurred.

Brennon was seated at a conference table next to his desk in a tastefully appointed office that was three times larger than any other office in the building. He wore his blue dress uniform, his way of fostering a connection with the front line troops.

He got to his feet to greet the three officers, then invited them to take a seat.

He looked directly at Gibson then switched his gaze to Donahue.

"Tom has briefed me on the state of your investigation," he said, "and I want to commend you both. You're doing a great job."

Donahue smiled. "Thanks, Chief."

Gibson simply nodded.

"Having said that, I must tell you that I received a call today from the Department of State." He consulted a notepad on the table in front of him. "From Assistant Undersecretary for Political Affairs…a man named Allen Rendleford."

He looked up and said, "He advises me that your suspect has diplomatic immunity…*complete* immunity. In fact, the word he used was *untouchable*…and for that reason, he tells me…no, make that he *ordered me*… to immediately cease any further investigation into this matter on the grounds that it infringes upon our country's national security interests."

Donahue was beside herself with disappointment, but her unhappiness quickly morphed into anger.

"But Chief, we think this guy murdered three girls that we know of, one of them the daughter of one of our own Lieutenants. We can't just walk away from this. We have to see it through. Something needs to—"

The Chief held up his hand, and it stopped her mid-sentence.

"Did I say we were going to walk away from this?"

Donahue bit her tongue. She'd done it again. She'd opened her mouth before she let him finish.

She gave him an embarrassed nod, took a deep breath, and kept her mouth shut.

The Chief continued, "He also said to me that *'our Allies'* will also be instructed to shut down their concurrent investigation *immediately*."

He leaned forward in his chair, arms resting on the table, his eyes moved back and forth between them.

"This places me in an awkward position. If this Mr. Rendleford is correct, the continuation of our investigation might put our country's national interest in jeopardy."

Uh, oh! Donahue could feel the pendulum swinging against her argument and towards Rendleford's. But the Chief wasn't through.

"So, I've given full consideration to the government's position, and I've concluded that national interest is Washington's problem, not ours. Our mandate is to investigate any crimes committed in LA and to make arrests for those crimes whenever we can."

He looked around the table, then gave Donahue a wink.

"Maybe it's not in our national interest to arrest this guy, but nobody has the right to tell me that we can't work a murder until we know who did it." He folded his hands on the table in front of him. "Besides, it really chaffs my ass when someone tries to order me around." He shook his head. "The arrogance of that prick. And what's this crap about *our Allies?* Is he referring to the Brits and the two cases that Tom mentioned, or is there something else about this case that I haven't been told?"

And that was when it hit her. Donahue sat up in her chair.

"He couldn't know about the British cases."

Everyone looked at her.

"We only got the call from my source at the Yard about—" She glanced at her watch. "—five hours ago!"

She turned to Gibson.

"No one knew about those cases, that is, unless someone here mentioned it, and that's unlikely."

"He brought up the phrase '*our Allies*' in our conversation," the Chief said, "so he knew about your investigation before he spoke with me."

She gave that some thought.

"Only one way." She looked at the Chief. "Someone must be tapping our phones."

The Chief pursed his lips and made fists with his hands. His mind was apparently made up.

"Okay. Here's what we're going to do." His gaze took in Donahue and Gibson. "I want the two of you to go to London and talk to your people at Scotland Yard and see if you can get copies of the British case investigations. Once we know where we stand with the Brits, call me, and we'll decide if a trip to Istanbul is warranted."

Donahue and Gibson both nodded.

Elwood said, "What do you want us to do about the phones, Chief?"

"Assume that they're being tapped. Get everyone's phones checked: work, home, and cell. If you find anything, I want to know right away."

He shifted his glance back and forth between them. "Get yourself new cell phones. If the Fed's are tapping our lines, they're going to wish they hadn't."

The meeting was over, and the three detectives got to their feet. As they headed towards the door, the Chief said to Donahue, "I would suggest that the two of you get over to London quickly. This guy at the State Department seems to have a very long reach, so I'm guessing that the sooner you get there and get what you need, the better."

Donahue nodded. "We're on our way."

* * * *

They wandered back downstairs to the squad room. As Elwood peeled off and went to his office, he said, "I've got a contact over at DEA (Drug Enforcement Administration). I'll give him a call and see what we can do about a sweep of the phones."

Gibson nodded. "We'll take care of the rest."

When they arrived back at their desks, Gibson said to Donahue, "Get a new phone using someone else's name on the account." He gave her a wry grin. "Perhaps Doctor Zachary will set one up for you under his name?"

"Cute," she said with a tight-lipped grin, "but that might end up being too cozy."

Gibson raised a brow. "Too cozy? As in relationship wise?"

Donahue vigorously shook her head.

"No, what I'm saying is that these guys might be monitoring his calls, too."

"I hadn't thought of that." Gibson's expression became solemn. "Guess I'm gonna have to do a better job of thinking this through."

Donahue was still seething. The idea that her phone calls were being listened to was outrageous. From her experience with wiretaps, she knew that a warrant wouldn't get past a judge without probable cause to believe that someone was actually committing a crime. But she'd committed no crime; she was merely doing her job, and if the tap was supposedly authorized for national security reasons, then the process was clearly abusive.

But how was she going to prove that her calls were being tapped?

And then it hit her. She turned to Gibson. "I think I know how to prove what the Fed's are doing. I'll be right back."

She walked down the hallway, in search of Thompson, who had taken over an interview room where she could get a lot of her paperwork done without interruption. But when Thompson heard what Donahue had in mind, she flashed a smile.

"It's a good idea, Jen. Want to use my phone?"

Donahue nodded. On Thompson's cell, the first thing she did was call a travel agent, a girlfriend from college who booked tickets for her and Gibson on that evening's British Airway's, red-eye flight to London. The second call she made was to Chimlin Boonprasom, also known as Kimi, a detective acquaintance of hers who worked sex crimes in Bangkok, Thailand.

Prior to working homicide, Donahue had attended an international conference on pedophiles which was held in Amsterdam. It was there that she met the diminutive Thai detective and they had been frequently corresponding ever since.

"Kimi? Hi! It's Jennifer Donahue. I'm sorry to call you at home. I hope I didn't wake you?"

"Jennifer?" Kimi's voice was heavy and sounded confused, and Donahue sensed that she had been asleep.

"I'm sorry I woke you up," she said. "I can call back later if you like?"

"No, it's okay." Kimi now seemed to be fully awake. "Is everything okay?"

"Everything's fine," Donahue replied, "but I need to ask you for a really big favor."

She explained that she was in the middle of a major investigation involving a political figure with diplomatic immunity, and how her superiors believed that her office and cell phones were being tapped. She asked Kimi to help her create an investigative diversion, and when she filled her in on what she wanted her to say, Kimi wholeheartedly agreed to play her role.

Her next call on Thompson's cell phone was to DI Mark Grayson of Scotland Yard. She gave him the details of her British Airway's flight, then asked him to meet them at the plane.

"Of course," he said. "By the way, please bring along the rough data for your DNA profile. Our lab folks want to see it all before they declare a positive match."

"Not a problem, and if it's okay with you, I'd like the same from you when we get there."

"I'll have it ready," he replied.

"One more thing," she told him. "An Undersecretary of State named Rendleford had been doing all he can to kill this investigation. We think he's got a tap on our phones because he told our Chief that you guys would be told to kill it as well."

"Would be told?" Grayson smirked. "Cheeky bastard isn't he? Well, I appreciate the head's up. I'll see you tomorrow morning."

He rang off the line, and Donahue passed the cell phone back to Thompson.

"So what's next?" Thompson asked.

"Now it's time to make a few calls that will send a certain Fed in the wrong direction."

She headed out the door and back to her office where she used the phone on her desk to book two economy tickets to Bangkok for late the following day.

"Bangkok?" Gibson, who had overheard her making the reservations, scratched his head. "What's going on?"

"You'll see," she replied. "I'm running a little test to see if our phones are really being tapped.

She then placed another call to Detective Boonprasom in Bangkok, and when Kimi picked up, she sounded wide awake.

Donahue put the call on the speaker so that Gibson could listen in.

"Kimi? Hi, it's Jennifer Donahue. I was calling to see if you had a chance to search through your unsolved homicide cases?"

Kimi kept her tone of voice both even and measured.

"We found five unsolved homicides, all of them matching the MO you sent us. We'd like to get a look at the DNA sample you have on your suspect. Can you send it to us?

"I'll do you one better," Donahue replied. She looked up at Gibson and smiled. "My partner and I will be taking a flight from here to Bangkok tomorrow evening. We'll bring the rough data along so that your people can run a comparison with what you've got on your cases." She paused for effect. "By the way, did you determine if the Prince was in your country during the times of your homicides?"

Kimi took a moment before answering.

"That part of the investigation is still pending, but so far we've determined that he made four weekend-trips here that would place him in Bangkok at the time of four of our cases. We're still checking with our immigration department to see if he was here when the fifth killing occurred."

"Okay." Donahue was openly grinning. She then gave her the flight information, and Kimi agreed to meet them when they arrived.

When she hung up the phone, Gibson was laughing.

“That’s going to really piss them off,” he said.

“I hope so,” Donahue replied. “In the meantime, we’re heading out to London tonight, and if Rendleford’s people were listening in on my call to Kimi and the airlines, and if they’re serious about thwarting our investigation, they might try to intercept us when we try to get on the plane to Bangkok.” She shook her head and laughed. “And by then, we should already be arriving in London.”

Donahue got up and gestured with her chin towards the Captain’s office.

“Should we let him know what I’ve done?”

“That would be prudent.”

Gibson stood up and checked his watch. “I’m going to head over to Cedars and see Claudie to make sure that I’ve got things covered there.”

“Give her my best.”

He put on his hat. “I’ll see you at the plane.”

TWENTY-NINE

On her way home to pack, Donahue made a detour to the West Los Angeles station house to meet with Lieutenant Michael Ryson. She found him doing some paperwork at his desk and he looked up when she entered his office.

"Detective Donahue?" His eyes grew wide with surprise. "Hey, what's up? Grab a seat."

She took a chair in front of his desk.

"I wanted to get back to you about where we are in our investigation."

He seemed to relax a bit. He pushed the papers to the side and tilted back in his chair.

"It turns out that the DNA left behind in your daughter's case matches the DNA in two other homicides in metropolitan London."

Ryson bolted into an upright sitting position.

"Two others? Does that mean you know who did it?"

"We're not sure. We have a suspect, but we don't yet have a sample from him that we can use to run a comparison."

"Who is it?" he asked. His tone was clipped and brooked no dissent.

She thought it over, then decided to tell him the rest of the story.

"Back when your daughter was killed, there was a guy who used to hang out at the club; a known player and a ladies man. His name never came up in the initial investigation, but we got a line on him from the club manager who told us the guy stopped coming around after the night of the murder. I won't bore you with all the details now, but we tracked him down through a parking citation that was written on his car. His name is Prince Muhammad bin Abd al Aziz. And yes, he really is a prince." She shifted in her chair. "And that's part of our problem."

Ryson hung his head, seemingly overwhelmed by the fact that a suspect had finally been named. Donahue wasn't sure, but for a moment it appeared as though his eyes had begun to tear up.

She waited while he composed himself, and when he was ready, she said, "His father is Ambassador Prince Bandar bin Abd al Aziz, of the Royal House of Saud. And as it turns out, he is one of three major candidates in line to succeed the current king as the next ruler of Saudi Arabia."

Ryson hardly moved. In fact, to Donahue, it looked as if he'd actually stopped breathing. She watched his eyes, dark and brooding, and for the briefest of moments, they lost their luster, becoming the windows to a bottomless pit.

"When his father was here, both he and the son had complete diplomatic immunity. The son picked up a rape by drugging allegation about five months before your daughter was killed. The State Department stepped in and pulled all the records, and the case went nowhere. That's why the MO wasn't picked up by the system."

Donahue paused to give Ryson time to absorb what she was telling him. She watched his face, looking for clues as to what he was thinking, but the man was now in complete control of his emotions, and with the exception of his unblinking stare, which by the way was beginning to unnerve her, he never gave a clue as to what was coursing through his mind.

"What about the other two cases?" he finally asked.

"Both of them popped up in London." Her shoulders sagged. "Shortly after your daughter's murder, the son left the States and apparently returned to Saudi Arabia. His father was later posted as Ambassador to the United Kingdom, and the son joined him there. The two rape-murders they're looking at occurred while the father was stationed there."

Ryson had folded his arms across his chest and his head rocked forward and backward.

Donahue continued, "Gibson and I are headed off to London tonight to review their cases. The Yard is trying to dig up a DNA sample from the Prince by checking with doctors and dentists in the area, on the off chance that he had a procedure of some kind while he was there. But if that fails, the Chief will probably allow us to go from there to Istanbul, Turkey, where the father and son are now stationed."

"Can this guy be extradited from Turkey?" Ryson asked.

Donahue shook her head. "He has immunity from extradition and prosecution. If he's the one, we can't touch him."

Ryson pursed his lips. "Then all of this...all of your efforts...*are for nothing*?"

"Not exactly. If we can prove that he did it, we may be able to convince the State Department to intercede with the government of Saudi Arabia to try him for these killings in their own country."

"A lot of good that will do if his father becomes the King."

Donahue shrugged. He got the picture, and unfortunately, there was no way to sugar coat it.

Might as well tell him the rest of it.

"I've told you all of this because we're starting to feel some heat from the State Department. They seem to be actively working to block our investigation. In fact, Gibson and I are going out of here tonight partly to make sure that we get to see the cases in London before the State Department gets to their sources in London to put pressure on the Metropolitan Police to shut things down."

Ryson was incredulous.

"Why the hell would they want to do that?"

Donahue bit her lip. "I've been led to believe that the father's ascension to the throne is crucial to our national interest. I have no doubt that they believe that any efforts to go after the son might undermine that goal by producing a host of unforeseen consequences."

"What if we went to the press?" he asked.

She shook her head. "I can't even imagine the shit we'd be in."

"Well, I'm gonna think that one over," he told her.

"Lieutenant." Her tone of voice was now serious. "I've gone out on a limb here to keep you in the loop. In fact, I've probably told you some stuff I shouldn't have said, but I think you're owed the truth. If you do anything now or say anything to anyone about what we're doing, we might never be able to prove that the son is the man who killed your daughter." She looked into his eyes. "Please? Don't say anything to anyone, and in particular, don't say anything on the phone, either at work or personal."

He raised an eyebrow. "Are you suggesting that someone has tapped my phones?"

She didn't respond. Instead, she reached for her purse and got to her feet.

"I've got to get home and get packed. Please, keep what I've told you confidential."

The stern look on his face suddenly vanished. He got to his feet, came around the desk, and unexpectedly gave her a hug.

"I appreciate your coming over here and filling me in. I'm really impressed with what you've done on this case. You're all right, Donahue."

"Thanks," she said.

He broke off the hug and stepped back.

"This has been a long time coming. Will you let me know when you've matched his DNA with my daughter's case?"

"I will, and I trust that you'll keep what I've told you just between us?"

"Of course," he said with just a moment's hesitation. "I wouldn't do anything to interfere with your investigation."

She smiled and took a step back. "I'll be in touch with you just as soon as we get back."

THIRTY

The flight on British Airways was arduous and hard on his back, which caused Gibson to shift uncomfortably in his seat. He was not a big fan of long-distance flying, and as such, this one had him on edge.

In his youth, he'd flown several times across the Atlantic with the military, and several times on vacations with his wife, but those trips had occurred early in his marriage, before kids, when he was full of adventure and never in need of sleep. But youth had been fleeting, and over time, he'd become more set in his ways. And while he didn't really want to take this trip, he had no real choice. It came with the job.

His knees were pressed up against the back of the seat in front of him, and his head kept slipping off the foam rubber pillow. Dejected, he folded his arms across his chest and clutched at the paper-thin blanket.

Another thought that had him worried was derived from an article he had recently read about the risks associated with blood clots formed by sitting too long on international flights. To avoid becoming a medical statistic, he'd taken the aisle seat, the better for taking frequent walks without disrupting the other passengers. As a result of his overactive mind, he was reduced to taking fitful naps throughout the non-stop, eleven-hour flight.

Donahue was a different story. She enjoyed flying international, and the longer the trip, the better she liked it.

She approached it as an adventure, and after boarding the plane, she drank a little wine, ate the so-so meal that was served after takeoff, and watched a romantic comedy on the seat back screen. When that didn't tire her out, she skimmed through a couple of movie-gossip magazines, drank a great deal of water for hydration, then popped a sleeping pill. She put on a sleeping mask, said goodnight to Gibson, then racked up hours of dreamless sleep throughout the course of the journey.

When they touched down at Heathrow Airport on the outskirts of London, they were met by Detective Inspector (DI) Mark Grayson who guided them through Customs and Immigration before walking them to his car. Gibson settled in the back seat where he soon found himself dozing off, while Donahue, now wide-awake, decided it was time for her to check in with Elwood.

She pulled out her new cell phone and dialed his also new phone.

"Captain?" she said, " It's Jennifer Donahue."

"Are you on the ground yet?" Elwood asked.

"We just got in." She glanced out the window at the rolling countryside. "We're on the highway, heading into London."

Elwood cleared his throat. "I sent an undercover officer out to LAX to the departure gate for the Thailand flight, just to see if anything was amiss. Turns out that a contingent of Federal Agents showed up, and my UC says they were really pissed off when you and Gibson didn't show for the flight."

Donahue slowly shook her head. "I knew they were tapping my calls. Those slimy bastards!" But her momentary elation at being correct about the bugging was immediately tempered by her certainty that the Feds would blame her for the deception and that somewhere down the road, she was going to have to deal with a payback.

"I guess I can count on an IRS audit this year," she said.

Elwood laughed. "That wouldn't surprise me at all."

Donahue took a deep breath, then sighed. "So what's next?"

"I've talked to the Chief about what happened, and needless to say, he's not amused. He's got a meeting set up with the US Attorney in LA tomorrow afternoon to bring up the matter of the Federal government wiretapping our lines."

"Good, and just so you know, there was no sign of the Feds at our BA flight, so hopefully, it'll take them a while to track us down."

Elwood's voice took on a cautionary tone.

"Just don't mess around while you're there, Jen. The Feds may be playing catch-up for a while, but once they do, it's gonna be for real, and one doesn't need to be a psychic to know that this turf war we've started is far from being over."

When she hung up the phone, she explained to Grayson and Gibson what had happened in LA with the Feds; and she left nothing out.

Gibson, who'd been unable to catch a real nap, sat upright throughout her recitation.

When she was finished, Grayson said, "I was going to mention that MI6, our foreign intelligence service, has been contacted directly by your government."

Donahue leaned forward. "Wow! It didn't take them long to catch up after all." She looked over at Grayson. "Has that caused a problem for you?"

"Six came down pretty hard on my superiors at the Yard—something, I might add, they didn't appreciate. But when the shouting was through, I'm afraid to say that Six came out on top. I've been told that it went all the way to Downing Street, and the Prime Minister himself came down on the side of your government."

He turned his head and looked directly at Donahue.

"Officially, I've been advised that our investigation has been completely shut down, and as of last night, the entire matter is now covered by the Official Secrets Act." He smiled ruefully and placed a finger to his lips. "All very hush-hush now, I'm afraid, so our cooperation is over."

Donahue could not conceal the disappointment on her face. "Somehow, I just didn't think your people would fold that fast."

Grayson shrugged. "Your people have a very long reach."

Gibson, who'd been silent up to this point, felt his anger overcome his lethargy.

"So we've come all the way over here for nothing?"

Grayson maneuvered a lane change through the increasingly congested highway traffic, then he locked on to Gibson's eyes through the use of his rearview mirror.

"Your State Department has been provided with a copy of all of our crime reports," he said. "And when I gave them to Six, I was once again admonished that *officially*, we will no longer cooperate with you on this investigation."

Gibson folded his arms across his chest. He was fuming. "Like I said, all the way here for *nothing.*"

"I'm sorry, Detective Gibson, but from this point forward, I'm afraid that the Yard is off limits for the both of you."

Gibson shook his head. "Then you might as well turn around and take us back to the airport." He leaned forward towards Donahue and said, "We better get on to Istanbul before they shut us down with the Turks."

Donahue shook her head. "I don't get it. Why are both of our governments so willing to protect this guy?"

Grayson met her glance. "To understand that, you need only to consider the relationship that exists between the Royal House of Saud and your own President. He and the King have been friends for many years, and because of that, it's highly unlikely that your government would ever allow anything to publicly embarrass any member of the Royal Family, particularly someone as influential as Prince Bandar." He shook his head, clearly frustrated by the actions of his superiors. "No, I believe that both of our governments have the same idea. The information we mutually possess concerning his son has great currency only if Prince Bandar himself becomes the next King."

"It's all about the oil," Gibson groused.

Donahue's mind drifted. She was trying to process what she was hearing, but at the same time, she was thinking ahead, trying to devise a way to go forward with the investigation.

Grayson picked up a sealed envelope from the seat between them and handed it to Donahue.

"What's this?" she asked.

"A complete set of our reports on the two homicides," he replied.

Donahue's surprise turned to a smile. "Thanks, Mark. I knew I could count on you."

"*Officially*," he said, pointing a finger in her direction, "I sent that envelope to you before I got the word about shutting things down."

Donahue nodded. "Understood."

"Good," he replied. He kept his eyes on the road. "Like you, I don't buy into all of the bollocks being tossed around by Six and your Department of State. If it turns out that Bandar's son is the one who killed those girls, then he ought to pay the price. It's as simple as that."

He looked over his shoulder at Gibson. "Someone needs to make him pay."

Gibson nodded. In his estimation, Grayson's stock with RHD had just gone up a big notch.

Donahue clutched the envelope to her chest. "Were your people able to locate any tissue or fluid samples from the son that would enable us to do an analysis of his DNA?"

Grayson shook his head. "I'm afraid not. You'll have to get what you need from some other source."

Donahue looked over her shoulder at Gibson. "Looks like we're going to Istanbul. You up for it?"

Gibson yawned. "Ask me after I get a few hours of sleep."

Grayson laughed. "That red eye flight is a killer. I've done it once or twice myself, and it takes me several weeks to readjust."

"Can you drop us off at a hotel?" Donahue asked. She gestured with her chin at Gibson. "The old guy gets cranky when he doesn't get his nap."

Grayson laughed. "I've booked you a room at the Dorchester Arms. Get a few hours sleep, then I'll pick you up around noon. I've got someone I want you to meet."

Donahue looked over in surprise.

"Who is it?"

A wry smile crossed Grayson's face.

"He's a former bodyguard for Mohammad, Bandar's son. He worked for the Royal Family while the Ambassador and his son were stationed here in London." He made eye contact with them both. "But you didn't find your way to him *from me*."

Donahue nodded. Behind her, she could tell that Gibson was smiling.

Grayson said, "Let me have your cell phone numbers in case I need to reach you."

Donahue jotted them down on the back of one of her cards and passed it over to Grayson.

"By the way," she asked, "Are we under surveillance?"

"Not yet," Grayson replied with a smile, "but the day is still young."

THIRTY-ONE

When noon arrived, Grayson was waiting for the two of them in a loading zone in front of the Dorchester Arms hotel. Gibson spotted him first, then led the way to the car.

"Feeling any better?" Grayson said to Gibson as he got into the front seat.

"Not really." His eyes were noticeably bloodshot, and his energy level was down. "I could have slept all day."

Grayson looked over the seat at Donahue who'd settled into the back.

"And how are you doing?" he asked.

"I'm fine," she said in a chipper tone.

Gibson groaned.

"I slept most of the way on the flight," she added with a quick glance over at Gibson.

"You look great," Grayson told her as he put the car in gear and drove through the streets of London to a pub on the lower east side. "It takes most people a day or two to get used to the change in time."

Gibson groaned again.

"Don't mind him," Donahue said. She shifted her gaze from Gibson to Grayson. "Old people. You know how that goes."

Grayson smiled. "I'll keep that in mind."

"So who are we meeting with, Mark?" she said.

"Fahd Abd al Rahman. He's a low ranking member of the Saudi Royal Family."

"Oh, wonderful," said Gibson as he stifled a yawn. "We get to deal with yet *another* prince."

When he looked back over the seat, Gibson spotted *that look*, the one that Donahue used to warn him to keep his feelings under control.

He then added, "I'm just saying…it seems like everyone we deal with on this case is a prince." He shifted his attention to Grayson. "You know, all Chief's, no Indians?"

Grayson laughed. "I take it that's an American colloquialism?" He glanced over at Gibson. "He's not a prince. He's too far down the ladder for a title. In fact, his closest relative in the chain of command is a distant third cousin of Prince Abd-al Rahman, who is currently the *Vice Minister of Defence and Aviation* under the Crown Prince Sultan.

"You've lost me." Gibson looked back at Donahue for affirmation. "I thought everyone in the country was part of one big happy family?"

Grayson shifted his eyes back to the road.

"The Head of the *House of Saud* is the King of Saudi Arabia who serves as the Head of State and monarch of the Kingdom. He holds almost absolute political power. He appoints ministers to his cabinet who supervise their respective ministries in his name. The key ministries of Defence, Interior, and Foreign Affairs are reserved for members of the *Al Saud* dynasty, as are most of the thirteen regional governorships. Most other portfolios have traditionally been given to commoners, often with junior *Al Saud* members serving as their deputies. Long-term political appointments, such as that of Crown Prince Sultan and the Minister of Defence and Aviation, have resulted in the creation of fiefdoms where senior princes have often appointed their own sons to senior positions within their own fiefdom. The guy I want you to meet is a distant third cousin of one of those political appointments, so while he's technically part of the Royal Family, he's quite far removed from any real seat of power."

"How many family members are there in the House of Saud?" Donahue asked.

"About seven thousand," Grayson said, "but most of the positions of power are wielded by the two hundred or so descendants of King Abdul Aziz."

"Seven-thousand?" A slow grin spread across Gibson's face. "Family birthday parties must be hell."

Donahue couldn't suppress a smile. Mr. Grumpy seemed to be coming around.

Grayson continued, "The sons of Abdul Aziz, the founder of the modern Saudi state, have so far been the only eligible candidates allowed to serve as King. There are twenty-two of them still alive, but they are getting really old, so the late King Fahd expanded the candidates to include the male progeny of King Abdul Aziz's sons. This has increased the pool to more than one hundred and fifty *eligibles*."

He looked back over the seat again at Donahue. "A committee of princes has been set up to vote on the viability of kings and the candidature of nominated crown princes. This committee includes all of the sons and some of the grandsons of the late King Abdul-Aziz. They vote for one of three princes nominated by the king as *Heirs Apparent*."

Donahue rolled her eyes. "So Ambassador Prince Bandar bin Abd al Aziz, the father of our suspect, is a member of that committee?"

"That's right," Grayson replied. "But more than that, Prince Bandar has been named by the current King as one of the Heirs Apparent, so he has a one in three chance of becoming the next king."

"And his son?" Gibson asked.

"The son, Muhammad, will one day be on the voting committee, and I would dare say, if his father becomes the next king, the son could one day end up being nominated himself as an Heir Apparent."

Gibson whistled. "I'm starting to get a feel for the bigger picture here."

"It's complicated," Grayson acknowledged. "If the father ends up King, most experts agree that relations with the West will continue to be good. And don't forget, that relationship is important beyond just the obvious reason concerning oil. The House of Saud carries a lot of sway with many other middle-eastern nations and groups. They've got very deep pockets that translate into influence, and that influence is a currency that the West sorely needs."

"I'm thinking we're stirring up a hornet's nest, Jen," said Gibson.

"That you have," Grayson agreed.

He parked the car at the curb in front of the *Black Dove*, a traditional English pub. Gibson and Donahue smartly followed him inside. Seated alone in the back of the pub with a plate of fish and chips was a young Saudi male who glanced over in their direction and nodded in response to Grayson's smile.

"Fahd, these are the two Detectives I told you about." He introduced Donahue and Gibson. "This is Fahd Abd al Rahman."

Abd al Rahman got to his feet, wiped his hands with a napkin, then shook their hands.

Grayson looked around, but there was no one else seated nearby.

"Mind if we join you?" he asked.

"No problem," Fahd said.

He resumed his seat while Donahue took the chair that was next to him. Gibson and Grayson pulled up chairs on the other side of the table.

The pub was a pleasant room; full of small, dark wooden tables and chairs, a long bar that ran along an interior wall, and big multi-paned windows that faced the street to better capture the late afternoon sun. It smelled of stale ale, fried foods, and cigarette smoke.

"Can I call you Fahd?" Donahue asked when she was settled.

He was working on a mouthful of battered fish, so his response was a nod of his head.

"Before we ask you about the Prince, I'd like to know a little bit about you?" she said.

The barkeep walked up, and for the moment the conversation switched as to whether or not they should order something to eat?

"How are those fish and chips?" Donahue asked.

Fahd wiped his lips with a paper napkin.

"Not bad, but stay away from the bangers and mash."

She nodded. "Fish and chips for me," she told the barkeep.

Gibson chimed in, "Just coffee for me."

And Grayson, not ordering for himself, waived the barkeep off.

Fahd turned towards Donahue.

"There's not much to say about me. I was raised in the Kingdom, came over here to study economics at Cambridge, but didn't like it much, so I dropped out for the time being and started going to work." Odd jobs, mostly. Nothing special."

Gibson raised an eyebrow. "I thought all of you Saudi men—particularly those of you getting educated in foreign countries—were financially set?"

Fahd smiled then shook his head. "Urban myth, Detective. My side of the family has no political power, so I have to work for a living."

"Accident of birth?" Gibson inquired.

Fahd nodded in agreement. "Clans within clans. "We're all still related, but there's only so many positions at the top. Those who are in power stay in power by keeping it within their own clan. The rest of us get a few privileges, but only enough to keep us from outright revolt." His dark eyes shifted to Donahue. "Much like the senior President Bush and after that, his son…no?"

Donahue was listening intently, but at the same time, she was sizing him up. Mid-twenties, thick black hair, narrow face, deep-set dark eyes, he was really quite handsome. Yet, there was an unsettled feel to him, a vibe that she realized she couldn't quite fathom. He was extremely bright, well educated, too, but beneath the calm exterior there burned a profoundly resentful male who would not forever tolerate the status quo.

Still-waters run deep, she thought. There was more to this guy than meets the eye.

"So you worked as a bodyguard for Prince Muhammad bin Abd al Aziz?"

He nodded. "I was with him for about six months. After that, I got myself a decent job as a doorman at a club over in Paddington." He smiled tightly. "Good tips and lots of birds. You can't beat that."

Donahue smiled. "I'm sure you can't. But did you have any special training for the bodyguard work, or did you just get the job because you were family?"

"I spent four years in *SANG*." When he noticed the blank stares on their faces, he said, "The Saudi Arabia National Guard."

Grayson interjected, "It's not like your National Guard, detectives. It's a tribal force forged out of those tribal elements loyal to the Saud Family. The SANG's mission is to protect the royal family from internal rebellion and the regular Saudi Army, should the need arise."

"How big is the SANG?" Gibson asked.

"About seventy-five thousand," Fahd replied.

Gibson rolled his eyes. "All that to protect one family?"

"Big family," Fahd said. He took a bite of the chips. "I was a lieutenant in a commando unit devoted to counter-insurgency."

Donahue's jaw went tight.

I was right! Still waters run very deep.

The barkeep arrived with her food and Gibson's coffee. She tasted the battered fish.

"Mmm, you're right," she told Fahd. "This is pretty good."

Fahd laughed. “Then you must be starving.”

That brought smiles from everyone.

Donahue said, “So why’d you leave the Prince’s employment in the first place? For someone with your training, it must have been a pretty easy job?”

Fahd studied her for a moment, and Donahue had the feeling that he was trying to assess how much she already knew.

“I didn’t like his attitude,” he said. “He was selfish, cheap, and a bully. He liked to stir up trouble, and when he did, we were left to clean up his messes.”

“What kind of messes?” Donahue pressed.

“Mostly fights. He would go into the clubs, toss around a lot of money, and use his title to impress the birds. He’d hit on anyone who matched his type, even if she was with some other guy.” He shook his head in lingering wonder. “I still don’t know why I put up with it for as long as I did. The money his father paid me wasn’t all that good.” He locked eyes with Donahue. “Bloody hell, I make more now as a doorman than I ever did working for the Prince. And there’s a lot less trouble now, too.”

“Were fights the only kind of problems the Prince created?” she asked.

Fahd didn’t answer right away. Instead, he seemed to be deciding how far he should go with his answer.

“There was always trouble with the birds,” he finally said.

“How so?” Donahue asked.

A slow smile appeared at the corners of Fahd’s mouth. “You’d be his type. He liked blonds, thin, and pretty. And he didn’t care much if they were single or married. Money, cars, the illusion of power, he’d do whatever it took to win ‘em over.” He looked down at his food. “And if all else failed, he wasn’t above putting a little something in their whiskey to make them more compliant.”

Donahue tried to keep the excitement out of her voice. “He drugged them?”

Fahd nodded. “He used the stuff that makes them go to sleep. I don’t remember the name.”

“GHB?” Donahue asked.

“Might have been,” Fahd replied.

“What happened when he drugged them?” Gibson asked.

Fahd looked down at his lap. It was clear to all present that he was reluctant to talk about the incidents of drugging or what his role in these crimes might have been.

He shifted his glance over to Grayson who gave him a nod, and this was not lost on Donahue.

Fahd said, "He'd wait for the girl to start feeling the effects, then he'd make a big show of helping her outside to get a breath of fresh air. One of us would get the car, and he'd put her in the front, then drive her off to his place for the rest of the night."

"Did you follow?" Gibson asked.

Fahd nodded. "By the time we'd catch up, he and the girl were usually already inside his flat. We'd stay in our car and wait outside until the morning."

"Did these girls ever complain?" Donahue asked.

"Not that I know of," Fahd said. "He told us, in the end, that they always took the money." He shrugged. "I guess he'd offer it to 'em when they woke up."

"How often did this happen?" Gibson asked.

Fahd gave it some thought.

"Not that often. Maybe once or twice a month. Usually, the birds would go with him willingly." He looked over at Donahue. "Money does strange things to women."

Donahue didn't respond. It saddened her that so many young girls could be bought if the price was right.

Gibson took a sip of his coffee, then said, "So why'd you quit your job?"

Fahd locked eyes with his. "His attitude."

Gibson raised a brow.

"He treated these women as whores. Not that they didn't deserve it, I mean, the ones who went off with him willingly. But the others? Bloody hell. They didn't have a say about what he did to them, and I didn't want to have any part of it, so I quit."

Donahue wasn't wholly convinced that an attack of conscience was Fahd's sole reason for leaving his job with the prince. Underneath it all, she thought she detected the barest hint of jealousy and admiration for the power that unlimited money could provide.

It must stick in his craw that but for an accident of birth, he might have been a man of unlimited power and means.

She looked over at Grayson and wondered if she should touch on his two homicides, but Grayson beat her to the punch.

"We've shown Fahd pictures of our two victims, but he can't remember either one of them specifically. On the other hand, he does remember one night when the Prince left a High Street club with a young blond but didn't take her back to his flat."

Fahd nodded. "He showed up the next morning. He said he took her to Browns. We left it at that."

"Browns is a five-star hotel here in London," Grayson said. "We checked. There was no registration for the night in question."

Donahue nodded. "And was that the night that one of your victims was attacked?"

Grayson nodded. "And killed." He gestured with his chin towards Fahd. "We've talked to him about both of our homicides. He's told us everything he knows."

Donahue turned back to Fahd. "Do you know if he liked to restrain the girls in any way?"

"Restrain?" Fahd asked. He looked from one to the other. "You mean, keep them there against their will?"

"Not that so much that as maybe tying them up, or something along those lines?"

She was doing her best not to put words in his mouth.

Fahr nodded. "He had a bunch of those plastic hand ties. I don't know what you'd call 'em, but the kind that coppers use when they're makin' lots of arrests. Anyway, I saw 'em in one of the tallboys in his bedroom."

Donahue's mind was reeling. If he purchased the Flexicuffs in bulk, perhaps they all had the same batch number? That would further tie the prince to their homicide case.

She looked over at Grayson who said, "The batch numbers on our two cases match. I was planning on telling you about that later."

She nodded and smiled inwardly.

Another nail in the coffin.

She studied Fahd. "Anything else you can add that might help us with our investigation?"

Fahd wiped his lips a final time and placed his paper napkin down on the table.

"Just this. If you try and go after him, watch out for his father. Crown Prince Bandar may be an ambassador and all that, but he's ruthless when it comes to protecting his future. He knows that his son is warped, that's one of the reasons he has bodyguards around him all the time. Not to protect him, but to keep him out of trouble. He wants the throne, and any hint of a scandal at any time could mean the end of his chances." He studied her for a moment. "The Royal Family is not immune to palace intrigue, and there are many among them who are jockeying for position should the Ambassador ever falter."

He pointed a finger at Donahue to make his point.

"Don't underestimate Bandar. Two homicide coppers from Los Angeles? They'd mean nothing to him or the people he would send who would willingly take you out."

Fahd got to his feet, smiled, and threw some bills down on the table.

"He doesn't care about his son," he said, "that is, unless the son does something stupid that would interfere with his plans. All he cares about is his power and what he has to do to keep it."

Fahd wished them good luck, then nodded slowly to Grayson before he made his way from the pub.

Donahue looked down at what remained of her now cold fish and chips and decided that she wasn't really all that hungry after all.

She pushed the plate away, then said to Grayson, "So? Who is he, Mark? That's not just *some kid* who works as a bodyguard."

Grayson smiled. He pulled out a bundle of notes and left the money for the check on the table.

"He's worked for us for the past two years. MI6 swears by him. He's a great resource in all matters concerning the House of Saud."

"So he's a spy?" Donahue asked.

Grayson shrugged but didn't answer.

"And his warning?"

"Take it to heart."

Donahue shook her head. "Well, Gibby. Not only have we stirred up an American hornet's nest, but it would also appear that we're now stirring up the entire Middle-East."

"*Protect and Serve...*" Gibson stated, "That's what we get paid for."

Donahue waited for Grayson to look in her direction. "Do you think the father knows that his son is a killer?"

"I doubt it," Grayson replied. "Too much of a potential liability to let him keep going."

"What do you think he'd do if he found out the truth about his boy?"

Grayson shot her a grin akin to that of a naughty schoolboy.

"Why do I have the feeling that we're going to find out?"

THIRTY-TWO

After a six-hour nap in adjacent rooms at the Dorchester Arms Hotel, Donahue and Gibson walked out of the building in search of a place to eat dinner. Gibson spotted a pub just across the street, and soon they were seated at a table by the window.

"I'm going to try the kidney pie," Donahue told him after briefly scanning the menu.

Gibson frowned. "Don't they have anything like steak or chicken? What is all this stuff, anyway? Bangers and mash?" He looked at Donahue over the top of the menu, and she gave him a smile.

"Bangers and mash, that's hot dogs and mashed potatoes…I think?" she told him.

Gibson closed up his menu. "Then bangers and mash it is."

They ordered their food along with a couple of ales, and when the drinks arrived, Gibson offered up a toast.

"Here's to stirring up a hornet's nest," he said. He took a large swallow of the ale, then nearly gagged.

"Ughhh!" He set the mug back down on their table. "This stuff is warm."

"They drink it that way over here," she said with a smile.

Gibson shuddered. "I can't imagine why." He picked up the mug and took another sip, then noticed that she was staring.

"What?" he said.

"You're still drinking it."

"I've been known to drink much worse." He saluted her with the mug, then took another swig.

"I just bet you have," she replied. "So where do we go from here?"

Gibson gave it some thought. "First thing I'd like to do is look over the Met's case files?"

"While you were sleeping I went through the stuff. You want a quick run down?" Donahue asked.

"You couldn't sleep?"

"I slept on the plane, remember?"

He smiled tightly. "Lay it on me."

She leaned forward in her chair.

"The first victim was named Patty Shaw, age twenty-three, a waitress at a club in Knightsbridge. She left work one night after her shift, and that's the last time anyone saw her alive."

"Family?"

"Mother, father, and two younger brothers. Father is a postal worker, mother works as a secretary for an accounting firm. Patty had a flat where she lived on her own. When she didn't show up for work, another waitress sent the police around to check things out. They found her tied to the bed."

"One hand or two?"

"Just one. A plastic tie. She was raped, and there was semen on her chest. Fresh bruising on her arms and face."

Gibson took out his notebook.

"Cause of death?"

"Manual strangulation. A DNA profile was made, and it matched with the semen from victim number two."

Gibson jotted down the salient facts in his notebook. He looked up.

"The plastic tie? Did it match with the serial number from our case?"

"Sure did. Same batch. And it matched with the one they found on Tracy O'Shea's wrist."

Donahue paused for a moment to take a sip of her ale.

When she put down the mug, she said, "Tracy O'Shea was born in Ireland, came to London five years ago. She's a little older, age twenty-nine. Married once, divorced, no children. Worked in a shop in Kensington Garden."

She paused in the recitation long enough to allow Gibson to catch up with his note-taking.

"She had a new boyfriend who was in Spain on business when she died. She worked her shift on a Saturday, and later that night she was seen at a club on Kings Road. She left alone around eleven-thirty. No one saw her again until the body was found on Tuesday."

Gibson cocked an eyebrow.

"Three days? Nobody missed her?"

She nodded. "She was off from work on Sunday and Monday, and with the boyfriend out of town, no one checked up."

Gibson made another entry into his notebook.

Donahue continued. "Late Tuesday afternoon, when she hadn't shown up at work, the employer went over to her house. He would care for her cats when she was on vacation, so he had a key. He spotted the body in her bedroom, backed out, and immediately called the police."

"Did he have an alibi?" Gibson asked.

"He's eighty-six years old," she said. "Besides that, his DNA didn't match."

Gibson laughed. "I guess that clears him."

The food arrived, and they spent the next twenty minutes talking about London and what they wished they had time to see. Gibson grumbled for a while about the fact that the hot dogs he thought he was getting were really English sausages, but he ate them anyway.

When the dishes were cleared, Donahue said, "Both women were blonds, five-five and five-six respectively. It seems he has a penchant for blonds."

Gibson nodded. "Well, unless you want to look over the crime scenes, I'm thinking we should probably give Tom a call and see if he wants us to go straight to Istanbul?"

"I agree. It's pretty clear we won't get any more cooperation from the British authorities."

Gibson nodded. "Your guy, Grayson? He went out on a limb for us with that informant."

"I know. He's a squared-away guy."

They paid for their meal, left the pub, and headed back towards the hotel.

"Where to now?" Gibson asked.

"Let's go to the bar in the hotel lobby," she replied. "I could use a real drink while I try to get in touch with Grayson."

Gibson smiled. "Now you're talking."

They had started across the street when her cell phone rang. "It's Grayson," she said, as she put the phone up to her ear. She stopped on the sidewalk to take the call.

Grayson said, "MI6 came by this afternoon and collected our complete files on the two murders. They had us sign copies of the Official Secrets Act, so as of now, the investigation is closed. We're forbidden to talk about it with anyone or to release any copies of the reports."

Donahue's eyes widened. "Do they know that you gave us a set of the reports?"

"They haven't asked me that question, and I haven't volunteered that information to them *yet*. But when they do, I will have to tell them the truth. So I would like to suggest that you and Detective Gibson leave the country as soon as possible before they pay you a visit and demand that you give them back."

Donahue rolled her eyes. Grayson was right. With both the US and UK governments doing their best to shut down the case, they had, at best, a tiny window of opportunity, and if they wanted to get things done, they were going to have to act fast.

Their course of action was obvious, get over to Istanbul, get their sample, and hightail it back to the States.

"Thanks for the heads-up, Mark," she said. "We'll be out of here on the very next plane."

"Good luck. Take this guy down if it's him."

"We'll do our best. Oh, and while I'm thinking of it, do you have any contacts with the authorities in Istanbul? We don't know anyone over there."

"I do," he said. "Barak Tuzil, Istanbul Police, very high-ranking. Tell him I told you to call. Here's his number. Are you ready?"

When she said she was, he read it off, and she put it into her cell.

"Thanks again, Mark. I'll let you know how this turns out."

"Please do. And watch your back. It looks like someone really wants your case to go away. "

* * * *

They bypassed the hotel bar and instead went directly to their rooms. In the hallway just outside her door, Donahue told Gibson, “I’ll call the airport and see if I can book us a flight. I think there’s one at seven am, so if I can get it, we should probably plan on leaving here at about…what do you think… four a.m.?”

Gibson grunted. “Won’t matter much. I won’t get any sleep. I’m wide awake now.”

“Just the same, set an alarm or ask for a wake-up call.”

“Yes, mommy,” Gibson said with a smile.

Donahue looked over and smiled back.

“Sorry.”

“While you’re doing that,” he said with a nod, “let me have the reports that Grayson gave us? I’ll stop by the front desk and see if they’ve got a business center where I can get them scanned and emailed to Elwood.” He gave her a wink that said *just in case.*

“Good idea! I’ll get them for you.” She inserted her key, opened the door to her room, and Gibson followed her in.

The files that Grayson had given them were still sitting on the table where she’d left them. She breathed a sigh of relief. Apparently, MI6 was still unaware that Grayson had given them a set. She picked up the pages, turned around, then handed them over to Gibson.

“I’ll call your room and let you know if I got us a flight and what time we have to leave,” she said.

“Shouldn’t we call that guy in Istanbul…what’s his name…*Tuzil?* Maybe we should let him know we’re coming?”

“I’ll try.” She glanced at her watch. “It’s pretty late. We may have to wait until we get there.”

Gibson headed towards the door.

“I’m going to stop at the bar down in the lobby. Wanna join me after you make your calls?”

She shook her head. “I think I’ll try to get some sleep.” She gave him a quizzical look. “Don’t you have to pack?”

“I never unpacked.” He gave her a wink. “Much faster that way.”

THIRTY-THREE

Donahue and Gibson were not prepared for what they encountered when their plane touched down at Istanbul's Ataturk International Airport, for it was a thoroughly modern facility with floor to ceiling, multi-story glass walls, skyways, and spacious passenger terminals serving dozens of major airlines from all over the world.

While the plane taxied up to the terminal, Donahue turned to Gibson and whispered, "This was not what I expected. I guess I thought there were going to be camels, bazaars and lots of tents...*but this place is so modern*." She shook her head. "God! I feel really foolish."

Gibson nodded. "It's not what I expected, either." He was seated next to the window and had been studying the city as they came in for a landing. "Did you see all the minarets? They're everywhere, sticking up all over the city. They look like missile silos."

When they disembarked from the plane, they were met by a uniformed police officer in black fatigues and a bulletproof vest who wore a submachine gun strapped across his chest. His black knit watch cap bore the insignia of the Intelligence Branch, and after looking carefully at their passports, he escorted them through customs where they picked up their bags, and to a waiting SUV that bore the lettered markings of the Istanbul Police.

As their bags were being loaded into the vehicle, Donahue pulled a handkerchief from her purse and wiped at her brow. The sun was still low in the sky, but a heavy cloud cover moving in from the Bosporus Strait was causing the humidity to rise.

It was then that a series of thoughts began to flood her mind:

I'm in Istanbul, a fabled city in an ancient country, at a spot which is the crossroads between the East and the West...

It's so exotic here! I love it!

As the vehicle pulled away from the curb, it was followed by two motorcycles, each bearing two uniformed officers, all four of whom were armed with machine guns.

After clearing a trip to Istanbul with their Captain, Donahue reached Tuzil on the phone before they boarded their flight. He agreed to meet with them and told her that he would arrange to have somebody greet them at the airport, but she had no idea they were going to end up with their own motorcade.

Their driver, a young man no older than twenty-nine, spoke fluent English, and he was only too happy to expound upon the wonders of Istanbul. He pointed out large office buildings, fine hotels, and rows of high-rise apartment complexes. He explained that even the poorest of its citizens were guaranteed housing, a fact that didn't get past the detectives who worked in a city where homelessness was of epidemic proportions.

"Do all of your officers carry automatic weapons?" she asked.

"But of course," the driver replied. "We are a secular country, but we are ninety-eight percent Muslim, and there are some who would use terrorism to thwart the will of the people. They would like to force us to become a religious state."

He negotiated a lane change through early morning traffic.

"Also, we must deal with the PKK, a Kurdish group that wants to take a piece of our country for their own." He looked up and caught Gibson's eye in the rearview mirror. "This city is a major hub for tourism, and we want to protect our visitors, so we must always be ready for all possible contingencies."

During the driver's mini-tour, when she glanced out the window at the famous Blue Mosque and the ancient Egyptian Obelisk that graced the Hippodrome Square right in front of the mosque, she felt her cheeks flush with embarrassment. Her preconceived idea about Turkey, the country, and this city, in particular, had been woefully ignorant. She made a promise to herself to get better informed about the world at large just as soon as she got back to the States.

When she asked the driver about Barak Tuzil, the young man told her that he was taking them directly to the Intelligence Branch where they would meet with Director Tuzil upon their arrival.

They pulled up in front of the headquarters building, a modern structure with pale, red, granite slab siding, lots of windows, and a gold seal above the front entrance way. The detectives were led through reinforced internal security doors, then metal detectors, before being guided to an elevator manned by another officer who took them to the third floor.

There was another security check before they were taken to the foyer that adjoined the corner office that bore the name of Barak Tuzil as the head of the Intelligence Branch for the entire city of Istanbul.

The receptionist offered them cups of strong, black, Turkish coffee, but both opted instead for bottles of cold water. Tuzil came out a few minutes later, introduced himself, then led them into his office.

Tall, heavy-set, big hands, he was well dressed in a dark suit and a crisp white shirt with a colorful print tie. His jet-black hair was just long enough to allow him to wear it in a short ponytail. His smile was warm and friendly, framed by a dark, thick mustache that ran to the corners of his mouth.

Once they were seated at a large conference table, he told his secretary that they were not to be disturbed. He offered them coffee, which both again declined, then directed his attention to Donahue.

"After you called, I spoke with our mutual friend, Inspector Grayson, who, by the way, has vouched for you completely. When I tried to find out what was going on, he advised me that he was precluded from discussing it in any way, so perhaps you can enlighten me as to what is the purpose for your visit?"

Donahue spent the next twenty minutes telling him everything about her case and what she knew of the ones that Grayson had discovered. She talked about the role of the US. Department of State, and their pressure on her and on MI6. When she revealed the name of their suspect, Tuzil frowned, but said nothing. Instead, he listened until she was finished before permitting himself the briefest of smiles.

"That's quite a story," he told them. "If I may make a suggestion?"

"Certainly," Donahue replied.

"Forget about pursuing this. Mine is a country that's poised on the verge of being invited to join the European Union. A scandal like this, one that involves the son of the possible future head-of-state of an oil-rich nation would not be good for our chances."

Donahue folded her arms across her chest. After Grayson's unqualified recommendation, she had expected Tuzil to be on their side, but apparently, he was just another bureaucrat who was concerned with his job and the best way to keep it.

But Tuzil was full of surprises.

"Having said that, and seeing from your reactions that you are intent on ignoring my advice, please tell me how I can assist you in bringing this matter to a successful conclusion?"

Donahue's anger turned to surprise. "You're actually going to help us?"

Tuzil smiled and ran a finger across his mustache.

"Of course I will, but first I need to know what you need?"

Donahue explained to him the purpose of their trip, to obtain a sample from Aziz that would enable them to profile his DNA.

"If he smokes, we might be able to get a cigarette butt, or a napkin, or something like that which would give us a sample of his DNA that we can take back to Los Angeles for testing."

"Just like CSI?" Tuzil said it with a smile. "I watch that show every week."

Donahue rolled her eyes. "Not exactly."

Tuzil frowned. "You mean you can't get a DNA profile within twenty minutes?"

She realized then that he was being facetious and she started to laugh.

"All we want is a sample," she finally said. "He likes the bars and clubs, so it shouldn't be too difficult to get a cigarette butt or an empty glass."

Tuzil said, "You realize that he has the same protections here that he had in your country?"

She nodded. "We may never be able to prosecute him ourselves, but perhaps his own country will do something once we have gathered all of the evidence."

"And if his DNA does not match your samples?"

"In that case, we will look elsewhere for the real killer."

Tuzil laughed and shook his head. "I see you are unfamiliar with the way politics are conducted outside of your own country."

"How so?" Gibson asked.

"If he is your killer, everyone who knows about this will use the results of your investigation to press forward with their own agendas." He studied them both. "In fact, I'm sure my own government would find a way to use this information for our own advantage."

"That's not our concern," said Donahue with a shake of her head. "We just do the investigation and let the chips fall where they may."

Tuzil looked puzzled.

Gibson clarified, "An American expression. It came from chopping wood. It means that you do your job, like chopping wood, and wherever the wood chips land, they will land."

"Ah," Tuzil nodded his understanding. "I like that saying. And are you ready for the consequences of what you plan to do?"

"For the most part," Gibson replied. "I suppose it could get ugly, but we'll just have to take that chance."

Tuzil put his hands together in the shape of a steeple and appeared to be lost in thought.

Donahue asked, "Do you have any unsolved rapes by drugging or unsolved rape homicides?"

"I'm sure we've got a few," Tuzil replied. "We get a lot of women flying in here from Russia and the former Soviet republics for the purpose of prostitution. There's always trouble swirling around them."

He locked his eyes with Donahue. "You said he used handcuffs?"

"That's right, plastic ones, the kind that comes in strips. We have the batch serial number, so if you have any homicide victims like that, we might be able to link your cases with ours?"

"I'll make the necessary inquiries," Tuzil said with a sigh. "Even though we're computerized, it might take us a little time to do a thorough case search."

"How long has Aziz been in your country?" Gibson asked.

"I don't know for sure, but it won't be difficult to find out."

There was a momentary silence between them.

"So how should we handle this?" Donahue asked.

Tuzil cocked his head and then smiled. "I will put some of my best people on him. We'll watch him for a while and see where he goes. And while we're waiting for him to go out, I'll arrange for you to be taken to a nearby hotel." He gave them a broad smile. "While you're waiting for us to figure out his schedule, I would encourage you to take in the sights. There are many things to see in this great city, and our food is beyond compare. Just leave me your cell phone numbers, and I will call you when we know what he is going to do."

Donahue smiled. "Thank you, Director. We appreciate the help."

Tuzil nodded. "It occurs to me that after you get your DNA sample, perhaps I could arrange a meeting with the Ambassador. I would imagine that if he was told what his son has done, he might ship the boy back home for prosecution in a tribal court."

Donahue shook her head. "Not from what I hear."

Tuzil gave her a puzzled look.

Gibson stood up. "I think we should tell you, Director, we were given a warning to be wary of the father. Our source has stated that he will do whatever it takes to protect his own reputation and his chance for the throne." Gibson shrugged. "Violence against us was not ruled out."

Tuzil's eyes narrowed. "So we must be concerned about your safety?"

Donahue nodded. "And yours."

The silence between them grew heavy as Tuzil considered this new complication.

"May Allah protect us all," he said.

* * * *

Two hours later, when they were settled in at their hotel, Donahue received a call on her cell phone.

In a soft voice, Tuzil said, "I have a team of detectives combing through our records for any unsolved homicides matching the MO of your case. Additionally, I have ordered a surveillance watch placed on Aziz. My people in the field report that he is currently still inside the Saudi consulate. They also say that he is escorted everywhere by two bodyguards, both of whom are armed."

"Is that legal here?" Donahue asked.

"They have permits," Tuzil replied. "An informant we have in their embassy has reported that Aziz frequents a number of nightspots. Along the coastline of the Bosphorus, he is known to go to *Pasha*, which is a huge, open-air club in *Ortakoy*. It has five restaurants, two dance-floors, and an entrance fee that my people tell me is nothing short of extortionate."

Donahue laughed. It sounded like some of the high-end clubs that she once patronized on the Sunset Strip in LA.

"The other clubs he prefers in that area are *Zihni*, and up the road from that,

Havana. Closer in town, he likes the *Roxy, Sefahathane, Hayal Kahvesi,* and a place called *Babylon.*"

Donahue chewed on her lip for a moment. "He really seems to get around. Perhaps Gibson and I should just follow him by ourselves? I really hate to have your people tied up on this."

Tuzil laughed. "I doubt if you or Detective Gibson could follow him by yourselves. And unless you can read our language, it's very likely that you'd lose him within a few blocks."

Donahue knew he was right. They were entirely out of their element in Istanbul, and they needed all the help they could get.

"Just remember, you are foreigners in this city. It would be easy for you to get into trouble if you don't have someone with you to keep you from making a big mistake."

It was a not-too-subtle reminder that they were on his turf and that he was the one in charge.

"I see your point. So what would you suggest?"

"I'll have my people follow him around, and once he settles in somewhere, I'll give you a call. Then, when you're ready, I'll personally go with you to make sure that everything goes well."

Donahue began to wonder if Tuzil was being pressured by the US or someone else to keep a watch on her activities? It would make sense, given that the Feds had leaned pretty hard on the Brits, so she should probably assume that they'd try the same with their allies, the Turks.

"That sounds like a good plan, Director. Thank you."

"Please, Detective Donahue," he said. "Call me Barak."

"I will, and you can call me Jen. And as long as we're now on a first name basis, I don't suppose you've been getting any pressure from our State Department?"

He was silent for a moment, which led her to believe that he'd been compromised, but when he responded, he quickly cleared things up.

"Your concern is understandable, but I can assure you that we have not yet heard from your government, and *when* we do, I will let you know."

Donahue breathed a sigh of relief. Was it possible they could get their DNA sample without interference from the Department of State?

"One more thing," Tuzil said. "I'm going to assume that neither you nor Detective Gibson is armed, for if you were, it would be a serious violation of our laws, and I'm afraid that even I would be powerless to help you if you were caught."

"We're not armed," she said, grateful that they'd left their weapons at home. "We're too smart for that."

"I'm sure you are," he replied. "Have a nice afternoon, and I will speak to you later tonight."

When he hung up, she debated whether or not to wake Gibson but decided instead to let him sleep. She was starting to feel the effects of the jet lag herself, and she realized that it wouldn't hurt for her to get a little more rest.

She turned on the TV, located the BBC broadcast, then stretched out on the bed, fully intending to watch the news while she rested. But almost immediately, she nodded off.

THIRTY-FOUR

At just after six pm, Donahue woke up from a fitful nap. She struggled to reach a level of consciousness that would enable her to know where she was. She quickly sat up, looked around, then picked up the phone.

"Did I wake you?" she asked when Gibson answered.

"I've been up for an hour," he said. "We need to talk."

She walked next door to his room and found the door cracked open in anticipation of her arrival. She knocked, stuck her head in, then noticed the suitcase laid-out on his bed.

"What's up?" she asked with a note of concern in her voice. "Something happen?"

He tossed a balled-up undershirt into the bag, then looked over in her direction.

"It's Claudette. She's taken a turn for the worse. I just got off the phone with her doctor. I need to get back to LA."

Donahue slumped down on the edge of the bed. "Oh, Gibby, *of course*. I'm so sorry. Is there anything I can do?"

He shook his head. "It was probably a stupid idea for me to come in the first place. I should have known that something like this could happen."

"Did the doctor say what's wrong?"

"Her blood pressure dropped significantly," he said as he zipped up his bag. "She may be bleeding internally. They're doing scans now, and if they have to operate, she'll be going in right away."

"It sounds like they're on top of it." She tried to offer encouragement. "She'll be okay. She's a very tough cookie."

He nodded, but he wasn't really listening.

"If I hurry, I can catch a flight out of here in about an hour. Tuzil is sending someone over to help me clear their airport security." He held her look again. "By the way, he's a pretty decent guy. Anyway, I called Tom and told him what's up, and he's sending someone out here to take my place. He or she should get here by tomorrow, sometime around mid-day."

"Don't worry about me," she said. "You just take care of Claudie. I'll get us our sample and head straight back."

Gibson lifted the suitcase off the bed, set it down on the floor, then sat down beside her.

"Tom doesn't want you to do this alone. He told me to tell you to wait for my replacement before you make contact. He wants to make sure that there are two people who could vouch for the method we used to get a sample."

Donahue nodded. "Okay, if that's what he wants. Did he say who he's going to send?"

"He didn't know." He locked eyes with her. "Look, Jen. I'm really sorry. I hate to leave you in this situation. I should have—"

"Don't worry about it," she said as she cut him off. She put a hand on his arm. "I'll be fine."

The room phone rang, and Gibson quickly picked it up. The desk clerk informed him that his driver, a policeman, was at the front desk.

Gibson hung up the phone. "Gotta go. My ride's downstairs."

Donahue stood up and gave him a hug. "She'll be okay. And you *will* call me when you get to LA and let me know what's going on… right?"

He nodded, picked up his suitcase, then made his way out the door.

* * * *

Back in her room, Donahue placed a call to Tuzil. She told him what was going on and that she had orders to wait for Gibson's replacement to arrive before moving in on Aziz.

Tuzil said he understood completely. He told her he would keep his people on Aziz to get a better handle on what they'd be facing. In the meantime, he suggested several restaurants she could go to for dinner, and he reminded her again to see the city if she had a chance.

She climbed back on top of her bed and thought over her recent conversations with Gibson. What kept coming back was their talk about relationships and how guilty he felt about his focus on work to the exclusion of the time he should have spent with his wife. He had learned his lesson the hard way. It was a lesson she decided that she didn't want to experience for herself.

She picked up her cell phone and placed a call to Zach. When he answered, she was pleasantly surprised.

"You picked up?" she said.

"Of course. How are you doing?"

"I'm fine. I was just thinking of you, and I wanted to hear your voice."

He was silent for a moment. "Is there anything in particular that you want me to say?"

"No. Nothing special."

There was silence on the other end of the line.

"Zach?" she said, and momentarily she wondered if the call had been dropped.

"Zach?" she repeated.

"I was trying to think of something to say that wasn't special?"

She laughed.

"How do you like Istanbul?"

"From what I've seen so far, it's beautiful and quite exotic."

He smiled. "So, now that we've got the small talk out of the way, do you think we could share a little phone sex?"

"What? Are you serious?"

"Of course I am. You know you want to..."

"Zach? I'm calling on an open line from a foreign country. Someone might be listening in."

"I'm willing to take that chance if you are?"

She laughed. "You're such a bad boy..."

THIRTY-FIVE

The next morning, after a night of deep sleep, Donahue had a breakfast consisting of yogurt, fresh fruit and walnuts, a cup of thick black coffee, and a piece of delicious pound cake. After breakfast, with nothing to do for the morning until Gibson's replacement showed up, she decided to take a walk in the downtown area. She wanted to see the city, but most of all, she wanted to get a look at the famous Blue Mosque.

Before leaving the hotel, she talked with the concierge about what she should be wearing in public. While a headscarf was not needed to go out on the streets, a dress code did exist for the mosque. She quickly put on the appropriate clothing, brought along a light sweater to cover her bare shoulders, and set out for what she hoped would be an adventure to write home about.

She walked away from her hotel down a winding hillside, past shops and restaurants, Turkish baths, and clothing stores. The streets were filled with people, most of them on their way to work, and any trepidations she might have had about being an American all alone in this foreign environment completely disappeared when she realized that there were thousands of tourists from all over the world wandering around the downtown area, visiting the mosque and other famous historical sites.

As she approached the mosque, she was pestered by a local man who tagged along beside her while he tried to get her to buy from him a collection of picture postcards. She politely refused—more than several times—then walked another dozen steps or so before she was surrounded by a group of local children on a field trip who wanted to know if she was from America? When she told them "yes" they burst into chatter, eager to show off their proficiency with English. When they later said goodbye, they ran off with their escorts, leaving Donahue free to make her way into the mosque.

It was then that she saw him; an older man, perhaps in his mid to late sixties. He had a dark beard and shoulder-length black hair. He stood off to her left, about forty feet away. His outfit was jeans, a cotton shirt, and a dark knee length overcoat.

He appeared to be watching her.

She noticed him first with her peripheral vision, but when she shifted her gaze to get a better look, he turned his back to her and disappeared into a nearby crowd.

Why was he interested in her? She was used to men staring at her, that happened to most women all of the time. But he had been more than looking; he was studying her, and considering that she was alone and in a strange land, she found it very unsettling.

Perhaps Tuzil was having her followed? It was indeed possible, but was it likely? She discarded that idea. It made no sense. But what about her own government? Had they tracked her down? It wouldn't have been hard to do, but if so, for what purpose?

The third alternative was one that she really didn't want to consider. Could word of their investigation have reached the ears of the Saudis?

She suddenly felt quite vulnerable and exposed without the reassuring comfort of a weapon.

She stayed rooted to the ground for another five minutes while she scanned the crowds, looking for the old man or anyone else who might show an interest in where she was going. But when the old man failed to resurface, she began to believe that her cop mentality had gotten the best of the moment.

She spun on her heels, made her way into the mosque, and spent almost an hour inside. The magnificence of the décor was both soothing and inspiring.

She left the Blue Mosque and walked in the humidity for almost a mile until she arrived at the *Hagia Sophia*. The guidebook she had picked up in the lobby of her hotel stated that the one-time basilica had been built in 532 AD, and was later converted to a mosque in 1453 AD, when the Ottoman Turks conquered the city. Now, as a museum, it was considered to be one of the finest examples of Byzantine architecture in the entire world.

She joined the crowd and made her way up the steps and into the Hagia.

It was then that she saw the old man again. He was thirty feet in front of her, standing off to the side, staring over in her direction.

She quickly turned around and went back out the way she came.

Who he was or who might have sent him was no longer her primary concern. All that mattered was her safety, and when *fight or flight* kicked in, she instinctively opted for the latter. Without a weapon in a foreign country and utterly alone, she knew she was at a distinct disadvantage. She no longer had doubts about his interest in her, and whether or not he was following her at the request of a government or just a run-of-the-mill stalker no longer made any difference. For her, it was now all about common sense. She was not in a position to risk a confrontation.

It figures that this would happen when Gibby wasn't around.

She reached the street and flagged down a taxi. She showed the driver a card with the name of her hotel, and minutes later, he dropped her off, unscathed.

Once in the lobby, she took up a position by the window to watch the street. He had spooked her badly, and she discovered that her hands were actually shaking. She stayed at the window for fifteen minutes, but there was no indication that he, or anyone else, had followed her back to the hotel.

She went up to her room, locked herself in, and settled in on top of her bed. She considered giving Tuzil a call, but then she hastily reconsidered. There was no proof that the man really posed a threat of any kind. In fact, the more she thought about it, the more she tended to dismiss the whole thing as the product of her overactive imagination.

Feeling just a little foolish about the way she'd reacted, she decided to venture out again if the opportunity presented itself, but in the meantime, still suffering from the throes of jet lag and a tension headache from the morning's incident, she lay back on the bed and took a little nap.

* * * *

A knock on the door slowly brought her around. She looked over at the bedside clock and noticed that she'd been asleep for almost five hours.

When she opened the door she felt her jaw drop. "Shari? They sent you?"

Shari Thompson was smiling from ear to ear. "The Captain didn't have to ask me twice."

Donahue stepped forward and gave her a hug. "But what about your kids?"

Thompson responded with a laugh. "My soon to be ex-husband isn't too happy with the situation, but it's good for him to get a taste of what I go through every day."

Donahue closed the door, and the two of them sat on the bed.

"So fill me in," Thompson said, and Donahue did, including the part about the pressure being applied by the American State Department; the impact it had on the Brits, and the informant's warning about the ruthlessness of the father of Aziz. Her recitation took nearly forty minutes.

Thompson rolled her eyes. "It looks like it's us against the world ...*again*. So what else is new?"

Donahue smiled. Having Thompson around would be fun, and she could count on her to watch her back. And thinking about that reminded her of the man that she'd seen that morning. Although she was sure it was nothing, she decided that she owed it to Thompson to tell her what was going on.

She felt more foolish by the moment as she described the old man and what had happened.

Thompson listened in silence, then said, "We'll keep an eye out for him when we go out, but if you're asking me what I think, it was probably just some guy smitten with your blond good looks." She smiled. "You know, you do have that effect on men."

Donahue rolled her eyes. "I know it sounds silly, but the way he was looking at me...it was more than that. I don't know. It just felt strange."

"Well, if you spot him again, let me know and I'll hit up his sorry ass. We'll find out exactly what he's up to."

Donahue got up and went over to the window. Throughout the city, a sound could be heard; the Muezzin's calling of the faithful to prayer. It was hauntingly beautiful and the two detectives listened attentively until it was over.

"That was great," Thompson said. "My God, I'm in Istanbul! I can't believe it!"

"That's how I felt yesterday."

Thompson picked up her purse. "I guess I'll go back to my room and get unpacked. Any idea of how you want to proceed from this point on?"

"Our contact here is a guy named Barak Tuzil. He's the Director of Intelligence for the Istanbul Police."

"Good guy?" Thompson asked.

"So far, but we'll see. Tuzil talks as if he's on board, but I have the feeling he can be leaned on, so we'll just have to wait and see. Anyway, he put his people on Aziz, and supposedly, if the guy goes out clubbing tonight, Tuzil will pick us up and take us there."

"Sounds good." Thompson looked at her watch. "I want to grab a quick shower. You wanna get some dinner when I'm dressed?"

Donahue nodded. "I'll knock on your door as soon as I'm ready. We can leave the hotel and go exploring."

"You think it's safe?"

"Wait until you see all the police. They even ride in tandem on motorcycles. This is a prime tourist area and they want to make sure that everything is copasetic."

Thompson nodded. "About an hour, then?"

Donahue said okay, and Thompson headed for the door.

"Hey, Shari?"

Thompson stopped and looked back.

"Be careful about using the phones."

Thompson nodded, then made her way from the room.

* * * *

Over a beautiful meal of lamb, grilled vegetables, and sweet tea, the two detectives managed to gossip about their lives and those of the people they worked with. When the conversation came back to the job at hand, Donahue told her about the crime reports she'd gotten from Grayson and the fact that they were located in her room.

"You think they're safe there?" Thompson asked.

"I hope so," Donahue replied. "Gibby had them scanned and he sent a set of them back to Elwood. If we lose our set, we can always get the boss to email us what we need. Anyway, when we get back to the room, you should probably look over the hard copies."

Thompson nodded, then took another bite of her lamb. "Why can't we get food like this back in LA?"

Donahue smiled. "If we search hard enough, I'll bet we can."

They were at a table by the front window that looked out over the street. Donahue happened to glance out and thought she noticed the old man she'd seen earlier in the day.

"Don't look out the window," she said to Thompson, "but across the street, standing under the green awning…I think it's the guy I was telling you about?"

And of course, Thompson immediately looked out, and as she did, the old man disappeared down the street and out of their view.

"I told you not to look," Donahue said.

Thompson smiled. "That's like locking two suspects in the back seat of a police car and telling them not to talk." She shook her head, but the smile remained. "Look, I'm sorry. It was involuntary, but I got a quick glimpse of him, and at least we know he's still out there. It looked to me like he was walking with a noticeable limp. When we head back to the hotel, he'll probably still be watching, and if he is, we'll grab him then."

Donahue attempted to suppress a laugh, but she couldn't. "You're some detective, Shari. Remind me not to bother telling you *not to look* anymore."

"We'll catch him," she said. "Just have a little faith."

Donahue thought for a moment, then said, "I think I'll bring this up with Tuzil. Maybe it's one of his people?"

"If not, then maybe he can help us find out who he is?"

* * * *

"He's on the move."

Tuzil called them at just after ten pm. "They've tracked him to a nightclub called *High End.* It's a techno dance club, popular with the eighteen to thirty-five age group."

"Has he gone inside?" Donahue asked.

"He has. If you'd like, I can be at your hotel in about ten minutes. I'll drive you over and point him out."

"We'll meet you down in front," she said.

As soon as he was off the line, she dialed up Shari's room, and the two of them agreed to meet downstairs.

Donahue got there first. She was wearing a black cocktail dress that barely showed any cleavage. Thompson arrived two minutes later, heels in hand, which she quickly put on in the lobby while they waited for Tuzil.

"I was ready to call it a night," Thompson said. "How do I look?"

She was dressed in a black leather, one-piece dress with black, strappy three-inch heels. Her long blond hair was recently curled, and the lobes of her ears sported large gold hoops.

"You look smokin' hot," Donahue said. "Are you ready to party?"

Thompson smiled. "Is the Pope a Catholic?"

A black car pulled up in front of the hotel, and the two detectives went outside and got in. Donahue introduced Thompson as Tuzil pulled away from the curb.

"Barak?" Donahue said when they were on the road, "Have you had anyone following me?"

"No," he said. "What's going on?"

"I spotted someone, an older man with long hair and a beard. He was at the Blue Mosque and then again at Hagia Sophia. I thought at first that it was just a coincidence, but we saw him tonight, near the hotel. He was watching us while we ate our dinner."

Tuzil seemed genuinely concerned.

"He might be a pickpocket, but then again, he could be a religious fanatic. Better not to take any chances. I'll have the two of you watched during the remainder of your stay, and perhaps we can find out who this person is?"

"Thank you," she said. "We appreciate that."

He nodded. "By the way, you both look very nice. You'll fit right in with the beautiful people."

Donahue smiled. They'd fit in all right...provided that they didn't try to speak. Their inability to speak Turkish was a dead giveaway.

He sped through traffic along a winding series of streets, and Donahue immediately realized how lucky they were to have their own personal guide. Had they tried this alone or gone in a cab, they would have no idea where they were going.

"Detective Thompson worked for a while in our Rape Special Unit," Donahue told him. "They specialized in rape-murders."

Tuzil looked over. "Perhaps you would consider talking to some of our investigators later? We can always use advice from someone with your expertise."

"I'd be happy to," Thompson replied.

"Excellent."

Tuzil said to Donahue, "He's got two bodyguards with him tonight. I've put three of my people inside, and I've got four others out in front and behind the club in case he decides to take off."

"You're not going to take him into custody, are you?" Donahue asked.

"I wasn't planning on it, but my people are there in case something goes wrong." He gave her a smile. "I wouldn't want anything to happen to either one of you."

"Well, we appreciate the thoughtfulness, but all we're going to do is get a cigarette butt if he smokes or maybe his glass if he has a drink. I don't think we'll have any trouble."

"Let's hope you're right, and once again, I trust that neither one of you is armed?"

"Does it look like we're carrying guns?" Donahue asked with a laugh.

Tuzil smiled. "I just wanted to make sure. Carrying an unauthorized weapon in this country would land you in prison for many years." His gaze shifted from one to the other. "You will be careful, yes?"

"Don't worry," Thompson said from the back seat. "Jen is in her element in clubs. We'll be fine."

Tuzil smiled. "When we get to the club, I'll get us all in and seated at a table. After that, you're on your own."

"Perfect," Donahue replied. "Once we have our sample, will you be driving us back?"

"But of course," he replied.

Donahue smiled. "If we get this over with quickly, then perhaps we can stop somewhere on the way back to the hotel and buy you a drink as our way of saying thanks for your help."

"That would be very nice," Tuzil said.

Thompson tapped Donahue on the shoulder. "Got a plan for when we get inside?"

"We can wing it. I'm thinking one of us can keep Aziz busy while the other one looks for a chance to get a sample."

"Sounds good," Thompson replied.

Tuzil pulled over in front of a well-lit club and parked his car at the curb. "You two stay in the car until I get things arranged. I'll be right back."

In less than two minutes, Tuzil was back, and they followed him into the club *High End.*

A taxi pulled up five car lengths behind them, and once they were past the front door and inside the club, a man climbed out of the back of the cab. Dressed in a dark business suit, his beard and mustache were now neatly trimmed, and his shoulder-length hair was pulled back in a tight ponytail.

He paid for the cab, watched it pull away, then took a quick walk around the block. If anyone was watching, he walked with a noticeable limp. He kept his eyes moving, noting the businesses that were still open, the location of a nearby cab stand, and the absence of surveillance cameras.

He was surprised to see two cars, one in front and one in back, each of which contained two men. Clearly, they were there as part of a surveillance on the club.

When he came back around to the front of the club, he walked inside and took a seat in a darkened corner of the room, one that was near the end of the bar.

THIRTY-SIX

Earlier that evening, when Prince Muhammad Abd al Aziz pulled up in front of the *High End*, it was in a black Bentley GT Continental, a present from a distant uncle of his who he suspected was trying to curry favor with Aziz's father, the Saudi Ambassador.

It was funny how things like that had happened. While the Prince and his father wanted for nothing material, there were many who tried to hedge their bets by plying his family with presents. Because his father could well end up as the next king, other members of the Royal Family, as well as outsiders, were only too willing to offer gifts that might later cause his father to look kindly on their business ambitions. And fortunately for Muhammad, many believed that a pathway to the father was one that led through the son.

He did little to discourage that kind of thinking, for he enjoyed the gifts. Currying influence was the way of the Kingdom, and for his part, Muhammad had his eye set on the post of Minister for Defense, one of the most lucrative of all the positions in the Family; and coincidentally, the very position that was currently held by the uncle who'd given him the gift of the Bentley.

Muhammad chuckled. His uncle would probably demand the car back if he knew that Muhammad had eyes on his job.

He stepped out of the Bentley and presented the key to the valet who promised to keep the car parked out in front. Muhammad's bodyguards pulled up right behind him in their Mercedes, meeting him at the curb before they walked with him up to the door of the club.

Because it was early there was still no line to get in.

Muhammad spotted the doorman.

"Yaz, my man!" It was a greeting he picked up from his time in America. "How's it goin'?"

Hayati Yazici, the young Turkish doorman, smiled broadly as the two bumped fists.

"Just fine, sir. And you?"

"I'm doing well." Muhammad leaned in towards Yazici and whispered, "If you see any good looking women out here, you be sure and send 'em over my way. Okay?"

Yazici winked, and Muhammad slipped him a generous tip.

"Enjoy yourself tonight, sir," Yazici said as he pocketed the money. He opened the door and stood aside while Muhammad and his bodyguards entered the club.

They hung out in the lobby while their eyes adjusted to the dimness of the lighting. Muhammad looked around. Most of the tables were occupied...many by couples, but there were tables with two or three girls.

He smiled at a pair of young women who were seated nearby. One of them smiled back.

"Did you see that?" he said to no one in particular.

One of the bodyguards, a Saudi named Gabir, said, "I don't know, Highness. She seems a little too fat, don't you think?"

Muhammad laughed. "You're right, Gabir. It's dark in here. That must be what confused me."

Muhammad walked into the main room, got his bearings, then nodded to people, mostly women, as he made his way to a stool at the far end of the bar.

He waived a greeting to one of the bartenders while his bodyguards convinced a nearby unassuming couple to move to other seats that were farther down the bar. Muhammad considered that corner of the club to be his base of operations, and as such, he preferred to have the space all to himself.

When the bartender came over, Muhammad ordered up tequila shooters for himself and his two bodyguards. When the bartender poured them out, Muhammad downed his right away, then called for another one.

"Leave the bottle," he told the bartender. "And bring me some extra shot glasses."

The bartender walked off to get the glasses as two dark-haired girls approached, both Turkish, one of whom was slightly overweight.

"The doorman told us to say hello," the thin girl said with a smile. She brushed a lock of hair behind her ear.

"And what is your name?" Muhammad asked.

"Arzu," she replied.

"Arzu?" A slow smile crossed his face. "Your name means *desire*, correct?"

The thin girl smiled.

"Ahh… I am right!" Muhammad turned to his companions. "I think Arzu desires me."

The bodyguards laughed.

Muhammad returned his attention to the girl. "Can I buy you a drink?"

The two girls exchanged a glance, then the thin one replied, "Sure. I'd like a martini."

Muhammad glanced over at the heavyset girl and gave her an inquiring look.

"And you?"

She smiled. "I'll take a rum and coke, please."

Muhammad nodded. "And what is your name?"

"*Mine*," she quickly replied.

Muhammad frowned in confusion. "Yes, yours," he said to clarify.

The two girls laughed before the heavyset one explained, "No. My name is *Mine.* I was named after a mountain near Mekke."

Muhammad started to laugh. "Your name suits you," he said. The two bodyguards joined in with the laughter, but the girls were clearly offended.

The heavyset girl, now thoroughly embarrassed, began to cry.

"C'mon," said her girlfriend, taking her arm. "Let's go." She turned to Muhammad. "We don't drink with pigs."

Muhammad laughed. "The only pig I see is your friend, the mountain."

The two girls stormed off amid a chorus of laughter from Muhammad and his two guards. When he once again had himself under control, Muhammad turned to Gabir and said, "Remind me when we leave to have a talk with Yaz. I think the poor guy needs to get his eyes checked."

The laughter resumed, and a few moments later, music came on and three beautiful women, all brunettes in their early twenties, made their way out on the dance floor.

Azir smiled. He pointed out the three women to his bodyguards, then got to his feet.

With the tequila bottle in one hand and four shot glasses in the other, he made his way over to the women, introduced himself, and after a few moments of conversation, he was pouring them shots while all four of them gyrated to the music.

THIRTY-SEVEN

Hayati Yazici watched with interest as Barak Tuzil led the two blond women up to the front of the club. As the doorman for a highly successful nightspot, he was required to recognize, on sight, any and all VIP's who showed up seeking entry to the facility.

He knew he'd seen the guy before, but he couldn't quite place him. The two women he was with were stunning; European in appearance, maybe even American. But nothing seemed to trigger a recollection, so he decided to fall back on his tried and true approach. Treat him as a VIP until he knew for sure he was not.

"Good evening, sir," he said in English.

Tuzil simply nodded.

Yazici continued to wrack his brain. He was usually pretty good at this. As a veteran of the club scene in Istanbul, he knew most of the regulars who made the scene. But try as he might, he just couldn't place this guy.

The car they drove up in was nothing special—a European Toyota—so the guy likely wasn't one of the *uber* rich. But the women were definitely westerners. He could tell by the shoes and the way they wore their clothing…too provocative to be Turkish. And western women very rarely hung out with other than VIPs.

When one of the women thanked him for opening the door, he detected her American accent.

Knew it, he thought.

He watched the women enter the club, and as Tuzil followed behind, Yazici noticed an earphone in his left ear.

Now that's interesting, he thought. *Could this guy be their security?*

But the guy looked to be too old for security work. Still, what other explanation could there be?

Good bodies, blond hair, western style…he thought about the money that he'd gotten from that spoiled-rotten Saudi, and it caused him to smile. When it was time for his break, and when his relief took over for him at the door, he would take a look around inside, and if the opportunity presented itself, he would have to see if he could steer the two women over for a meeting with Aziz.

Who knows? Perhaps that stuck-up little punk would give him another cash tip?

* * * *

Tuzil and the two women detectives were led by a waitress up a flight of stairs to the second level of the club. There was music coming from the dance floor, and it was so loud that it made ordinary conversation all but impossible. Along the way, they walked past dozens of young women and a few young men who passed them on the stairway coming down from the upper level. Everyone seemed intent on making their way to the dance floor.

Thompson shouted to Donahue "This place is seriously overcrowded."

The hostess offered them a table next to the railing that overlooked the dance floor and the bar below. They took their seats, and while Donahue peered over the railing, Thompson consulted briefly with Tuzil before ordering three beers and three glasses of bottled water.

"I can't find him, Barak," Donahue shouted over her shoulder. Her eyes continued to scan the crowd down below. "Can we find out from your people where he's seated?"

Tuzil spoke into a microphone attached to his right cuff sleeve. A few seconds later, he leaned over and said, "He's with his two bodyguards, somewhere over near the far end of the lower bar." He directed her gaze towards a corner of the room.

"What's he wearing," he whispered into the cuff microphone?

A few moments later, he nodded, then tapped Donahue on the arm.

"He's wearing black pants and a black long sleeve shirt, not tucked in. Sleeves rolled up several turns, and a large gold Rolex on his right wrist."

Donahue almost laughed at the Rolex reference. To her, the word Rolex was synonymous with Saudi.

She then studied the dance floor on the lower level. It was surrounded on three sides by tables and chairs, three deep in most spots, and the majority of them were filled with couples or small groups. Along the fourth wall was a long mirrored bar with thirty or so stools set in front. Most of the seats were taken, but at the end of the bar, a spot being watched over by two large men, were half a dozen stools, all empty.

Donahue watched as several couples and single males made their way over towards the empty stools. The two large men quickly turned them all away, forcing the men to place their drink orders at more crowded sections of the bar. After this happened three times in a row, Donahue realized that the large men were likely Aziz's bodyguards, throwing their weight around on behalf of the Prince.

"I think I found his bodyguards," she said to Thompson and Tuzil. "They're next to the bar where all those empty barstools are."

She then scanned the dance floor before settling on a group near the center.

"I think I found him," she said. "He's out on the dance floor with two or three girls. He's got a bottle in his hand."

Tuzil peered over the railing while Thompson stood up to get a good look.

"Yeah, I see him," Thompson said. "The guy that's dancing with the three brunettes."

"That's him," Donahue replied.

Tuzil craned his neck. "Okay. I see him, too." He then sat back down and caught Donahue's eye. "So, what do you have in mind?"

"Watch and wait," Donahue said. "We'll play it by ear."

* * * *

They watched from the upper deck as their subject danced provocatively with the three brunettes. The music was seventies rock, recorded by Turkish cover bands and spun by a local DJ. It blared loudly from two speakers on a turntable platform located on a stage at the far end of the club.

The *High End* was known for its light show, and throughout the dance numbers, the stage lights flashed from red to blue to green. At several points in the repetitive cycle, the colors disappeared, and a strobe light was used to create the illusion that the revelers were dancing in freeze-frame motion.

After what seemed like a good thirty minutes, the DJ took a break, and the house lights came back up.

Muhammad stood on the dance floor with the three brunettes, laughing and talking. He was too far away for Donahue to get a sense of what he was saying, but he started to gesture, and it appeared to her as if he was trying to convince the women to join him for a drink. The girl's locked eyes and a decision was made. They followed Aziz towards the bar.

The two bodyguards stood aside as Aziz and the women took seats on the bar stools. The four of them resumed talking, and Aziz was quick to pour them another round of shots.

Thompson caught Donahue's attention. "Shall we head for the bar and stir things up?"

"I'd feel better if he wasn't with those other women, said Donahue. "We may only get one shot at this."

Just then, a man walked up to their table. "How are you people enjoying the club?" he asked.

Donahue looked up. It was the doorman they'd seen when they first walked in.

"Just fine," she said, "but it's just a bit crowded."

"Popular place," he told her.

"I can tell," Donahue replied.

The man moved closer to Donahue. "Say, listen, I noticed that your gentleman friend here has an earpiece, so I assume he works as your security. If that's the case, and if you ladies are here to do some dancing, I have a friend downstairs that I know would love to meet you. Think you'd be interested?"

Oh, brother, Donahue thought. Now we have to put up with this?

"I don't think so," she said, "but thanks anyway."

"Are you sure?" the man asked. "He's a Saudi Prince, a member of the Royal Family. I'd be happy to make the introductions."

Donahue smiled. *Game changer! This was almost too good to be true.*

She looked over at Thompson who nodded.

Donahue looked up at the doorman. "A real Prince? Well, in that case, why not?"

"I'm Hayati Yazici," he said, "but everyone calls me Yaz."

"I'm Jen," Donahue said, "and this is my friend Shari."

Yaz nodded. "You come with me now, and I will make the introductions."

"In a moment, Yaz," said Donahue. "We'll meet you over by the stairs. I need to discuss a few things in private with my security officer. I'm sure you understand."

"Of course," Yaz told her. "I will wait for you by the bottom of the stairs."

When he wandered off, Donahue caught Tuzil's glance.

"We'll go down there with the bouncer. Can you stay up here and keep an eye on the bartender? If we end up ordering drinks, I'd like to know for sure that he isn't going to serve them spiked."

Tuzil glanced over the rail. "I should get closer. If you want. I can go down and—"

But Donahue shook her head. "Aziz's bodyguards won't let you get near that end of the bar. I was watching, and they've been keeping other people at bay." She gave him a weak smile. "You can see better from up here, Barak. Besides, Shari and I both worked undercover vice in the past. We can take care of ourselves."

Tuzil reluctantly settled back in his chair. Donahue leaned over and whispered, "Under no circumstances will we leave the building with Aziz or anyone else. So if something goes wrong—"

"I'll step in," he said.

Donahue put her hand on his shoulder then started off towards the staircase. Thompson was right behind her. As they made their way down to the first level, Thompson asked, "So how do you want to play it?"

Donahue whispered. "I'll get him out on the dance floor while you see if you can get us a sample."

"And if he goes for me?"

Donahue laughed. "Is this a contest?"

Thompson smiled. "No reason we can't have a little fun."

They reached the bottom of the staircase where they met up with Yaz who directed them across the now open dance floor.

Aziz was talking to the three brunettes and his bodyguards were off to one side. As Donahue approached his eyes drifted up and over in her direction. Yaz gave him a wave, and Aziz excused himself from the women he was with and made his way over to where Yaz and the two detectives were now standing.

Yaz smiled. "Prince Aziz," he began, "This is—"

Aziz brushed him off and went straight over to Donahue. "Ladies," he said as he held out his hand. "*Comment allez-vous*?"

Donahue cocked her head to one side. "I'm sorry, Prince Aziz, but we don't speak French."

"*Ah, ha!*" he said. "So you are an American. I recognize your accent. I also speak English."

"So I can tell," she replied.

Aziz laughed. He looked over at Thompson and his eyes took her in.

"Can I buy you ladies a drink?" he asked, returning his attention to Donahue.

Donahue flipped back her hair. "Are you really a prince?"

Aziz smiled. "I am Muhammad bin Abd al Aziz, and yes, I am a prince from the House of Saud." He held out his hand once again. "And you are…?"

This time Donahue took his hand.

"Jennifer Donahue," she said. "And this is my friend, Shari Thompson."

Muhammad took Donahue's hand and kissed the back of it. He nodded to Thompson but kept his attention on Donahue. He leaned in, and in a softer voice, he said, "Now that you know my name, what can I get you to drink?"

Donahue smiled at Thompson. "What do you think, Shari? Shall we go crazy and have a tequila shooter?"

Aziz smiled. "That's what I've been drinking."

Thompson nodded. "Well, then, let's get this party started!"

"Excellent!" Aziz pressed a large bill into Yaz's front shirt pocket, then indicated with a gesture for him to leave.

Yaz wandered off, and Aziz motioned for the women to follow him over to the bar.

When his bodyguard had chased away the three brunettes, Aziz gestured to the bartender who came over quickly.

"Nesri," he said, "We will have *Barrique* tequila shooters."

Nesri nodded.

Aziz turned back to face Donahue. "I believe you will like this brand. It is very smooth."

Donahue smiled. "We'll see." She withdrew her hand from his. "Do you live here in Istanbul?"

"I do," he replied. "I work at the Saudi embassy." His gaze shifted over to Thompson. "And do you ladies live here, too?"

Thompson shook her head. "We're on vacation. We'll only be here for another two nights."

Aziz seemed to give that some thought. "What a shame. This is such a beautiful city, and there's so much to see."

Donahue smiled. "I guess that means that we'll have to come back again and stay for a longer time."

"An excellent suggestion," Aziz replied.

The bartender returned and set three shot glasses down on the bar. He showed the bottle to Aziz who nodded and then began to pour.

Donahue felt herself begin to relax. She was in complete control of the situation. It was obvious that Aziz was enamored with her by the way he held her hand and would not let go. And if it weren't so serious, his fawning would be almost laughable.

Now that the bartender was pouring all three drinks from the same bottle, there was very little chance that the liquor would be spiked. This was going like clockwork, and all she needed to do was play it out and they'd have the sample they wanted for their DNA comparison.

Aziz picked up two of the shooters and handed them to Donahue and Thompson. He then picked up his own.

"Don't we get a wedge of lime?" Thompson asked.

Donahue laughed. "You'll have to forgive my friend," she said jokingly. "She still thinks she's back in the sorority house."

Thompson pouted. "I like it that way."

Aziz smiled and directed his attention to Thompson, "This is a very smooth tequila. You won't want to kill the taste with a wedge of lime."

"But I don't drink it to taste it," Thompson said. "I drink it to get buzzed."

Aziz picked up his glass. "If you don't like it straight the first time, I'll get you a lime for the next one."

"Fair enough," Thompson said.

Aziz raised his hand by way of a toast. "To a wonderful evening with two beautiful ladies."

Donahue smiled, and the three of them gulped down their shots.

"Wow!" Donahue put her glass back down on the bar. "That is smooth. What's it called again?"

Aziz set his glass down next to hers. "It's *Barrique de Ponciano Porfidio.* It's one of the finest tequilas in the world."

He looked over at Thompson who had a smile on her face.

"No lime for me. That was great," she said.

"How about another?" Aziz asked.

"Not yet," Donahue replied. "I came here to dance, and if I have too many shots too soon, I won't be able to walk."

Muhammad glanced over towards the DJ's corner then back at Donahue.

"He took a break," he told her. "I'm sure he'll start up again soon. In the meantime, why don't you tell me a little about yourself, Jennifer? Where do you live in the States?"

For the next ten minutes, they engaged in small talk. Donahue told him that she was a secretary for a real estate company in Los Angeles, and he hinted to her that he was a very important man at his embassy. While this was going on, Thompson, who pretended to feel left out, struck up a conversation with the two bodyguards. They were very receptive, and while she kept them entertained, she also kept her eye on the bar top and on Aziz's empty shot glass.

When Aziz decided they should have another drink, he signaled to the bartender to pour another round. But instead of using the old shot glasses, the bartender collected the used ones and laid out three more from behind the bar.

Thompson locked eyes with Donahue, and the two of them exchanged a frustrated glance. There was no way to retrieve the old glass now, so they'd have to keep their eyes on the new one.

Three more tequilas were poured, and soon thereafter, they were dispatched with fanfare. Aziz seemed highly animated, and he was quick to make reference to the fact that he was already several shots ahead of them.

Donahue felt a small buzz coming on, so she decided that the second shot would be her very last. But if they were going to get his glass, it would have to be soon.

The DJ wandered back to his stage above the dance floor, and Aziz gave Donahue a big smile.

"You said you wanted to dance?"

She smiled. "Let's do it."

* * * *

Tuzil continued to watch from his perch on the balcony. So far the bartender had been doing his job professionally, so he wasn't worried about the drinks being tampered with. He marveled at how easily the two women had made contact with Aziz. It shouldn't be surprising, considering the fact that both of them were very attractive, but they'd gotten close to a protected man without any effort at all.

There was a lesson to be learned from that, something he could take away for future investigations. Perhaps he should add a couple of attractive women to his intelligence squad?

A beautiful woman can do many things that a man could never accomplish.

His subordinates had been briefed that the two women detectives were going to make contact, and now they were all watching on heightened alert. It would all be over soon. The detectives would have their glass, and he could go home to his wife and his house full of kids.

He watched the DJ head back to the booth and sensed that Donahue and Thompson would soon be making their move.

"Stay attentive," he whispered to his people through his cuff microphone. "The lights will be going down."

* * * *

The DJ climbed up into his booth and began his next set with a song from Billy Idol, *Flesh for Fantasy*. The lights came down and switched to blue, and the dance floor began to fill up.

Aziz grabbed Donahue's hand and led her out to the dance floor. One of the bodyguards followed close behind while the other continued to talk to Shari Thompson.

"What's your friend doing?" Thompson asked, pointing to the one now standing by the dance floor.

"He's keeping an eye on the Prince," he replied.

She looked over at Aziz and feigned surprise. "He's really a prince?"

"That's right," the man answered. "We work for him."

"Are you bodyguards?" she asked, eyes widened.

Playing naive was so easy. It was just what this guy assumed her to be.

He nodded.

She smiled. "That sounds very exciting."

She glanced over at the bar where the empty shot glasses had been placed. Now was her chance.

"I'm going to get another shot," she told the bodyguard. "Can I get you one?"

"No," he said. "I better not. I'm still working."

She smiled. "Well, you go ahead then and work. I'll have a drink for both of us."

She touched his arm, turned, then moved closer to the bar. Placing her handbag on the bar top in front of her, she quickly looked around, then palmed Aziz's empty shot glass and slipped it into her purse.

Now, to cover what she had done, she waived to the bartender. When he came over, she said, "Can I get another tequila?"

The bartender smiled, collected the two remaining empty shot glasses, and poured her one in a fresh glass.

She thanked him, turned around, and downed the shot.

"Woohoo!" she said aloud as she smiled to herself. *That dirtbag of a prince might be a killer, but man does he know his tequilas.*

* * * *

When they reached an open spot on the dance floor, Donahue began to dance. Aziz joined in, and to Donahue's surprise, he wasn't bad. He had all the moves down, shaking his hips and a two-step slide. She gave him a smile and did some shaking of her own.

He was occupied for the moment, and she hoped that Shari had used this opportunity to get his glass off the counter. She looked over towards the bar, but the lights were down so low that she couldn't see Shari against the darkened backdrop. She didn't worry too much, because the longer the dance went on, the higher the likelihood was that Thompson would have time to act.

* * * *

The suited man with the beard was still seated at the bar. He slipped off the barstool and made his way out through the crowd and onto the center of the dance floor. He no longer limped.

He danced alone but kept his eyes glued on Donahue and Aziz. The darkness of the club and the alternating blue and red floodlights were instrumental in providing him with complete anonymity. The crowd swallowed him up; a crowd so dense that no one would know that he was dancing alone.

When the lighting switched over to strobe, he moved quickly through the crowd towards Donahue and Aziz.

* * * *

Shari had the glass in her purse, so it was time to pull the plug on this charade. She wanted to gesture to Donahue, but it was too dark to see her buried somewhere in the crowd. Bored with remaining on the sideline, she made her way out to the dance floor to let her partner know that it was time to go.

* * * *

With her back to Aziz, Donahue continued to dance, and when the strobe began to pulse, she did a twist around in a slow circle, admiring the other dancers, seemingly caught in the freeze-frame as the light gave the illusion of stop action.

The music was loud, too loud to be heard without screaming, and it reminded her of her days in college, a time in her life more carefree and wild—

She was still facing away from Aziz when she first spotted the face of a bearded man. He was in the crowd dancing, but he was looking right at her. In the chaos of the dancing and the strobing lights, it was hard for her to focus on his form, but each time the white strobe came back on, she could see that he was getting closer to where she was.

She wasn't sure why he stood out among all the faces she saw. Perhaps it was the scare she had earlier in the day with the bearded man who she was sure had been watching her? Then again, it might be one of Tuzil's people, coming out to make sure that she was okay. But whatever the reason, she was aware of him now, so each time the strobe went on, she made a point of trying to keep track of his whereabouts.

In one of the freeze-frame moments, she saw his face full on—and specifically his eyes—and it gave her a moment's pause. They were dark and intense, devoid of all warmth. She'd seen eyes like that many times before. They were the eyes of a person who was dead inside.

Seemingly out of nowhere, Thompson appeared at her side. Donahue spotted her in her peripheral vision and momentarily turned her head to face her. Shari smiled and winked, then said something that Donahue was unable to hear. But the smile Thompson had given her said everything. They had their glass and could leave.

In the next instant, man with the beard was right behind her, and in a moment of darkness between the strobe flashes, she felt her body being shoved forward, directly into that of Thompson who was still trying to speak.

Still on her feet, she spun around to see who crashed into her, and when the strobe light flashed once again, she recognized the face as that of the same old man who had followed her earlier during the day.

What the hell? He got cleaned up...

He was much better groomed than he'd been before, but it was his eyes that gave him away.

He turned away from her and shifted his gaze to Aziz, and that was when it hit her. She'd seen him before...and it was then that she realized exactly who he was.

* * * *

He had pushed Donahue out of his way with his left hand, before taking a step forward towards Aziz who now faced him head-on with a look of surprised annoyance on his face.

The old man swung upwards with his right hand and buried an ice pick into Aziz's groin.

Aziz buckled from the blow, bent forward, mouth open, and let out a strangled scream that struggled to be heard. The man pulled back on the ice pick, which severed the connection to Aziz, then swung it again, this time overhand, landing a blow to the side of Aziz's neck.

It must have penetrated the carotid artery, for his blood— in sync with his heartbeat—came out in spurts that were all but invisible to those nearby. But in the flash of the strobe, Donahue could see the first of the airborne splashes of what looked to her like a dark black liquid. It was hauntingly beautiful, even mesmerizing, as new patterns took shape and seemed to hang without effort in the air during those very brief moments of time which were frozen in the flash of the strobes.

Aziz pitched forward and dropped face down on the floor.

* * * *

In the next few moments, pandemonium prevailed. Dancers began to slip on the blood, then a woman tripped over the body of Aziz and let out a piercing scream.

Donahue instinctively reached for the bearded man, but he slipped through the crowd and out of her grasp.

* * * *

Thompson didn't see what had happened to Aziz, but she spotted a body on the floor. It was hard to tell what was happening. The strobes were still going, and so was the loud music.

A fight? Did someone trip? What in God's name had happened?

Alarm bells went off in her mind.

Her first thought was for her partner. She grabbed for Donahue's arm, then pulled her back against herself to shield her from whatever it was that seemed to be going horribly wrong.

* * * *

As the crowd around them seemed to move away, the two bodyguards shoved people aside to get to Aziz. Now on the ground and still face down, Gabir was the one who reached him first. He used his body to shield Aziz while he tried to make sense of what had happened.

His partner, more proactive and even more concerned, pulled out his gun and waved it towards the crowd.

* * * *

From his perch at the rail on the balcony, Tuzil saw the commotion break out on the dance floor. It was impossible to see what was going on, but people seemed to be reacting to something, and he strained his eyes in the ever-changing lighting to find out what it was?

"Can anyone see what's going on down there?" he said into his microphone.

Screams broke out, people began to scatter, and he could now discern what looked like a body that was down on the dance floor.

Tuzil struggled to process what was going on in the moments of light that were flashed by the strobe.

Panic on the dance floor spread throughout the club, and within a few moments, everyone down below him was in motion.

Someone shouted..."*Gun!*"

Tuzil began speaking rapidly, hoping that his people could hear what he was saying.

"Move in! Move in! Something has happened! Someone down there has a gun!"

* * * *

When Thompson heard the word "gun" screamed out by a woman nearby, she pulled Donahue away from Aziz, but to her surprise, it was as if they were caught in a river current. Before she could react, the two of them were propelled from the dance floor and out towards the street as a sea of people swirled around them, forcing them towards the door.

It was impossible to prevent what was happening, so Thompson held onto Donahue's arm with a death grip. Panic was taking hold, and it was now just a question of survival.

Could they stay on their feet and avoid being trampled?

* * * *

At some point, the lights came back up, and Tuzil took in the scene below. Aziz was lying on the ground, face down, and it looked like blood was smeared all over the floor. Someone was kneeling over him, yelling. Another man stood nearby, bent over in a crouch, one arm outstretched, with a handgun pointed towards the disappearing crowd.

The sea of people below him was moving towards the exit at frightening speed. He saw Donahue and Thompson in the middle of the crowd, moving with the others towards the door.

His own people appeared to be moving towards Aziz, but fighting against the actions of the crowd was keeping them from getting there quickly.

His mind was churning. Who was the man with the gun? An assailant? And why were Donahue and Thompson leaving the scene? Could they have had a hand in this?

Too much, too fast! It was out of control.

He yelled into his microphone, and with his free hand he drew out his weapon.

"Man with a gun near the body on the floor. I'll try to keep him covered from up here."

To the officers in the unmarked cars outside he said, "The two subjects are leaving the club. They're in the crowd, both are blonds...one in black leather and the other in a black dress. Detain them both, use caution."

He drew down on the man with the gun and watched as his people approached with weapons in their hands.

He could hear his men and women shouting from down below.

"Polis!...Polis!"

The Saudi bodyguards were not fools, and the one with the gun quickly dropped his weapon. He raised his hands, as did his companion, and both of them yelled for an ambulance.

Four plainclothes officers were now on the scene. One checked on Aziz's condition while the others cuffed the bodyguards and put them down on the floor.

The officer with Aziz looked up at Tuzil and shook his head.

Tuzil sighed. "Call for medical services," he said into his microphone. The last thing he needed was a claim by the Saudi's that he hadn't requested any medical care.

While the call went out, Tuzil made his way down the stairway and picked his way to the dance floor through overturned pieces of furniture.

"Seal this off," he said to one of his men. "I want a full crime scene workup."

One of the officers called him by name. He pointed to an ice pick lying on the floor. It was covered in blood.

"Don't let anyone touch it," Tuzil said. He stood over it and looked at the handle. "I'm going to want it printed."

He then spoke into his microphone. "Are the two blond women in custody?"

"Yes, sir," came the answer in his earpiece. "They're in our car."

"Keep them separated," he yelled. "I don't want them sharing details of their stories." Frustrated, he rubbed a hand across his forehead.

Will my people ever learn?

"Take them to the station in separate cars," he added.

He then looked down at the two prisoners on the floor.

"Get them down to the station and keep them separate," he said to a subordinate. "Once I've got this scene under control, we'll meet up and see where we're at?"

Tuzil looked at his watch and thought of the notifications he was going to have to make. It was going to be a very long night.

THIRTY-EIGHT

Donahue shivered. She was seated on a metal chair in a windowless interrogation room in the basement of police headquarters in downtown Istanbul. Her hands were cuffed behind her back, and a Turkish policewoman, in black uniform pants and shirt, stood post with her back to the door, watching over Donahue through dark, narrowed eyes.

Donahue flexed her fingers to encourage circulation, then arched her back in a stretch. She'd been sitting in this room for almost four hours, and except for an escorted trip to the ladies room, she'd been alone for nearly five hours with only her thoughts to keep her occupied.

Aziz was dead…she knew that much, and on her way over in the police car, she'd given a description of the man who'd done it. But since that time, no one had been in to see her, and there was no sign of Tuzil or anyone else that could vouch for the legitimacy of her presence at the scene, or for that matter, the presence of her partner.

As she thought about Thompson, she wondered how she was doing? They'd been together for the first few minutes after their initial detention, but shortly after that, they were separated, and she hadn't seen hide nor hair of Shari since that time.

She asked several times to be allowed to call the American embassy, but the guard at the door had ignored her request. And to make matters worse, she was freezing in her cocktail dress and was experiencing goose-bumps. She was sure that someone had intentionally lowered the temperature on the air conditioning, and her sheer cocktail dress did little to keep her warm.

She was just about to ask the guard for a jacket or a blanket when Barak Tuzil walked into the room.

"Take off her cuffs," he said to the guard. The woman moved in behind her, and the cuffs were quickly removed.

Tuzil placed a laptop computer on the table and pulled up a particular screen. When someone knocked on the door, the guard swung it open, and Thompson appeared, hands cuffed behind her back. A second guard who was with her had her sit in a chair next to Donahue.

"You okay?" Donahue asked.

Thompson nodded sharply. "I've had better nights out on the town."

Despite their situation, Donahue smiled.

Tuzil waited for Thompson's cuffs to be removed, then turned to the guards. "Will one of you please get our guests some blankets and something warm to drink?" He glanced over at Donahue and Thompson. "Coffee? Perhaps some tea?"

Donahue noted this change of attitude.

"Tea, please," she said, and Thompson nodded her concurrence with the order. She was busy rubbing her wrists to alleviate the numbing tightness of the cuffs.

"Two teas," Tuzil said to the guards, and both of them quickly disappeared.

He settled into a chair that was next to them and said, "I have a tape I want to play for you. I think you'll find it quite interesting."

He turned the computer towards them, and a video image of the crowded club's dance floor began to play.

Donahue and Thompson watched in fascination. It showed Donahue dancing with Aziz; Thompson's approach from one side; and the mysterious bearded man as he danced his way through the crowd.

When the strobe light came on, Donahue suddenly realized that the moments without light had provided the killer with an almost perfect opportunity to strike out at Aziz while those around remained oblivious to what was going on.

The bearded man had used his arm to muscle Donahue out of the way, then had stepped around her to confront Aziz. In one swift movement, his hand came up in a roundhouse, underhand motion and appeared to hit Aziz in the area of the stomach or groin. When Aziz doubled over, the hand pulled back and swung around in an overhand circle, coming down from the top. Aziz's hands shot up to his neck as the bearded man turned and slipped out of view. It was then that Aziz dropped down to his knees before falling face-forward to the floor.

The tape ended with the lights coming up as the crowd surged away and raced towards the doors.

Donahue looked up. "He stabbed him twice?"

"That's correct," Tuzil said. "We think the first blow was to the groin, and when Muhammad grabbed for his privates, he exposed his upper body. The killer put the second strike into the side of his neck."

"What was the weapon?" Thompson asked.

"An ice-pick. We recovered it from the floor near the body." Tuzil shrugged. "As you can see, the tape is not very clear, but for our purposes, it did help eliminate the two of you as suspects."

He looked at them both with narrowed eyes and Donahue met his glance.

"Suspects?" Donahue was incredulous. "You thought we had something to do with his murder?"

Tuzil smiled wanly. "Not me personally, but until we sorted things out, we had to detain you." He studied their skeptical reactions. "I'm sure you would have done the same thing if our roles were reversed."

Thompson scoffed. She was clearly upset. "If they were reversed, you wouldn't have been kept in handcuffs in a freezing cold basement."

"I'm sorry," Tuzil said, "but there were those above my pay grade who suggested that you might have used our cooperation to get yourselves close to Aziz." He shrugged. "I had to deal with a lot of speculation until someone discovered that the murder was on tape."

Donahue accepted Tuzil's explanation, but she too wasn't happy with the way things had gone.

"Did you manage to catch him?" she asked.

Tuzil shook his head. "He got away from the club before our people could seal it off." He leaned forward and started another digitalized tape. "There was a camera by the door. The lighting was a little better."

They watched as the bearded man made his way past several people still entering the club. And as he hit the street, he appeared to be followed by a mass exodus of panicked people who pushed and shoved their way from the building. In that crowd, Donahue and Thompson could be clearly seen as the surging crowd carried them forward and through the front doors.

When the tape ended, Donahue sighed.

Tuzil noticed her reaction. "Did you recognize this man?"

Donahue nodded. "He was the man I told you about, the one that followed me when I was walking around by the Blue Mosque and at the Hagai Sophia."

Tuzil rubbed at the stubble on his unshaven face. "Perhaps he followed you to the club?"

"Unless he had inside help?"

"Meaning?"

"Meaning that someone on your squad might have tipped him off, or perhaps he was monitoring your radio transmissions?"

Tuzil thought it over, then nodded. "I can vouch for my people, but you may be right about our frequency being monitored. That wouldn't be too difficult to do."

Thompson shifted her weight in her seat and crossed her arms. "Any leads from the club?"

"There were no prints on the ice pick and apparently he didn't order a drink, so I'm afraid we got nothing." He looked from one to the other. "I've stationed men at the airport and at the train station, but no one matching his description has been spotted. We're going through our Customs photos right now, everyone who entered the country since a week before your arrival, but so far, no luck."

"The beard could be a fake," Donahue suggested.

"If that's the case," said Tuzil with a shrug, "then I suspect we might never find out who did it."

Donahue caught something in his tone, a hint of resignation, as though he didn't believe they really had much chance at all of an arrest.

The door opened up, and the two guards returned with blankets and three cups of tea. Additionally, one of the guards brought in their purses, setting them down on the table.

Donahue wrapped the blanket over her shoulders while Thompson examined the contents of her purse.

"What happens now?" Donahue asked as she reached for her cup of tea. "Are we free to go?"

"You are," he replied.

Thompson placed her purse back on the table and folded her arms across her chest.

"Can we get a blood sample from the body to close out our case? It would be nice if we could have something to take back with us, considering that your people have taken Aziz's shot glass from my purse."

"I'm afraid a blood sample will not be possible." Tuzil leaned back in his chair. "The Saudi government has already taken possession of the body." He looked at his watch. "In fact, I've been told that the Ambassador will be escorting his son back to the Kingdom later tonight."

Tuzil reached into his pocket and pulled out a sealed plastic bag. In it was the glass that had come from Thompson's purse.

"We did not book this into evidence when we brought you in," he said. He handed it over to Thompson. "It should provide you with the DNA you need. But remember, you did not get this from me."

Donahue gave him a questioning look.

Why did he say it was not itemized? What was going on here?

"Did I miss something, Barak?" she asked. "Why all the cloak and dagger? The man is dead."

"Cloak and dagger?" Tuzil frowned.

"Intrigue," Thompson added. "Why does it feel like something is going on here that you're not talking about?"

Tuzil smiled. "You are very perceptive, detective, and you are correct. There is a much bigger plan at work here, one that concerns both of our governments." He winked. "It is beyond my pay grade and beyond yours as well."

Thompson looked over at Donahue. "Sounds like we're going to be kept in the dark."

Donahue got to her feet.

"If we're done here, I'd like to get a shower and some sleep. Any chance you can arrange for someone to give us a ride back to the hotel?"

Tuzil's turned to the guards, spoke softly in Turkish, and watched them disappear from the room.

"They will arrange for your transport back to the hotel, but I would suggest that you leave Istanbul as soon as you can."

"Leave?" Thompson got to her feet. "Why would you suggest that? We've done nothing wrong."

Tuzil kept his voice even. "You were here to investigate the son of an

Ambassador from a foreign country. That, by itself, will lead to some difficult and embarrassing questions. But when we consider the fact that the target of your investigation was murdered in your presence? Well…" His shoulders came up in a shrug. "…I'm afraid that what we have here is an international incident, and I suspect that it would be better for you if you were not still here when the fallout rolls downhill."

"But we—"

"He's right," Donahue said, cutting Thompson off. "We've done nothing wrong, but we could end up here for weeks or months answering questions that should never be asked."

Tuzil looked at her with a new sense of admiration. "I see that you understand me, Detective Donahue."

Donahue nodded. "Still, I'd like to get that shower and some sleep. Is it okay if we catch a flight later in the day?"

"The next one-stop flight leaves today at three p.m." Tuzil glanced at his watch. "You should be able to get a little sleep before it's time to leave."

Thompson rolled her eyes. "I guess that settles that." She looked over at Donahue. "Shall we go?"

Tuzil led them upstairs to the lobby of the station, and at the front door, he pulled Donahue aside while Thompson made her way to the car.

Tuzil faced her. "I do not think the timing of the killing was coincidental, and I also believe that you know a great deal more than you're telling me."

Donahue shot him a look. "And it would appear that you know a great deal more than you're telling me."

Tuzil kept his eyes locked on hers. He lowered his voice to a near whisper.

"I am a man who believes in the law and in the system, but I also believe in justice." He glanced around. There was no one else around within earshot. "My people have uncovered the murder of a Russian prostitute that matches very specifically the M.O. of your killings. The plastic cuff that was used to bind her wrist to the bed frame bears the same serial number as the batch used in the other cases."

Donahue's eyes widened. "Was there any DNA?"

He shook his head. "There was no semen, but we did find a trace of saliva on one of her breasts." He winked. "It will be tested against a blood sample that we removed from the floor of the nightclub."

Silence settled in between them.

Donahue's mind was racing. They had taken a sample of Aziz's blood from the scene of the stabbing. For all of his posturing, the Turkish authorities were intending to get some answers, even if they had to do it under the table.

"Why are you telling me this?" she asked softly.

"I want you to understand that I am not wholly unsympathetic to your desire to bring out the truth, but sometimes there are reasons to withhold the facts... reasons that better serve the public."

"But..." she began.

"Look, detective, I believe in a sense of symmetry, and tonight it would appear that a certain form of justice was reached in this case." His expression softened. "I would not be surprised if my people did little more than go through the motions of a follow-up investigation."

Donahue's face registered her surprise.

Were all their efforts to track down the bearded man really nothing more than a sham?

"If you do know who did this," he said, "perhaps it would be better for everyone concerned if you did not reveal what you know."

She thought about this warning and realized with certainty that she was playing in a pond that was out of her depth.

"Will our presence here and the details of our investigation become known to the Saudi Ambassador?"

Tuzil shook his head. "My superiors and I believe that this unfortunate killing was an act of Muslim extremism directed at the Royal House of Saud."

The light came on, and Donahue finally got a sense of where this was going.

Tuzil caught the recognition in her eyes and said, "In the long term, it will be better for both of our countries if we maintain this position. Wouldn't you agree?"

Donahue nodded slowly. "So, I'm gonna guess that you've already heard from our US Department of State?"

"To say they are not happy would be an understatement. And that reminds me, your Captain in Los Angeles would like you to call him as soon as you can."

Donahue blinked slowly. What had started out as a simple cold case had turned into a major catastrophe. What she needed right now was some sleep. Only then might she be able to make sense of it all.

She held out her hand. "Thanks for everything, Barak. If you're ever in LA, I'd be happy to buy you dinner."

Tuzil smiled. "I hope someday you will return and get a chance to enjoy the hospitality and beauty of my country."

"Someday, but not anytime soon. Right?"

Tuzil winked, then reached for the door.

"By the way," Donahue said, "you mentioned the serial number on the plastic handcuffs. How did you get your hands on the crime reports from LA and London?"

Tuzil gave her an embarrassed smile. "While you were being detained, we searched your rooms."

"Why am I not surprised."

"Incidentally," he added, "the British government has requested that we return the London reports to them, and of course, my government has already complied."

Her eyes narrowed. "You've been very busy."

"However, we did scan a copy for our own internal purposes, just as your Detective Gibson did before he boarded his plane."

Donahue could only shrug. They'd been under surveillance the entire time they'd been in Istanbul, and that brought up a troubling thought.

As they walked out to the curb in front of the building, Donahue said, "Tell me something, Barak. Since you've been watching me so closely, how is it that your team didn't pick up on the old man who was following me around?"

Tuzil briefly closed his eyes. "Who says we didn't?"

"You're letting him go, aren't you? Because he doesn't fit with your Muslim terrorist scenario?"

Tuzil sighed. "You're talents are wasted as a police officer, detective. You should look into a career in the diplomatic services."

Donahue frowned. "And the Brits and my government are on board with this?"

"It is best for all concerned if it ends here and now."

"Well, I will say this. You're nothing if not thorough."

His eyes shifted to the car parked at the curb. "Your driver is waiting. Get some rest and have a nice flight, Jennifer. I hope someday to see you again."

* * * *

"Captain? It's Jen Donahue."

"Where are you?" Elwood asked. The phone connection was loud and clear.

"Shari and I are at the airport in Istanbul. Our flight for LA leaves in two hours. I'm sorry I couldn't call sooner, but our host strongly insisted that we get packed and get out of Dodge right away." She looked around. The two officers who'd been with them since they'd left the police headquarters were twenty feet away, just standing and watching.

She nodded to one of them who nodded back.

"In fact, we've got a pair of minders standing right nearby, so I can't say much right now."

Elwood leaned back in his chair. "Are you okay?"

"We're fine. For having spent time in custody in a Turkish jail, I suppose Shari and I should be grateful that it's not like it was in *Midnight Express*."

She was referring to a film made in 1978 about an American's harrowing time in a Turkish prison for possession of unlawful drugs.

Elwood laughed. "I see that it hasn't impacted your sense of humor." He was silent for a moment. "We've got a lot of questions at this end, but they'll keep until you get back."

Donahue sighed. She'd be put through the wringer when she got back. Of that she was certain.

"How's Gibby's wife?" It was her real reason for having called in the first place.

"She had a setback of some kind. Gib's not talking much about it, but when I spoke with him last night, he told me she was holding her own."

Donahue sighed. '*Holding her own*' was better than *losing ground.* At least something was going right.

"I'm sorry about the mess here, Boss. Anything you need to know before I have to hang up?"

"Not really. The Chief received a call from your buddy Rendleford over at State. From what I understand, he was pushing to get you fired. That man's got a wild hair up his ass."

"Is my job on the line?"

Elwood laughed. "To quote the Chief…'*I told him he could fuck off and mind his own business.*'"

Donahue smiled. The Chief had just earned her undying respect.

"One small thing," Elwood told her. "No comment needed, but your buddy demanded that the Chief turn over a piece of evidence that came from the scene."

Donahue was taken aback. *Did Tuzil set them up?* He didn't strike her as someone that duplicitous. It was then that she remembered that there had been two guards in the room when he gave them the shot glass. Maybe one of them said something that somehow made its way back to State.

She looked over at the two watchdogs who were talking between themselves. "If that's the case, we might have a problem when we land in LA."

"I'll send a few of our guys over to meet the plane," Elwood said. "Just don't get up in their faces."

"Thanks, Tom. We'll give you a call when we land."

She hung up the phone. Thompson was seated nearby with a cup of coffee in her hand.

"Are we cool?" Thompson asked.

"Not exactly."

Donahue sat down and put her carry-on bag on the floor in front of her. "That asshole from the State Department has been bending the Chief's ear. He demanded that I lose my job."

"I wouldn't worry about that, Jen. You've done nothing wrong."

Donahue shrugged. "Nevertheless, we've got to be cautious, Shari. You never know what this guy is capable of doing. He seems to have a pretty long reach."

Then it struck her. There was a way around Rendleford and what she knew he had in mind.

She leaned over to Thompson and whispered, “Do you still have the shot glass in your purse?”

“Yeah.” Thompson studied her face. “Why?”

Donahue whispered her concerns and her plan, and when the recitation was over, Thompson smiled wickedly.

“What have you gotten me into, Jen? All I wanted was a little vacation time away from the job and my kids.” She slowly got to her feet. “Be careful what you wish for… right?”

For the benefit of the watchers, Thompson said, ”As long as we’ve got time, I’m going to do a little souvenir shopping. You want to come with me?”

“Nope.” Donahue leaned back in her seat. “I’m beat, so I think I’ll just hang right here.”

Thompson nodded.

She walked over to the watchers. “Hey, guys. I’m going to go into that souvenir shop over there to get a few things to take back to my kids. And after that, I’m gonna get a fresh cup of American coffee over at Starbucks. Is that okay?”

The smaller of the two men smiled. “You can do whatever you like, detective. All we have to do is see that you make it on the plane.

Thompson nodded. *Yeah, right.*

“Don’t worry about that,” she said. “My almost ex-husband wants me home as soon as possible. Wouldn’t you think a grown man could handle a few rambunctious kids?”

The two guards laughed.

“If I leave my bag with Detective Donahue, would you guys mind keeping an eye on it?”

They looked at each other, and one of them nodded.

“Thanks.”

And then, seemingly as an afterthought, she added, “Would either one of you like a cup of American coffee? It’s not as good as Turkish, but it’s still pretty good? And, as a thank you for driving us over here, it would be my treat?”

Both of them nodded their thanks.

“You take it black?” she asked them.

"Sugar, please," said the taller of the two.

"Black's fine for me," replied the other one.

"Okay." She smiled broadly. "I'll be right back."

Donahue watched Thompson as she headed into the duty-free shop and it was all she could do to keep from smiling. Leave it to Shari to charm the two guards. It might have screwed things up if one of them had gone along.

* * * *

Fifteen minutes later, after delivering the cups of Starbucks to the two grateful watchers, Thompson resumed her seat next to Donahue.

"It's done," she said as she took a sip of her coffee.

Donahue smiled...one less thing to worry about.

Across the room, one of the watchers put his hand up to his ear, looked over in their direction, then started towards them.

"Uh, oh!" said Thompson as she leaned back in her seat. "Don't look now, but one of the babysitters is coming this way."

Donahue turned just as the watcher walked up.

"Detective Donahue, would you mind coming with me?"

"Why?" Donahue asked.

The watcher shrugged. "This way," he said.

She got to her feet and reached for her carry-on bag.

"You can leave that here," he said. "We'll keep an eye on it for you."

She turned towards Thompson. "If you don't hear from me in twenty minutes, call Tuzil."

Thompson nodded. She watched Donahue walk off with the watcher and thought...*What in the hell is it now?*

THIRTY-NINE

The watcher led Donahue through a security door and down a long hallway that was closed to the public. When they came to a steel door, he stopped, punched in a security code, then stood to the side as the door slid open.

"I will wait for you here," he said.

Donahue nodded. She took a deep breath, then walked through the door.

She had entered a meeting room of some kind, with an oversized table, at least a dozen chairs, and a view of the busy tarmac where planes were parked at the gates.

Standing off to the side of the table was a single, well-dressed, swarthy male. He watched her enter, then gestured to her to take a seat. When she did, he moved around the table to take a chair very close to her, never breaking off his penetrating gaze.

Donahue immediately sized him up. A designer suit, muted silk tie, jet black hair, and a short, dark beard...he was definitely Saudi, with an uncanny resemblance to Prince Muhammad.

"Do you know who I am?" He spoke in perfect English with a trace of a British accent.

"You bear a striking resemblance to Prince Muhammad bin Abd al Aziz," she replied.

He held her glance. "He was my son."

Donahue sighed. "You have my condolences, Mr. Ambassador."

"Thank you," he replied. "I was told that you were a true professional, detective, so I will come right to the point." He folded his hands on the table. "I would like to hear from you about the conduct of my son."

Donahue felt her breath catch in her throat. What the hell was going on? How did the Ambassador learn of their investigation? And how was this meeting arranged? And what should she do? Should she tell him what she knew about his son? How would he take it? And what about the *bigger picture?* What about the

State Department? The Turks? The Brits?

Barak had told her that the Allies were all in agreement; the killing would be blamed on a Muslim terrorist. They wanted leverage over this man, leverage that could affect the economic security of all of their nations.

What the hell was she supposed to say?

"Mr. Ambassador, I don't feel comfortable being here."

"I understand," he said after a moment, "but I have heard some things about my son that are very troubling, and that is why I need for you to tell me the truth."

Donahue pursed her lips and frowned. "I'm sorry, Mr. Ambassador, but I can't discuss my investigation with you."

The Ambassador inhaled deeply. "I'm sure you've been spoken to, detective. I know what's at stake here. There are people in your government as well as others who believe that they can use my son's behavior before his death as a way to influence my government and me. However, I can assure you, that will not occur."

He leaned back in his chair, and it was at that moment that Donahue saw a truly broken man; a father who was mourning the loss of a son he thought he had known; a father who would stop at nothing to learn the truth.

And who were his sources?

His information was awfully good, and it was pretty clear that it was coming from the highest of levels, so he probably already knew that his son was suspected of being involved in a series of murders, and if he knew that already, then all he really wanted was official confirmation, and as a parent, he deserved just that.

As far as she knew, this man wasn't involved in his son's crimes, so why should he be treated as if he were?

Because someone in her government had bigger plans?

Screw that!

Screw them all!

To hell with her own State Department, and in particular, that bastard Allen Rendleford. He had undermined her work at every turn, subverted justice, and pushed her boss to fire her for doing her job. She owed him nothing, and as far as she was concerned, she wouldn't be part of any plan—government sponsored or otherwise—that would involve the extortion of this particular man, or for that matter, anyone else.

"All right, Mr. Ambassador. If you want to know the truth, I will tell you. But in exchange, I want to know who your source is? I need to know who I can trust."

The Ambassador seemed to give it some thought. "You are thinking it is Director Tuzil, but I assure you, it is not. The intelligence service from my country has penetrated the Turkish police. Our sources are many and varied, and for that reason, I seek confirmation of the rumors that my people have heard."

"You mentioned director Tuzil," Donahue said. "Is he the one who arranged for this meeting?"

The Ambassador nodded. "He is a trusted friend, but on a professional level only. I asked him to arrange this introduction because I was told that he had been working with you."

"Then why don't you just ask him about my investigation?"

"Because he has told me in no uncertain terms that it is your investigation."

To Donahue, that made sense. Go straight to the horses' mouth.

"All right," she said, reluctantly. "You want to know the truth? Your son raped and murdered a young girl in Los Angeles, and after you took him to Great Britain with you, he killed two more. And, since you've been here in Istanbul, the Turkish police suspect that he may have killed again."

The Ambassador put his hands over his eyes and began to weep; softly at first, then louder.

"I had no idea," he finally said. "He was always a difficult boy; willful, disobedient. But this?" He struggled with his thoughts, then caught her glance. "There was a girl in Los Angeles who said my son had raped her. Was that true? At the time, your government assured me that the charges were groundless."

Donahue snorted. "A man in the State Department named Rendleford threatened to deport the young woman to Moscow if she went forward with the claim. But your son raped her, Mr. Ambassador, of that you can be sure."

"And you have evidence for all of this?"

Donahue nodded. She explained about the DNA match between the LA and British cases, the use of the flexible handcuffs with the same batch number on the LA, British, and Turkish victims, and the claim made by an unnamed bodyguard source that his son was into drugging young girls in bars, then taking them back to his residence for sex.

When her recitation was finished, she waited for the Ambassador to say something, but he was silent. Obviously, the nature and details of the crimes committed by his son had him reeling, so she waited in her chair while he processed what she'd told him.

Finally, he said, "I'm so sorry about this. Can you provide me with the names and addresses of his victims and their surviving family members?"

"Why?" she asked. "What good would it do?"

"Reparations," he answered quickly. "It won't make up for what he's done, but it might make things a little easier for them."

She studied his face but could detect no guile.

"All right," she said. "I'll make arrangements to get that information to you." As an aside, she added, "You do know that my government and the others wanted to keep this information from you?"

"Why would they do that?" he asked.

"I'm not an expert on foreign relations, but it's my understanding that someday you might be King, and I think that the idea may have been that publicizing the truth about your son might damage your chances, and that was something they want to avoid."

The Ambassador smiled and shook his head.

"Whoever the Council's choice is for King, my country will maintain our relationship with our Allies. It is the only way that we can continue to remain on the throne." He shook his head. "No, what they seek is leverage over me; leverage they won't have if another is selected."

He pursed his lips. "Your State Department is very devious. I will have to address that after my son is in the ground."

"You didn't hear it from me," she said. "I'm already in enough trouble as it is."

He nodded. "Only Director Tuzil and I know about this meeting, and he can be trusted to keep it quiet." He studied her face. "I will have to find out from Tuzil what they planned to say about my son's killer?"

"I was told that they are planning to say that your son was killed by a Muslim extremist." She shrugged. "But who knows for sure?"

"That would make sense," the Ambassador replied. He leaned forward in his chair. "If my people felt that we were under attack by the more radical elements of our religion, they might be more inclined to align themselves with the requests of your country to crack down on extremist groups." He looked around for a moment. "Perhaps the death of my son was Allah's wish after all. Do you know the identity of the killer?"

Donahue got to her feet and raised her hands in surrender.

"This is all too heavy for me, Mr. Ambassador. I'm just a cop, doing my job." She looked at her watch. "I need to get back to my partner. I told her to call out the troops if I didn't get in touch with her in twenty minutes."

"I understand." He got to his feet and extended his hand. "Thank you for being honest with me, Detective Donahue. I commend you for doing your job, and if there's anything I can ever do for you, either personally or professionally, just give me a call."

He handed her an embossed business card. "If you ever need anything, just call and leave your name and a number, and I will get back to you right away."

With that, he walked over to a nearby glass door and punched a code into the keypad lock. The door swung open far enough for Donahue to see several members of his personal security detail standing just outside. The Ambassador walked out, and the door closed behind him, leaving Donahue alone with her thoughts.

Well, you've done it now!

She walked over to the steel door and decided she would keep her meeting with the Ambassador a secret from everyone, including Shari Thompson.

No sense getting her or anyone else involved.

FORTY

Their flight was more than an hour late getting into LA, and when it landed, Donahue and Thompson were greeted by four FBI agents who escorted them into a waiting room at the Tom Bradley International Terminal.

"What about Customs?" Thompson asked. "Don't we have to go there first?"

An agent in a dark blue suit quietly told her, "It's been taken care of."

The room was set up for interviews. There was a metal table, four chairs, four windowless walls, and a closed circuit camera in the upper right corner that Donahue suspected was on.

"What are we doing here?" Donahue asked.

"You'll be told in a few moments," said the tallest of the four. "In the meantime, why don't you both take a seat?"

"This is bullshit," Thompson said. "You've got no right to detain us. I've got kids at home that are waiting for me. I'm outta here."

"Sit down." The tallest of the agents pointed at a chair as if he was a parent schooling a child.

Thompson glared. "You must be the guy in charge. That's good, because I never forget a face, and when this is all over, I'm going to personally track you down and make sure that you end up being named in my lawsuit."

One of the agents laughed but quickly stopped when the tall one glowered.

The door to the room swung open, and in walked two more suited men.

"Looks like this is turning into a Brooks Brother's convention," Thompson said to Donahue. Then, "Shouldn't you boys be out solving bank robberies instead of wasting our time in here?"

The biggest of the two newcomers, a strikingly handsome man with short, dark hair, said, "I'm Frank Toledo, Department of State, and this is Jason Anders, US Attorney's Office, out of Washington DC."

Donahue smiled at Anders before addressing her remarks to Toledo.

"Well, Frank, I take it Rendleford couldn't make it, so he sent you instead?"

Toledo nodded. "Considering the problems you've caused this country, Detective Donahue, I wouldn't expect you to be so glib."

"What you expect of me doesn't matter one wit, Frank. Why are you detaining us? We've broken no laws."

"You were previously warned not to pursue your investigation of Prince Muhammad bin Abd al Aziz, yet you continued to do so to the detriment of this country's foreign policy."

"Spare me the lecture," said Donahue, but for all her bravado, she was starting to worry. It was clear that these guys were seriously pissed. "You still haven't told me why we're being detained?"

Toldeo removed his glasses, cleaned the lenses with a soft cloth, then put them back on.

"You can make this easy or difficult for yourselves, it makes no difference to me."

"What is it you want?" Donahue asked.

"I want the shot glass you brought back with you from Istanbul," Toledo said.

"You can't have it," Thompson said, a touch of anger in her tone. "It's evidence in our criminal case."

"You are no longer involved in the investigation of that case," Toledo said. "We want that shot glass."

Thompson folded her arms across her chest. "Not a chance, and I want a lawyer."

Toldeo turned to Agent Anders. "They're all yours."

Anders placed his briefcase down on the table and pulled out a four-page document. He showed it to Donahue.

"This is a search warrant signed by Justice LeAnn Griffin, Federal District Court of Appeals, directing us to conduct a search of your persons and your possessions for a shot glass once used by Prince Muhammad bin Abd al Aziz. Now, you can hand it over without further delay, or I'll bring in a female agent who I can assure you has been instructed to conduct a very thorough search."

He handed Donahue the warrant which she immediately read before dropping it down on the table.

"You realize that you're interfering with a criminal investigation," she told him.

Anders smiled. "As you've been told, we're taking over your investigation on the basis of national security interest."

Donahue looked at Thompson. "We've got no choice, Shari. Show them your purse."

"It's not there," she said. "I think I left it in Istanbul."

Donahue rolled her eyes, "You did what?"

Thompson shrugged.

Anders was growing tired of the delay. "Your purse, Detective Thompson."

She reluctantly handed it over to Toledo.

He opened it up, rummaged around, then pulled out a sealed plastic bag. Inside was a shot glass.

The agent glanced over at Anders, then back at Thompson.

"Left it in Istanbul…*my ass*."

"And a large ass it is," Thompson retorted.

The agent shot her a look, then held the bag up to the light. Then, to no one in particular, he said, "The glass says *Istanbul* on it?"

"A souvenir," Thompson replied. "It was for my husband."

"Yeah, right." Toledo slipped the bag with the shot glass into Anders briefcase then handed her back her purse.

"Can we go now?" Donahue asked with a note of agitation.

"Not yet," Anders replied. He pulled two more documents out of his briefcase. "You are hereby served with an order to show cause. There is a hearing scheduled next week in Federal court on the national security implications related to this investigation. You are directed to appear with counsel at that time, and you will note, that in the interim, the two of you are precluded from discussing any aspect of the investigation of Prince Muhammad bin Abd al Aziz with anyone other than your attorneys."

"You muzzling us?" Thompson asked.

Anders smiled. "Absolutely! Should you release any information about this case to anyone at any time, you will be in direct violation of this order. And I can assure you, if details of this case get out, the Justice Department will pursue contempt proceedings against you, and the two of you *will* end up going to prison."

Donahue placed her copy in her purse and said, "C'mon, Shari. Our luggage is waiting at the carousel."

Thompson picked up her purse and her carry-on bag. She looked over at Anders, and as a parting shot, she said, "You will be hearing from my attorney."

* * * *

The two of them walked out of the conference room and followed the signs to the luggage carousels. Standing at the one where their luggage had come in were two LAPD detectives and a Customs agent. Their bags were on a table placed nearby.

"Hi, boys," Donahue tapped one of them on the shoulder.

Richard Bengtson, a detective from Robbery-Homicide Division, quickly turned around at the sound of her voice, and she could see that he was visibly upset.

"Where the hell have you been?" he said.

"Oh, look, Shari," Donahue teased, "our protectors are guarding our bags."

"They should have been watching our backs," Thompson replied.

Bengtson groused, "We've been waiting here since before your plane touched down."

"Your concern is touching, Rich," Thompson said, "but you were out-foxed by the Feds. They intercepted us just as we stepped off the plane."

Bengtson's partner, Rick Jackson, usually the silent one, raised an eyebrow.

"Did they work you over?"

"Rubber hoses and needles under my nails. But I want to go on record right now saying that my partner, Detective Donahue, was the first one to scream and spill her guts."

"They threatened a full body cavity search," Donahue said, "so, of course, I folded."

She began to laugh, as did Thompson, and Jackson asked, "What's so funny?"

"Not here," Donahue told him under her breath. She turned to the Customs agent.

"We good to go?"

The Customs agent, who had overheard their conversation, nodded. "You ladies are crazy, but you're cleared. Welcome back to the States."

Donahue smiled. It was good to be back at home where she understood the rules of the game.

FORTY-ONE

Bengtson and Jackson drove them straight down to the Police Administration Building. While in the car, Donahue made a call to Zachary, but as usual, she got his machine.

"Hi, babe," she said. "I'm back in LA and on my way to the office. Call me later when you get this message."

She put away her phone and looked over at Thompson. "You gonna call your ex?"

"Not yet," Thompson said with a laugh. "Until I walk through the front door of my house, I'm still on vacation, and if I give him a call, all I'm going to hear is whining about the kids and how hard it's been for him... *blah, blah, blah.*"

Donahue laughed.

At the station, the four of them took one of the elevators to the fifth floor. While Bengtson and Jackson went straight to their desks, Donahue and Thompson walked directly to the door of the Captain's office where they found Tommy Elwood, seated in his chair, feet on the desk, his phone to his ear.

He looked up, waved them in, and gestured to the two chairs in front of his desk.

"Welcome back," he said when he hung up the phone. His feet came off the desk and he leaned forward. "You guys okay?"

"Tired," said Donahue, "but none the worse for wear."

"That's good." He caught Thompson's glance. "Thanks for filling in for Gibson. I know this didn't exactly go the way it was planned but your help was greatly appreciated."

Donahue said, "Speaking of Gibby, how's Claudette?"

"Like I told you, the last time I spoke with him he said she was resting comfortably. She had some kind of setback, but he didn't go into details. The squad sent her a flower arrangement, and we added your names to the card."

"Thanks," Donahue said.

"Who do we see about kicking in?" Thompson asked.

"See my secretary," Elwood replied. "She collected the money."

Thompson nodded.

Elwood leaned back in his chair. "So, what happened? All I heard was that your suspect got himself killed?"

Donahue started at the beginning and filled him in on their association with Tuzil, the tracking of Aziz to the nightclub by Tuzil's people, and the method used by the bearded man to get close enough to Aziz to shank him with an ice pick. She glossed over the details of their detention, and concluded with their release and being escorted to the airport. She elected not to mention her meeting with the Saudi Ambassador.

When she was finished, Elwood asked, "Do they have any idea who did the killing?"

"If so, they're not saying, but they've got a few working theories."

Elwood cocked an eyebrow. "Like what?"

"Like a Muslim extremist, intent on the overthrow of the Royal House of Saud, or someone with a grudge against the Ambassador or his son."

"Well, that narrows it down," Elwood said with a guffaw. "That's a suspect list that would include more than half of the Middle-East."

Donahue smiled. "Whoever he is, the guy slipped through their fingers. Tuzil told me that they covered the airports and trains, but no one stood out."

Elwood rubbed at his chin. "I don't suppose they let you have a blood sample from the body?"

Thompson shook her head. "The body was released to his father before they even let us out of jail."

She looked over at Donahue, and the two of them started to laugh.

Elwood gave them a quizzical look.

Donahue explained, "It occurred to me that Rendleford might try to seize the shot glass we got from Aziz at the bar."

"Did he?" Elwood asked.

Donahue deferred to Thompson. "While we were waiting for our flight out of Istanbul, I purchased a designer purse from the Duty-Free Shop." Thompson smiled broadly. "I put Aziz's shot glass inside it, and got the store to agree to ship it through customs directly to my home."

Elwood smiled. "Smart. But what if they check your mail?"

Thompson shook her head. "They won't. They'll be content with the shot glass that we gave them when we got off the plane at LAX."

Donahue could see the confusion on Elwood's face.

"It's like this, Tom. When Shari bought the purse, she also bought a shot glass at the Duty-Free shop that she sealed in a clear plastic bag. She put it in the purse she was carrying for the flight back here."

"I spit in it, too," Thompson added.

Donahue rolled her eyes. "You didn't?"

Thompson smiled. "I wanted to make sure that they got a little DNA."

Elwood laughed, then shook his head.

"You realize, of course, that you've tampered with evidence in a federal investigation. They'll come down on you hard when they realize what you've done."

"Screw them," Donahue said. "This is our case and our evidence. And as soon as that purse shows up, we'll have the lab get us a DNA profile, and then we'll know for sure, once and for all, whether or not Aziz is the one who killed Carrie Ann Ryson."

"But Shari lied to the FBI," Elwood said, "and that's a crime."

"Actually, I told them the truth," said Shari. "I said I left the shot glass they wanted in Istanbul, which I did, and I told them the one they confiscated was a souvenir, which it was."

Elwood smiled broadly. Technically, she was right. She had told the truth.

"But the case is over," he said. "He's dead, and no one cares about it anymore."

Donahue frowned. "I care, Tom, and I would think that the parents of the girls who were killed would still care."

Elwood raised his hands in surrender. "Point taken. Okay, I'll brief the Chief and let him know what's going on." He smiled tightly. "I'm sure he'll appreciate your little shot glass switch, but there's bound to be some fallout from that stunt that I don't think he's going to be too pleased about it."

"There already is," Donahue said.

"What are you talking about?"

"Fallout."

Donahue produced the paperwork from her purse and handed it over to Elwood.

"The US Attorney hit me up with a search warrant and an order to show cause at a hearing scheduled in federal court next week. Oh, and the paperwork also includes a gag order preventing Shari, Gibby and I from disclosing any details about our investigation to anyone, which technically, I suppose, includes you."

Elwood read it over slowly.

"It says here that the case has national security implications." He looked up at his detectives. "What a crock!"

He dropped the paperwork on the desk, then mused, "These guys mean business, don't they?"

"Afraid so," Donahue replied. "For what it's worth, I'm sorry about the shot glass thing. I can see now that it's only going to make things worse."

"No apology necessary, Jen," said Elwood with a shake of his head. "You were doing your job. Besides, we can lay it all off on Thompson, and you'll find yourself in the clear."

"Hey, I'm right here," Thompson said. She shot them both a pouty look and placed her hands on her hips. A smile spread over her face. "Would this be a good time to put in for reimbursement for the purse I used to wrap up the shot glass?"

Elwood tried to repress his smile. "Sure, why not? Just make sure that you do it in triplicate, and don't submit the forms unless every line is filled out."

"All right!" She looked over at Donahue. "See? Didn't I tell you he was the best?"

Elwood leaned back in his chair. "Of course, you know it will never leave my desk, but I wouldn't want to discourage you from taking your best shot."

Thompson looked over at Donahue and shook her head. "See? Didn't I tell you he was nothing but an old, stubborn grouch?"

Donahue and Elwood laughed until there were tears in both of their eyes.

When his composure returned, Elwood said, "Why don't the two of you take off? Go home, unpack and get some sleep. I'll see you in here tomorrow morning, and we'll go through a detailed debriefing about what happened on the night that Aziz was killed."

"You've got a deal." Donahue wasted no time as she got to her feet. "But what about the subpoena?"

"I'll talk to the Chief, and he can make the call to the City Attorney. I suspect that they would have jurisdiction in this matter."

As they started for the door, Elwood added, "In the meantime, don't discuss the case with anyone."

Donahue nodded. "Don't worry, I won't."

"And you?" Elwood looked directly at Thompson.

"What case?" she replied.

"Good answer."

Donahue smiled, "I think I may stop by the hospital and see Claudette and Gibby. Anything you want me to pass on?"

"Just give them my best," Elwood said. "And tell Gib not to worry about us. We'll hold down the fort until he's ready to come back."

They walked from his office, back into the squad room, and Donahue said, "I don't imagine that we've seen the last of the feds."

Thompson smiled. "How pissed do you think they'll be when they find out about the shot glass?"

"Knowing this guy Rendleford, he'll probably try to have us thrown into jail."

"I was thinking that, too." Thompson said with a frown. "We've really done it this time, haven't we?"

"We are in the right on this one, Shari. I don't buy into the ethics of the idea that they want to use the son's crimes as a way to extort his father into sending the US more oil, or whatever else they think they can get away with. We're doing our job the best way we know how. That's all there is to it. End of story."

Thompson snorted. "Nice speech, Jen. Maybe they'll let us share a jail cell?"

"In that case, I just hope you don't snore."

FORTY-TWO

Donahue drove directly to Cedars Sinai Medical Center in West Los Angeles. After parking in the nearest available lot, and grousing to herself about the ten dollar parking fee, she made her way into the building, up the elevator, to the room being used by Gibson's wife.

Claudette was resting comfortably in a single patient room. Her eyes came open when Donahue walked in.

Donahue stepped up to the bed and stroked her on the arm.

"Hi, Claudie! How are you feeling?"

Claudette smiled. "I'm doing much better, Jen. The doctor says I can go home tomorrow."

"That's great!" Donahue took her hand. "I was so worried when I didn't hear anything from your husband."

"That man." Claudette rolled her eyes. "He's been hanging around here like a lost puppy. I have no idea what to do with him." She lowered her voice. "He's even talking about retiring."

Donahue's eyes widened. "Is that what you want him to do?"

"God, no!" she replied. "He'd drive me crazy." She shook her head. "As soon as I get back on my feet I want him to get back to work. He wouldn't be happy if he wasn't solving cases. That's what he does."

"I know," Donahue replied. The thought of Gibson pulling the pin and leaving the department had her seriously concerned. "I'll talk to him."

"Good!" Claudette shifted her weight in the bed. "You talk some sense into him, Jennifer. Maybe he'll listen to you. Lord knows...he doesn't pay any attention to what I have to say."

At that moment, Gibson made his way into the room with a Styrofoam cup of coffee in his hand.

"Hey, Jen," he said when he saw her. "You're back."

"I just got in a few hours ago. I wanted to see how Claudette was doing before I went home."

"She's doing fine," he said. He glanced over at his wife. "Did she tell you they said she may get to go home tomorrow morning?"

Donahue nodded. She squeezed Claudette's hand. "I can't stay. I've got to get home and get some sleep. I'll call you tomorrow, and if you're released, I'll try and come by and pay you a visit."

"You don't need to, sweetheart," Claudette said. She squeezed her hand back. "I'm going to be just fine."

"Okay, then. Can I borrow your husband for a few moments?"

"Of course, and tell him what you think about this retirement nonsense."

Donahue smiled. She led Gibson down a hallway and into an empty surgical waiting room. They sat together on a couch.

"Has she been bending your ear about my pulling the pin?" he asked.

"She doesn't want you to do it. Says you'll drive her crazy if you're hanging out at home."

"What do you think?"

"You serious?"

"Yeah." He took a sip of coffee. "I'd like to know what you think?"

"She's right. You'll drive her crazy."

He smirked. "I knew you'd say that." He eyed her carefully. "So what did you want to see me about?"

"First off, how is she *really* doing? You didn't bother to call and let me know."

A sheepish look spread over his face. "I'm sorry about that, Jen. It turns out she had an irregular heartbeat; one chamber beating faster than the others. They gave her a beta-blocker, and now it looks like that chamber is in sync with the others. Her doctor says she's gonna be fine."

Donahue started to relax. "That's great! Thank God. Now, if you've got a moment, can we talk a little business?"

"Sure."

"I wanted to fill you in on what happened in Istanbul. Shari and I got a DNA sample from a shot glass Aziz used the night he was killed. We'll be sending it out in the next few days to the lab, but I'm confident it's going to come back as a match."

"No surprise there."

She went on to tell him about the seizure by the feds of the souvenir shot glass and the court order for her and Thompson to appear in court.

"I know about that," he said. "I got served with one myself this morning."

Donahue studied him carefully.

"Then I should also tell you this. Before I left Istanbul, Tuzil told me that as far as his country is concerned, the investigation of Aziz's death is now a closed subject."

"They're not going to investigate?" Gibson's eyes went wide.

"Apparently not. Tuzil says that the US, Turkey, the Brits and the Saudi's are comfortable with the idea that the killer was a Muslim extremist. That will give the Saudis a good reason to go after their homegrown terrorists, something that turns out to be in the best interest of everyone concerned."

Gibson shook his head in amazement. "So they turn the death of a scumbag like Aziz into a positive?" He locked eyes with Donahue. "Looks like everybody wins."

"Not exactly."

She debated whether or not to say anything further, then abruptly made up her mind. She lowered her voice.

"I know who killed Aziz."

Gibson didn't speak but stayed focused on her face.

"I recognized him out on the dance floor."

Gibson held her stare. "I'd say you've got a bit of a dilemma on your hands."

He got to his feet, crossed over to the window, and admired the view of the city below before turning back.

"And you're telling me this…*why*?"

"Because I don't know what I'm supposed to do?"

She got to her feet, walked over to the window, and stood next to him.

"I don't like being in this position."

Gibson kept his expression blank. "Sounds like you could throw a real monkey wrench into their carefully constructed plan?"

"I know...*and for what?"*

"How about for justice?" he said.

Donahue almost laughed.

"*Justice*? I should turn in a guy for taking out a serial killer who had the entire system gamed? Where's the justice in that?"

Gibson rubbed at the stubble on his chin. "Would he do it again?"

It was a simple question and right on point. Would someone who had led an otherwise exemplary life do something like this again? She already knew the answer to that. The killing of Aziz was clearly situational. It wasn't the start of a pattern of conduct. It was justice catching up with a guy who otherwise couldn't be touched by the system.

A sad smile crept over her face. "I think I know what I have to do."

Gibson nodded. "Just make sure you've thought it through."

"I will." She walked back to the couch and picked up her purse. "You coming in tomorrow?"

He turned and gave her a nod.

"Once I get Claudette settled in at the house, I might try to come by if it's not too late?"

"Okay. I'll see you then."

FORTY-THREE

Donahue, Gibson, Thompson, and Elwood walked over to the Federal Courthouse which was only two blocks from their offices in the Police Administration Building. After showing their identification to Federal Marshals and surrendering their firearms at the security checkpoint, they took the elevator to the third floor and entered the courtroom where their case was going to be handled.

Seated at the counsel table was Donald Vincent, their attorney, who was a high-ranking City Attorney and a former police lieutenant who now specialized in cases that involved police officers. Tall and lean, with a full head of short, gray hair, he gestured to the four of them to take a seat in front of the railing in chairs that had been placed there precisely to accommodate their presence.

At the other end of the table was a Deputy US Attorney named Eric Sherman, and next to him was Frank Toledo, the representative from the Department of State who had taken the shot glass from Thompson at the airport.

Toledo looked over as they took their seats and gave them a nod.

Thompson smiled, then mumbled under her breath, "Found any interesting DNA this week?"

"Shh," whispered Donahue. "Let's not make this any worse than it already is."

"You're right. I'll keep my mouth shut."

Gibson leaned forward to engage Vincent in a conversation while Elwood amused himself by giving Thompson a brand new toothbrush. It was a not-so-veiled reference to the possibility of her ending up incarcerated by the close of the day.

The court clerk, who was seated at a desk just below the one that would be occupied by the judge, got to her feet and waived to Frank Toledo, gesturing to him that he was wanted on the phone.

Toledo nodded, got to his feet, and wandered over to take the call.

Donahue watched him with interest. He seemed intent on what he was being told, and several times he looked over in her direction. After a few moments of very brief conversation, he hung up the phone and returned to the counsel table.

He huddled briefly with Sherman who glanced up to look at Donahue. He seemed visibly shaken.

A few moments later, a law clerk from the US Attorney's Office arrived in the courtroom and handed Sherman a piece of paper. Sherman read it, then passed it over to Toledo. When Toledo had finished reading what was on the page, he trotted over to the phone, made a call, spoke briefly to someone, then returned to his seat.

To Donahue's way of thinking, he did not appear to be a happy camper. She nudged Gibson. "Something's going on." She told him what she'd seen, but before Gibson could respond, the Marshall called the courtroom to order, and Judge LeAnn Griffin took the bench.

A severe looking woman, with short gray hair and a thin, angular face, she leaned forward in her chair and shuffled through some papers which she studied through a pair of bifocals that perched on the tip of her nose.

"Good morning ladies and gentlemen." She looked down from the bench directly at Sherman. "In the matter of the United States Government versus the Los Angeles Police Department and defendants Donahue, Gibson, and Thompson, is the government ready to proceed in the show-cause hearing?"

Sherman got to his feet.

"Your Honor, might we adjourn this matter to your chambers? I've just received some information by telephone which I need to bring to the attention of the court and counsel."

Judge Griffin did not look pleased, but she acquiesced. "I'll see counsel for both parties in my chambers."

She got to her feet, left the bench, and was followed shortly after that by Sherman.

Don Vincent got to his feet.

"Do we go with you?" Gibson asked.

Vincent shook his head. "Counsel only. When I come out, I'll fill you in if I'm allowed to."

He disappeared through a door at the side of the courtroom that led to the judge's chambers.

Thompson got to her feet. She walked over to Toledo and said, "Do you know what's going on?"

He looked up at her, frowned, then shrugged.

She smiled. "That bad, huh?" She walked back to the others and took her seat.

"You're flirting with danger," Donahue whispered. "These boys have a very long memory."

Thompson leaned forward and mouthed the words, "Fuck 'em if they can't take a joke."

Gibson, who'd been watching this exchange, slowly got to his feet.

"You're going to get us twenty years, Shari," he said.

"Where are you going?" Donahue asked.

"As far away from Thompson as I can get." He looked back at them and winked. "When lightning strikes, I don't want to be anywhere near her."

He started across the courtroom toward a drinking fountain when Vincent and Sherman appeared at the doorway, followed a moment later by the judge.

"Resume your seats," the Marshall called out, and everyone went back to their places.

Donahue leaned forward to speak with Vincent, but he motioned that he'd talk to her later. She settled into her chair and waited for the judge to speak.

"In the matter of the Government versus the Los Angeles Police Department, we're back on the record." She looked over the top of her glasses.

"Mr. Sherman? I believe you wish to address the court on the record?"

Sherman slowly got to his feet.

"You're Honor," he began, "the Government is withdrawing our Motion to Show Cause. I have been advised by my office that we are not pursuing the national security implications of this case."

A low murmuring could be heard throughout the courtroom as the gist of what he said sank in.

"Very well." The judge looked over at the City Attorney.

"Mr. Vincent? Do you have anything to add?"

Vincent got to his feet.

"No, your Honor. I'm sure my clients are satisfied with this outcome."

The judge made a notation in her file. "This case is dismissed."

She looked down at Donahue and the others. "Detectives, you are free to go. This court apologizes to you for the time you've wasted coming over here. Hopefully, in the future, the government will know what they want to do well in advance of this court taking the bench."

She quickly stood and walked out of the courtroom as everyone else got to their feet.

"What the hell just happened?" Elwood asked.

Vincent walked over. "The case was dismissed."

Elwood rolled his eyes. "I know that, Don. But why?"

Vincent produced a piece of paper that he held up for them to see.

"Apparently, UPI and AP just put out a wire story that Mr. Sherman produced a copy of in chambers. After he read it to the court, he advised the judge that this case was now moot and they would not be going forward."

"What did it say?" Thompson asked.

Vincent passed it to Donahue who read it to the others.

Ambassador to Turkey, Prince Muhammad bin Abd al Aziz of Saudi Arabia, revealed today that his son, who one week ago was killed in Istanbul, Turkey, was the subject of a criminal investigation being conducted by law enforcement authorities in the United States, Great Britain, and Turkey. His son, Prince Muhammad bin Abd al Aziz, an ambassadorial representative of Saudi Arabia, was suspected of being a serial killer who was believed to be responsible for rapes and murder in both the United States and Europe.

The Ambassador said that he believes that the killing of his son was perpetrated by someone who was angered because his son was covered under the umbrella of diplomatic immunity while in the countries where the murders occurred. During his remarks, the Ambassador stated, "My country has always dealt harshly with those who commit these types of crimes and had this information been made known to us, my son would have been sent home for the purpose of standing trial for these offenses."

When asked if his son would have been punished if convicted, the Ambassador stated, "Of course. He (the son) violated the basic tenants of the Koran. My country would not hesitate to carry out the ultimate punishment (the death penalty) for anyone guilty of such egregious personal conduct."

The Ambassador stated that he has been in contact with the appropriate parties within the Turkish government and that as a father and as a representative of the Saudi government, he is not seeking an investigation into the identity of his son's killer.

"The killing was Allah's will. My son was guilty of terrible acts, and as a member of the Royal House of Saud, his actions are not above the law. The punishment for his crimes was appropriate."

The Ambassador went on to apologize to the victims' families, his countrymen, and to the world at large for the actions of his son.

He concluded his remarks by thanking the authorities involved in the investigation of the facts surrounding the conduct of his son, and he stated that his representatives are contacting the families of the victims to whom he will personally offer his most profound apologies. He added that he intends to make financial reparations to the families of those involved.

"Well, what do you know? He did it!" said Donahue who shook her head as she handed the wire copy back to Don Vincent.

Gibson gave her a questioning look. "What are you talking about?"

Donahue flushed. "Nothing. Forget it."

But Gibson held her glance.

"I'll tell you later," she finally said.

She looked across the counsel table at Toledo, then whispered to Thompson, "I'd give anything to see the look on Rendleford's face right now. As the architect of this mess, he's probably pissed as hell at the outcome."

Vincent, who overheard her remark, turned to face her and lowered his voice.

"Allen Rendleford is no longer with the State Department."

Donahue's eyes went wide. "What happened?"

"Sherman mentioned it in chambers. He told the judge that he confirmed by phone this morning that Rendleford had been asked to resign, and apparently, he did."

"You're kidding?" She couldn't hide the wonder on her face.

"No reason was given," Vincent said, "but Sherman told me in the hallway that the President, who is a good friend of certain members of the Royal House of Saud, was the one who personally demanded that Rendleford submit his resignation." He gave her a smile and a wink. "We live in strange times, detective."

Donahue rolled her eyes. "Boy, I'll say."

When the congratulations were over, Elwood and Thompson left for their office, while Donahue and Gibson remained behind to chat with well-wishers who came by to watch the proceedings. When they finally left the building to walk back to the station, Gibson said, "Are you gonna tell me now?"

"Tell you what?" she asked.

Gibson gave her that *you know what I'm talking about* look.

"Oh, that." She took a deep breath and met his glance. "I didn't mention this before, but the Ambassador and I had a meeting in Istanbul while Shari and I were waiting for our plane."

"And you didn't think it was important enough to mention?"

"It was a confidential meeting," she replied. "But I guess it doesn't matter now, so I can tell you." She stopped walking and turned to face him. "I told him about his son and what he'd done. The man was truly shocked. He said he had no idea, and I believed him. He said he would contact the victim's families and offer reparations, which it looks like he's planning to do."

Gibson cocked his head. "So what was this stuff about asking the Turks not to look into the identity of his son's killer? Did you have something to do with that?"

"Not at all. I never told him that I knew who did it. My guess is he wanted to end it there, and you've got to admit, he's pretty smart. By putting it all out there, he can move on without any fear that the other countries—or even his own countrymen—would be able to use the information against him."

"There goes the US leverage for oil." Gibson sighed. "Oh, well, I suppose ten dollars a gallon won't be all that bad."

"Don't blame that on me," Donahue said with just a hint of laughter in her tone. "Besides, we only get about ten percent of our oil from Saudi Arabia."

Gibson pondered that thought.

"One more question," he finally said. "Why do you suppose the President would ask for Rendleford's resignation?"

Donahue momentarily looked away.

"Mmm...because I just might have mentioned to the Ambassador that

Rendleford covered up his son's first rape case, and that perhaps he wouldn't have killed anyone if Rendleford had stayed out of it and simply told the Ambassador the truth."

Gibson smiled. "Wow, Jen! You don't mess around. Remind me to always stay in your good graces."

"That's the truth," she said with a measure of pride. "It really doesn't pay to mess with me."

They walked in silence for a while before Gibson asked, "Have you decided what you're going to do about that other matter?"

"Which other matter?" she asked.

Gibson frowned. "Is there more than one?"

Donahue nodded. "I'm going to talk with Zach this evening. It's time for me to move on."

"You sure about that?" he said.

"I'm sure. We've reached a serious impasse, and I've come to realize that if Zach really was the one that I wanted to be with for the rest of my life, I would have been willing to do whatever it takes to make it happen. But I'm not, and to pretend otherwise is to do both of us a disservice."

Gibson took a few moments to absorb what she said. It sounded as if she'd thought things through and knew what was really in her heart. He couldn't fault her for that, in fact, he admired the fact that she had the strength to move forward with her life in this manner.

"I've got your back," he said.

"Thanks, Gib. I knew you would."

"And that other little matter? Do you know what you're going to do?"

She shook her head. "I'm still waiting for the lab results on the DNA. After that, I'll make up my mind."

EPILOGUE

Three weeks later, Donahue pulled up at a Spanish style, middle-class tract home in the city of Calabasas. On the border of Ventura and Los Angeles Counties, this sleepy Los Angeles suburb, nestled in the Western foothills of the San Fernando Valley, was home to mostly well-to-do professionals, including lawyers, judges, doctors, and more than a few cops.

She parked at the curb, rechecked the address again, then got out of her unmarked Ford and made her way to the front door.

She rang the bell, and while she waited, she looked around. Kids toys were left out in driveways up and down the street, a sure indication that most of the inhabitants were very young families.

When the door was opened, Lieutenant Mike Ryson couldn't hide his surprise.

"Detective Donahue." He stared past her towards the street, as if he expected to see other officers nearby.

"Hello, Lieutenant. I thought I'd drop by to talk to you about our progress in the investigation of your daughter's killer."

Ryson appeared relieved.

"C'mon in," he said. He opened the door wider and stood aside to let Donahue enter his house.

It was air-conditioned, a relief from the warm winds that flowed into the Valley from the high desert. Ryson led her into the living room.

"Can I get you a soda or a beer or something?" he asked.

"Thanks anyway. I'm fine."

He gestured for her to take a seat on the couch and he sat in a nearby chair.

Donahue leaned forward. "I wanted to let you know what we discovered. The DNA results are back. The sample we picked up in Turkey from Aziz was a positive match with what we found on your daughter. I won't bore you with the numbers, but the likelihood of it being anyone else would be in the twenty-seven billion to one range."

"So there's no doubt?" Ryson asked.

"No doubt. Aziz is the one who attacked and killed Carrie Ann."

She watched him intently, but aside from a small sigh, he didn't reveal any emotion. Instead, he said, "Well, I guess that finally puts it to rest."

"What you may not know is that the British government has conclusively linked him to two victims who suffered the same fate as Carrie Ann. Additionally, I heard from my contact in Turkey. They took a sample of blood from Aziz's body, and their lab has been able to connect him to a murder in Istanbul. That means he was good for at least four killings. There may be more, but it's going to end right there."

Ryson leaned back in his chair. Donahue couldn't imagine how he was feeling. Having your daughter murdered was beyond comprehension, and knowing who did it, while providing one part of the answer, was never enough for those who were left behind to pick up the pieces.

"Such a waste," he said. He got to his feet, walked into the kitchen and returned with a couple of bottles of beer.

"You sure I can't offer you one?"

She thought about it, then acquiesced.

He opened the beers, handed her one, then took a long pull from his own.

Donahue continued, "I thought you might also like to know that the makeup and the beard you had on in Istanbul was very effective. And 'the old man posture and limp?' It fooled everyone."

He stopped drinking his beer and studied her intently. "Are you wearing a wire?" he asked.

"No."

He got up again, left the room, and when he returned he had a piece of equipment in his hand.

He turned it on and held it out in front of her, searching for an electronic signal. When he was satisfied that she wasn't broadcasting their conversation, he returned to his seat.

"Why are you asking me about this?" he said.

"I'm not sure. I have no intention of turning you in. The Turks won't pursue it, and the kid's father considers the matter closed, so sending you to some god-forsaken Turkish hell-hole prison doesn't seem to make any sense."

"So, I guess I didn't fool you?"

Her smile had no mirth. "It was your eyes, Lieutenant, the intensity. I knew it almost right away."

"I thought you might have figured it out, but when I didn't get stopped at the airport, and when nothing happened once I got home, I started to believe that I got away with it."

She reached for her beer and took a small sip.

"You must have used a false passport. I checked with Customs and Immigration, and they didn't have you coming or going."

"Passports are easy enough to come by," he replied, "if you know the right people."

She smiled. "So, you lost the beard, and while they were looking for an older man, you passed as someone who was much younger."

He nodded. "By the way, did you spot me at the Blue Mosque?"

"I did, and later at the Hagia Sophia, but I didn't know who you were at the time."

"I wanted to see who you were meeting with. I was going to follow you to Aziz."

"Did you follow us that night?" she asked.

"Actually, no." He rubbed at the stubble on his chin. "You were being followed by the Turkish police throughout your entire visit."

He pulled out a pack of Marlboro cigarettes and lit one up.

"When you came by my office and told me you were headed to London, I caught a flight directly to Turkey. I went right to the Saudi Embassy, and I followed Aziz for a couple of nights until I got a sense of his habits."

Donahue coughed from the cigarette smoke, and Ryson quickly put it out.

"Sorry," he said.

"I'm just not used to the smoke," she said.

Ryson slouched back in his chair and drank a little more of his beer.

"Where was I?" he asked.

"You followed Aziz?" she replied.

"Right. Once I knew his habits, getting to him wasn't difficult."

"But why did you do it while we were there? It increased your risk of getting caught."

"I had no choice. I was afraid that time was running out. If you didn't arrest him, I figured the Turks might jump the gun." He cocked his head. "If they expelled him from the country, I realized that once he was back in Saudi Arabia, nothing would happen and I'd never get close." He shut his eyes for a moment as if reliving what had happened. "I saw my chance, and I took it," he said.

Donahue nodded. There was very little of value in questioning him further. She hadn't expected him to tell her anything in the first place, and the fact that he did had surprised her. He was obviously a man of conscience, and what he did was likely giving him trouble. But she was sure that it was strictly situational, and when the system completely fails, sometimes something outside the norm is needed to restore the balance.

She had thought that confronting him would be something she'd find satisfying, but in truth, it just seemed sad and sordid. He had killed the man who murdered his daughter, and if she ever had a child and had been in his situation, she knew that she likely would do the same thing.

"So what's next for you?" she asked.

He shrugged. "I'll do another year, maybe less, then I'm going to move to Montana. I need to get away from this city and the scum we have to deal with."

A broken, bitter man, she thought.

"Good luck, Lieutenant." She got to her feet. "I don't expect I'll be seeing you again."

He stood up and walked her to the door.

She stepped outside. "Oh, by the way, if I were you, I wouldn't visit Turkey again. I'm pretty sure the Turkish authorities were on to you that night. My source wouldn't confirm it, but he strongly hinted as much. Anyway, if the political climate ever changes, you might find yourself rotting in one of their jails."

She turned away and walked to her car.

* * * *

While cruising down the 101 freeway on her way back to downtown LA, she dialed Thompson on her phone.

"Hey, you," she said when Thompson picked up. "Are we still on for dinner tonight?"

"Girls night out, hell yeah!"

"Good, because I've discovered a Turkish restaurant over in Hollywood, and I'm pretty sure you're gonna love the food."

* * * *

www.ingramcontent.com/pod-product-compliance
Lightning Source LLC
LaVergne TN
LVHW091033080826
845145LV00002B/480

* 9 7 8 1 7 3 3 5 1 6 0 0 6 *